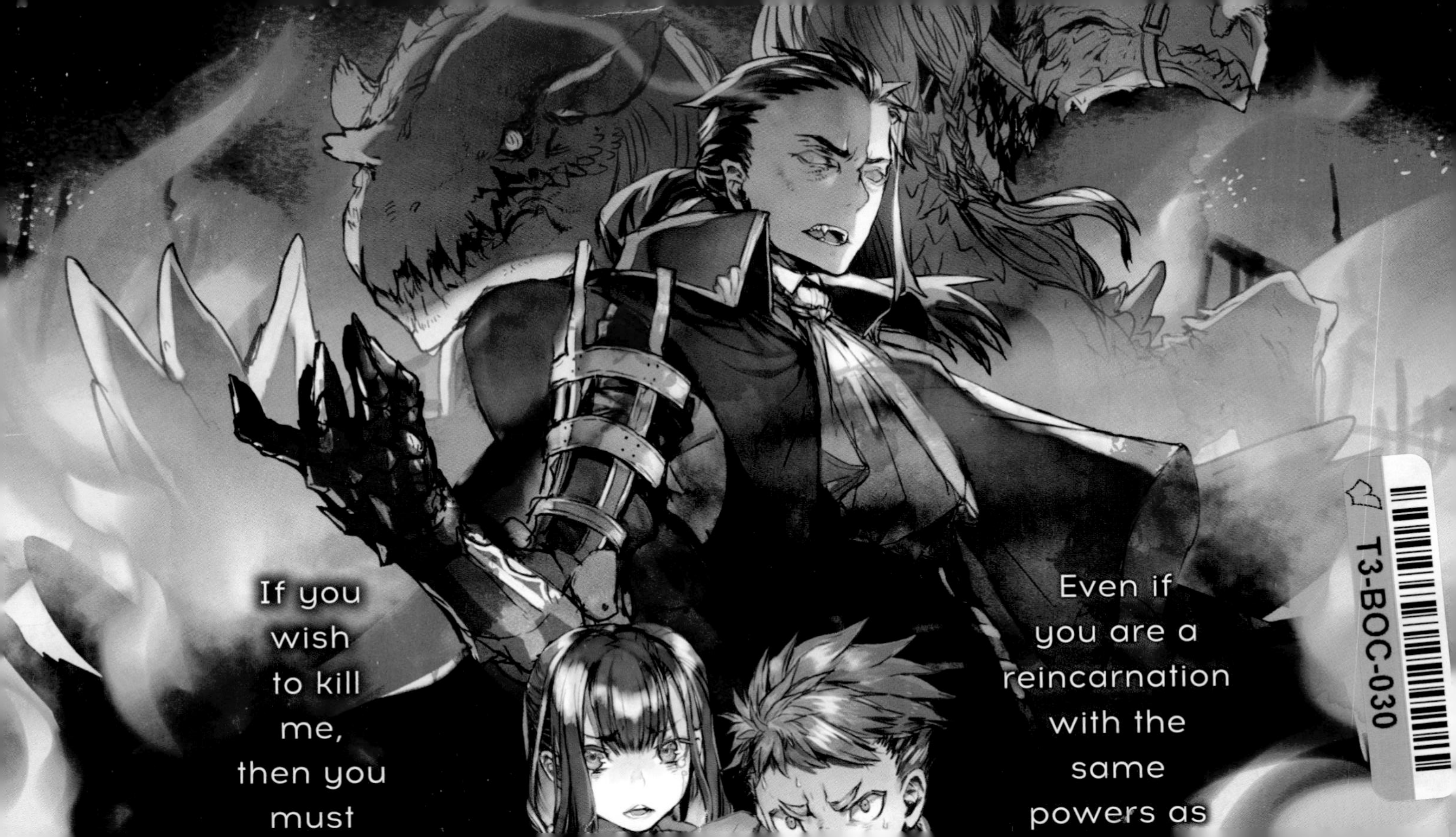
Even if you are a reincarnation with the same powers as
If you wish to kill me, then you must

surpass me in strength. I will oppose you with everything I have.
my young mistress, I will not lose so easily.

So I'm a Spider, So What?

10

OKINA BABA

Illustration by TSUKASA KIRYU

New York

So I'm a Spider, So What?, Vol. 10

Okina Baba

Translation by Jenny McKeon
Cover art by Tsukasa Kiryu

KUMO DESUGA, NANIKA? Vol. 10

First published in Japan in 2019 by KADOKAWA CORPORATION, Tokyo.
English translation rights arranged with KADOKAWA CORPORATION, Tokyo, through TUTTLE-MORI AGENCY, INC., Tokyo.

Yen On
150 West 30th Street, 19th Floor
New York, NY 10001

Visit us at yenpress.com
facebook.com/yenpress
twitter.com/yenpress
yenpress.tumblr.com
instagram.com/yenpress

First Yen On Edition: November 2020

Library of Congress Cataloging-in-Publication Data
Names: Baba, Okina, author. | Kiryu, Tsukasa, illustrator. | McKeon, Jenny, translator.
Title: So I'm a spider, so what? / Okina Baba ; illustration by Tsukasa Kiryu ; translation by Jenny McKeon.
Other titles: Kumo desuga nanika. English | So I am a spider, so what?
Description: First Yen On edition. | New York, NY : Yen On, 2017–
Identifiers: LCCN 2017034911 | ISBN 9780316412896 (v. 1 : pbk.) | ISBN 9780316442886 (v. 2 : pbk.) | ISBN 9780316442909 (v. 3 : pbk.) | ISBN 9780316442916 (v. 4 : pbk.) | ISBN 9781975301941 (v. 5 : pbk.) | ISBN 9781975301965 (v. 6 : pbk.) | ISBN 9781975301989 (v. 7 : pbk.) | ISBN 9781975398996 (v. 8 : pbk.) | ISBN 9781975310349 (v. 9 : pbk.) | ISBN 9781975310363 (v. 10 : pbk.)
Subjects: CYAC: Magic—Fiction. | Spiders—Fiction. | Monsters—Fiction. | Prisons—Fiction. | Escapes—Fiction. | Fantasy.
Classification: LCC PZ7.1.O44 So 2017 | DDC [Fic]—dc23
LC record available at https://lccn.loc.gov/2017034911

ISBNs: 978-1-9753-1036-3 (paperback)
978-1-9753-1037-0 (ebook)

10 9 8 7 6 5 4 3

LSC-C

Printed in the United States of America

contents

Prologue Thus a Goddess Was Born

A long, long time ago…

The world was considerably advanced.

There were machines everywhere that made people's lives easier.

But the people of the past committed a grave error.

They laid their hands on the forbidden power source, MA energy, which they should have never trifled with.

A certain woman explained the dangers to them and urged them to refrain from using it, but they paid her no heed.

After all, MA energy could make their lives even better than they already were.

But all that awaited them was destruction.

By the time they had realized their mistake and tried to right their wrongs, it was all far too late.

The end was fast approaching.

As they wept in despair, the people discovered a single ray of hope.

A means of saving the world by sacrificing a single woman.

That woman was the very person who had warned them of the dangers of MA energy.

As the people changed their tune and begged her to save them, she nonetheless agreed.

And so she became the sacrifice that would keep the world alive.

The people called her a goddess and worshipped her.

1 Let's Set a Goal

The scents of richly steeped tea and sweet confections mingle with the aromas from the flowers that decorate my room.

The smells are all wildly different yet somehow harmonize perfectly.

Even that was intentional, I bet.

The folks who run the duke's mansion are something else.

Right now, we're having our customary tea party.

The attendees are Vampy; three of the puppet-spider sisters: Sael, Riel, and Fiel; and me.

Also, Mr. Oni, who's looking very uncomfortable.

Just us six.

The mansion servants scattered as soon as they were done setting things up, as usual.

Well, I guess I can't blame them, since we generally give off a *Don't mess with us* aura to the staff.

Even if that wasn't the case, they probably couldn't bear the awkward atmosphere in here.

Yeah. You could cut the tension with a knife, mostly thanks to Vampy, who's staring daggers at Mr. Oni.

As she continues to glare at him in silence, Mr. Oni looks increasingly bewildered as to what he should do.

I guess these two are never going to get along at this point.

I mean, they've already tried to kill each other twice.

Mr. Oni was in a state of insanity thanks to the ultrapowerful Wrath skill and its terrible side effects.

While he was on a rampage, Vampy and I fought him twice, nearly losing our lives both times.

Huh? You're saying that in the second fight, I totally owned him with a super-cheap strategy?

Doesn't ring a bell.

Anyway, Mr. Oni and Vampy have a pretty nasty history.

On top of that, Vampy was beaten to a pulp and nearly died the first time, and I interfered the second time, so there hasn't been a clear winner.

Although I'm pretty sure our little bloodsucker would've lost if I hadn't intervened.

But that reality probably just makes her hate Mr. Oni even more, since she's a really sore loser.

Which brings us to the current standoff.

Unreal.

If you're gonna fight, just do it already.

Just don't ruin my rest-and-relaxation time!

Why do I have to put up with an atmosphere so depressing that I can barely even taste my tea and pastries?

Now that my stomach capacity has shrunk drastically, I only get so many opportunities to enjoy tasty food!

Ughhh, no waaaay.

Mr. Oni seems to be begging for a lifeline with all the desperate looks he's giving me, but I ignore them.

Our tea parties are typically held in silence.

And thanks to the merciless teachings of the mansion's Spartan instructor, we now have impeccable manners, which means our eating and drinking are totally silent, too.

Not a word and not a sound. That's gotta look weird to anybody but us.

But the puppet spiders and I never really talk, so naturally, Vampy also has nothing to say.

Mr. Oni seems to have picked up on this, so he doesn't try to make conversation, either.

Is it just peer pressure?

We keep drinking tea and eating pastries in tense silence.

Aren't tea parties supposed to be a little more lighthearted?

Oh, but then again, apparently noble tea parties often include people scheming, thinly veiled threats, information bartering, and so on. Just thinking about it makes my stomach hurt.

So I guess this equally stomachache-inducing atmosphere might be dead-on for a tea party!

Incidentally, that conclusion's mostly based on my personal views and assumptions, so don't go taking my word for it, folks!

Ahhh, that's the ticket. At times like this, you've just gotta avoid reality by getting lost in thought.

Until I figure things out, Mr. Oni will have to suffer a little while longer.

That said, it isn't as if I'm wrestling with the meaning of life or anything.

I'm just deciding what to do next.

Now, that might be a big deal if I was coming up with some crazy future plan, but it's nothing that deep.

You know how in Japan, high school second-years get that form to fill out their career prospects and start worrying about their futures? It's like that.

Once they become third-years, there are college-entrance exams or job hunts or whatever waiting for them, like it or not.

So when second-years start to think about the future, they've still got some time to figure things out.

This is basically the same idea. I don't need to rush to make a decision, but I'm gonna have to face the music eventually.

Maybe I'm biased, but I doubt there are that many second-year high school kids who have a clear vision of their future.

Most of them are probably just thinking, *I guess I'll go to college or whatever and then get a job or whatever,* right?

And more often than not, that's exactly what happens.

It's just like my current situation.

If things go on the way they are now, my future likely consists of being snatched up by D and turned into some kind of subordinate.

Getting hired straight out of high school! Way to go, me!

Yeah. D seems to really like me, so if I don't do something soon, she'll probably slowly but surely turn me into her pet.

It's not like D has actually said that explicitly, but as far as I can tell, that's exactly the kind of thing she'd do.

It's like when you get a job offer thanks to your parents' connections.

If I stay on this path, I'll just keep wandering aimlessly through life, get scouted by D, and end up on her payroll.

Is that a bad thing? No, not really.

D is a god who manipulates the incredibly complex magical conjuring known as the "system" without batting an eye, and now that I've met her in person, I know for a fact how unfathomable she is.

As I am now—no, no matter how strong I might get going forward—I can't even imagine a future in which I could possibly beat her.

I don't know anything about the world of gods, so having one take me under her wing would actually be a pretty sweet situation for me, wouldn't it?

I am technically a god, after all (LMAO)!

A brand-new god—freshly deified and still wet behind the ears.

And between the system and me swallowing that continent-destroying bomb or whatever, I took a highly irregular route to godhood, so my combat ability is currently weaker than it was before I became a god.

Not that I know what the *regular* route to godhood is anyway.

But at the very least, I'm guessing it isn't leveling up a bunch thanks to a gamelike system, then swallowing a continent-destroying bomb.

Anyway.

I'm technically a god now, but I don't feel like one in the slightest.

The sheer amount of energy swirling inside me is definitely godlike, though.

As you may have gathered, the energy I absorbed from that continent-destroying bomb is...well, enough to destroy a continent, duh.

So for people in the know, or at least deities in the know, it's easy to tell that I'm a god.

What would happen if I wandered off to some other planet, then?

Well, I'd get found by the gods of that planet.

Seems inevitable?

Now, if they were happy to just peacefully coexist, that'd be fine and dandy.

But from their perspective, I'm essentially a trespasser, so I wouldn't be surprised if they attacked me without so much as a hello.

I mean, even when I left the Great Elroe Labyrinth, the Demon Lord attacked me right away.

That's when I learned exactly how dangerous it is to leave your home turf.

Then again, the Demon Lord was already targeting me personally, so it wasn't really about me leaving the labyrinth, not exactly.

But still, as long as I stay on this planet, no random unknown god is going to come down from on high to attack me for no reason.

This place is under D's jurisdiction.

The powerful magic of the system covers the surface of the entire planet, and as you know, the party responsible is none other than D.

That means D literally rules the world.

Even when she's not actually here, trying to mess with this planet would be the same as picking a fight with her.

So as long as I'm on this planet, I'm automatically borrowing D's might.

You could even say that I'm under her protection.

So taking a step out from that safety zone requires a lot of courage for a newbie god like me.

I don't know anything about godhood, so if I was to leave D's sphere of influence, it'd be like an acrobat doing a crazy trapeze trick without a safety net during their first day on the job.

I could die. Easily.

So currently, I have no plans for leaving this planet, aka D's area of authority.

Honestly, it makes becoming D's stay-at-home housewife or whatever all the more tempting, in terms of my personal safety anyway.

In fact, I don't think I have any other options at the moment.

Especially considering how bad it would be if I did anything to get on her bad side.

Considering everything that's happened so far, I have no idea what D might do to me if I tick her off.

I'm scared that it would be worse than anything I could possibly imagine.

It's just, I dunno…

That's also the biggest problem with the idea of working for D.

Like, she definitely has a mean streak.

Take, for instance, the way she toys with a certain person's heart using the system or all the times she's maliciously meddled with me.

She doesn't call herself an evil god for nothing.

And when I actually saw D with my own eyes, she was even scarier than my worst fears somehow.

Would I really be all right living and working under someone so impossible to understand?

...I can't say that I would.

Huh?

Wait, am I screwed no matter what I do?

...No, of course I'm not. I'm not, okay?

Let's just go with that. Yeah.

Either way, it doesn't change the fact that there's nothing I can do right this instant.

I just have to keep doing whatever I can, here on this planet where I can act freely.

Whether I ultimately let D recruit me in the future, or whether I choose to reject her, I'm in no position to make any decisions right now.

I don't have enough knowledge or power for that.

Which means my first course of action is to acquire more of both.

So basically, the same thing I've been doing all along.

I need to regain the strength I enjoyed back to when I still had the support of the system, or ideally get even better.

On paper, my specs are definitely higher now, so I should be able to do everything I did with the system and more.

Honestly, I'm not too worried about that.

I can tell I'm making progress every day, even if it's happening super-gradually.

Compared to the overwhelming anxiety I felt when I couldn't even produce thread, with no idea if I'd ever get my powers back, any progress is way better than none at all.

The more time passes, the stronger I'll get. That much I know for sure.

But that's not to say that I've got no worries whatsoever.

As long as I stay on this planet, I don't have to fear any unknown gods attacking me, but there are gods I *do* know that are kinda worrying and other sketchy characters, too.

The god in question is Güli-güli, and the sketchy character is Potimas.

No matter what I do—or don't do—these guys will probably keep taking actions that affect the course of the entire world.

Right. Even if I just keep living my life normally, the world won't stop changing.

Even as a god (LOL), there are still ways I can be killed, and not just by other gods.

That Potimas jerk is well aware of that much.

His machine army plays by its own rules, outside the system.

Even I have the rule-breaking art of teleportation under my belt, but I still can't let my guard down.

Sure, I can use my teleportation to transport enemies into dangerous areas, warp myself to safety, or do all sorts of other stuff.

That's why I'm almost 100 percent confident I wouldn't lose to any enemy who operates within the system at this point.

As long as the Demon Lord doesn't use her crazy speed to land a hit on me before I can react or something like that.

But the mysterious barrier Potimas uses might even be able to stop me from teleporting.

And the only plays I've really got right now are that and my thread.

Without teleportation, I'd have virtually no way of winning.

Also, Potimas is the Demon Lord's sworn enemy, and I'm clearly part of her faction right now.

It's not like I owe her my firstborn, but the Demon Lord has done a lot for me.

She's protected and supported me so much, even when I lost my powers.

So I do think I should work for her at least until I repay that debt.

Which means it's basically a done deal that I'll end up fighting Potimas eventually, so I gotta come up with some kind of strategy.

Hmm. I mean, I guess it *is* pretty simple.

That thing is called a "barrier," so it probably affects a limited space, right?

In theory, all I really have to do is make sure I'm on the other side of that limit.

In other words, I just have to avoid getting near him.

Gotta stay outside the barrier's range, attack from a distance, and take him down.

Easy peasy.

And as long as I put my aforementioned mad teleportation skills to use, I can move around as much as I want.

The only problem is that I don't have a long-range attack right now!

But I've got a few ideas, so all I have to do is follow through on at least one of them.

Then I should be able to deal with Potimas...to a certain extent. I hope.

But, like...

Defeating Potimas isn't the Demon Lord's goal.

I mean, I'm sure it's *one* of them, but her true goal is way grander than that.

She wants to do something about this world that's teetering on the brink of destruction.

Basically, she wants to save it, I guess.

But that'll be tough, even for someone like the Demon Lord.

Strong as she might be, she's not a god.

Güli-güli is an actual god, and even he's just standing by and watching, so I doubt a non-god like the Demon Lord can do much about it.

And yeah, I guess I'd like to do something about it myself, if I can.

This place is my current safe zone, so I need it to last or I'll have nowhere to go.

What, Earth?

I mean, yeah, that's an option, but that's also where D is.

D's the kind of person I want to see only once in a while. Once in a very, very loooong while.

If I started seeing her all the time, it'd be bad in more ways than one.

It's like a black hole, in a way.

You know it'd be terrible if you got sucked in, but you can't help being drawn toward it anyway.

No, I gotta make sure I keep some distance between us.

Hmmmm.

At this rate, the Demon Lord might work herself to death before she can accomplish anything. Someone's gonna have to deal with that.

Ugh. This is tough.

There's so much stuff I want to do, but there's only one of me!

Dammit. If only I could make two or three more bodies.

...Huh? Wait, I *can* do that, can't I?

If I just use the basic idea of the Egg-Laying skill to make a sort of clone, then use the concept of Parallel Minds to put part of my brain in there...

If anything, I'd just have to make sure I can control it so I don't have another runaway Parallel Minds incident like before, right?

...Could be worth a try.

All right.

My short-term goal is to figure out how to make clones.

My medium-term goal is to help the Demon Lord.

And my long-term goal is...to get strong enough to escape D.

Yeah. I really should get away from her, I think.

I've always done the most to resist anyone who's tried to exploit me, whether it was Mother or the Demon Lord or anyone else.

The Demon Lord and I are pretty much allies at this point, so it's not like she's in charge of me or anything.

But it's not gonna be that easy with D.

If I go to where she is, I'll more than likely end up serving under her.

Does that really measure up to the standards I've been living by all this time?

My problem is, the more I interact with D, the more I start to think that maybe it wouldn't be so bad.

That's why I need to put some distance between D and me, so I can think things through rationally.

What really scares me is that at this rate, I might just accept my fate for the simple reason that I know I can't run away.

So I have to get strong enough that I *can* run away and figure things out then.

Will I actually run away or not?

Ugh, no, that's all wrong!

If I'm that wimpy about it now, then when the time comes, I'm totally just gonna be like, *Well, I CAN run away now, but I guess I don't really NEED to.*

I've gotta be firm here: I WILL get away.

No matter what happens.

I'll commit everything I've got, body and soul, to making sure I escape at any cost.

Okay. I just gotta keep telling myself that if I fail, I'm probably dead.

Just as I'm able to gather my thoughts, the door violently flies open.

There's only one moron around here who would bust into my room without knocking like that.

“’Scuse me.”

“You are *not* excused. Please leave.”

Just as I thought, it was Mr. Deadbeat himself.

And Vampy immediately starts picking a fight with him.

Why do these two get along so poorly?

I think Vampy might hate him even more than she hates Mr. Oni.

Well, I mean. I hate Mr. Deadbeat, too, but still.

“How many times do I hafta tell ya? I got no business with you, brat! Besides, this is *my* damn house! Or do you not remember that, either, birdbrain?!”

“Can you blame me when I always have to deal with an idiot whose brain is even smaller than a bird’s? I have to at least try to sink to your level, or you won’t even understand what I’m saying. It’s not like you can grasp civilized speech.”

“…”

“…”

This is the part where a little girl and a grown-ass man get into a glaring contest.

BOY, SURE IS PEACEFUL AROUND HERE.

“Um, shouldn’t we stop them?” Mr. Oni leans over and whispers to me.

“Hey! Who the hell is that?!”

Mr. Oni’s movements catch Deadbeat’s eye, and he sets his sights on us instead.

“The hell is going on here?! No one told me this guy was gonna be here! This is my house, dammit. Why is some jackass I don’t even know sitting around like he owns the place?! You better tell me quick, or I swear I’ll throw you out myself!”

“Erm…”

Deadbeat closes in on Mr. Oni, who just looks baffled.

Makes sense. Mr. Oni doesn’t speak demon.

He has no idea what Deadbeat is saying.

“He has permission to be here, I’ll have you know. From Miss Ariel and from your elder brother, too, I’d imagine.”

“Huh?”

Deadbeat scowls when Vampy brings up the Demon Lord’s name.

It’s true, though. The Demon Lord met Mr. Oni right after he regained his sanity, and I’m sure the head butler has already informed the master of the house, Deadbeat’s older brother, Balto.

Since the Demon Lord gave permission for him to be here, Balto can't exactly go against her wishes.

And that being the case, Balto's deadbeat younger brother certainly doesn't have the power to kick him out, either.

"Tch! Why doesn't anyone tell me stuff like this? Dammit!"

Deadbeat smacks the table angrily.

Not hard enough to break it, fortunately, but it does spill some liquid from one of the teacups.

Excuse me. That was my tea.

Does this guy exist only to make my life miserable or what?

"Listen up, you. If you got permission, I ain't gonna try to kick you out. But I think I at least got the right to know what you're doing here. So out with it. Who are you, and why are you in my damn house?"

Deadbeat peppers him with questions, but of course Mr. Oni can't understand a single thing he's saying.

He looks to Vampy and me helplessly for assistance.

Deadbeat doesn't seem to like that. He grabs Mr. Oni by the horns, literally.

"What's with these stupid accessories anyway? You think it makes you look cool? Well, guess what? You just look stupid!"

Uh, those aren't accessories, buddy.

...Also, are you really one to talk?

"Hmm? He doesn't look nearly as ridiculous as you, though."

There goes Vampy, saying things she should be keeping to herself, as usual.

It must have just been a knee-jerk response. Once she realizes what she said, she claps a hand to her mouth.

The puppet spiders all freeze, and the maids watching from the hallway all gasp.

Look, there are some things in this world that you're just not supposed to point out, no matter how much you might want to.

Like when your boss is obviously wearing a toupee.

And equally high on that list is Deadbeat's god-awful fashion sense.

Even Vampy, who's practically his nemesis, has never gone that far.

Until now.

But now that it's been said, there's no going back!

We have to face the facts.

Deadbeat always looks completely ridiculous!

I dunno how to explain it, but none of the clothes he wears ever looks good together, let alone on him.

You might call his fashion "eccentric"—if you were trying to be nice—but the truth is that his outfit choices are usually so bizarre that he always ends up looking really stupid.

I get that you're trying to pull off a unique look, but it's just not working for you, sweetie.

"Hmph. A brat like you just doesn't get how cool this look is!"

...And yet, Deadbeat just seems triumphant after Vampy's comment.

I'm sorry. I never know what sort of face to make at times like this.

Like, am I allowed to smile?

No, I'm pretty sure that'd be a bad move.

Everyone else seems to feel the same way: They're all wearing strange expressions.

The puppet spiders have changed from their default expression to a super-serious one.

You guys don't have to go out of your way to change your faces right now!

I can't tell from that reaction if you're trying to be considerate or just being smarmy little jerks!

"...If you say so. Anyway, he doesn't understand demon language, so you're not going to get through to him that way." Vampy probably sensed that pushing the topic any further would be fruitless, so she forcibly changes the subject back to Mr. Oni. "And I should point out that those horns aren't accessories, either. He's a humanoid monster known as an oni."

"A what?!"

At the word *monster*, Deadbeat's hand flies to the hilt of the sword hanging from his waist.

"Were you even listening? Miss Ariel, the *Demon Lord*, personally approved his staying here. So you understand what would happen if you laid a hand on him, yes?"

"Urgh...," Deadbeat groans.

He keeps glaring at Mr. Oni for a few more seconds, then reluctantly pulls his hand away from his weapon.

But it's clear from his grim expression that he still has his guard raised.

"In that case, I really gotta know what's going on here. I hate to say it, brat, but I need you to translate for me."

He plops himself down in an empty seat, barking an order at Vampy.

I'll give him this—it was the right decision not to bother asking me, at least.

But saying it like that to Vampy was a BIG mistake.

"Oh? But he understands human just fine. Why not ask him yourself?"

See? Vampy is already smirking as she launches her counterattack.

There are two major languages in this world: human and demon.

Despite how big the world is, if you master those two languages, you can communicate with just about anyone.

Sure, there are local dialects and expressions and things like that, but it's sort of like the Kansai dialect in Japanese. As long as you've mastered the basic language, you can more or less figure out the rest.

But Deadbeat is asking her to translate.

Demanding, no less.

If you think about it, that can only really mean one thing.

"Go on, then. Why don't you ask him whatever you want to know? His name? Where he's from? How he wound up here? You want to know, don't you? Go ahead and ask. In the human tongue."

Vampy grins gleefully, the wicked expression of a bully.

Her sadistic streak is showing on her face.

She's more of a demon than any demon here.

Well, I guess technically she's a vampire.

"Grrrgh...!"

Deadbeat turns bright red and grinds his teeth.

Normally he would storm out angrily if he got humiliated this badly, but he's being weirdly persistent today...

Deadbeat glances at me and then at Mr. Oni.

Hmmmm? What's the deal?

"I...don't speak human. Translate for me."

Shaking with embarrassment, Deadbeat manages to spit out the words through clenched teeth.

Yeah, I figured.

Otherwise, he wouldn't keep refusing to speak in the face of all that mockery.

"Oh? Oh my, *really*? Good heavens, but you're from the noble family of a demon duke! Who would have thought you couldn't even speak human?! I'm so, *so* sorry. Never in my wildest dreams would I have guessed such a thing!"

Vampy twists the knife!

It's super-effective on Deadbeat's heart!

That's gotta hurt.

"Just translate already, dammit!"

"Don't you mean *pretty please, with a cherry on top?*"

Vampy isn't letting up!

Deadbeat is no longer breathing!

This is brutal stuff.

"Pretty...please! With... With a cherry on top!"

Yiiiikes.

I've never actually seen someone turn red as a lobster from sheer rage and embarrassment before.

Is he gonna be all right?

Hasn't all the blood rushed to his head by now?

"Well, I suppose if you really insist."

Evidently satisfied, or perhaps guessing that Deadbeat is going to snap if she pushes him any further, Vampy smiles as brightly as the sun and finally agrees to interpret for him.

At this point, however, Mr. Oni is practically curled up into a ball, looking like he wants to sink into the floor.

He can't understand their conversation, since they're speaking demon, but he must have figured out from the atmosphere that he's somehow responsible.

Mr. Oni might have taken the most damage in this fight.

"Damn, buddy, that's rough!"

For some reason, Deadbeat is now crying manly tears as he claps Mr. Oni on the shoulder.

Once Vampy agreed to interpret, their conversation went fairly smoothly.

She took her role surprisingly seriously, acting as their go-between without adding a single snide comment of her own.

Maybe she got her fill of picking on Deadbeat for the day.

There are a few parts of the story that have to be omitted: how we went to stop Mr. Oni at the request of the administrator Güli-güli, the valley on the other side of the Mystic Mountains, and stuff like that. But otherwise, the explanation Deadbeat gets is mostly accurate.

The only fabricated bits are that Mr. Oni traveled through the Mystic Mountains on his own and that we took him in once he found his way out and collapsed from exhaustion.

We came up with that cover story together ahead of time, so it's no problem.

So once he gets the gist of Mr. Oni's story, this is Deadbeat's reaction.

"I guess you got no other choice, then. You gotta go eventually, but for now you're welcome here as long as you need."

Deadbeat makes a loud, gross sniffling sound, exaggeratedly blowing his nose!

Vampy looks revolted.

Even the puppet spiders are a little disturbed, but obviously the one who's most uncomfortable is Mr. Oni, who's experiencing all this up close.

Huh. This is kind of unexpected.

I haven't known Deadbeat for long, so it's not like I had a perfect grasp of his personality, but I always kinda had him pegged as a pompous ass who didn't have much else going on.

Now that he's reacting like the antihero of a delinquent manga—a big jerk with a heart of gold—I kinda don't know what to think.

Like, who knew he was that kind of character?

He struck me more as a small-time thug.

But I guess he's actually a pretty important guy in the demon world, so he's not really small-time in the first place. In fact, he probably has underlings of his own.

I dunno if those underlings actually respect him, but most of the staff here seems to be fond of him, at the very least.

Yeah, you heard me. Aside from the head butler, the mansion staff are usually plenty willing to help out Deadbeat.

For one thing, he keeps visiting us every damn day, even though the head butler instructed the staff to keep him away.

If Deadbeat was forcing the staff to obey him, they'd probably be reporting it to their boss.

But there hasn't been a peep from the head butler, so either they're not tattling on him or the head butler's in on it, too.

Either way, someone is definitely helping him behind the scenes.

Which means Deadbeat might actually be surprisingly nice to his underlings.

Not that I care either way.

Yeah. It's way too late for Deadbeat to improve his standing in my eyes.

"If you got nowhere to go, I can hire you, y'know? You must be pretty strong if you crossed the Mystic Mountains on your own. How 'bout it? Wanna join my army?"

Boy, he sure changed his tune quickly after hearing Mr. Oni's sob story.

Mr. Oni still seems uncomfortable, but once Vampy translates for him, he responds by requesting some time to think about it.

Yeah, that's not the kinda thing you can decide right away.

Not to mention, if he's gonna work for a demon, he'd probably have to learn their language.

He'd have to start there.

"Well, just lemme know if you need anything."

With that, Deadbeat cheerfully takes his leave.

He's kinda presenting himself as a big-brother figure.

I, uh. I don't know how to feel about this.

"What in the world was that?"

Looks like Vampy feels the same way.

At any rate, this means Deadbeat approves of Mr. Oni being here now, so at least he'll be able to keep staying in the mansion without a problem.

"Where to go from here...?"

After Deadbeat leaves, Mr. Oni murmurs to himself, lost in thought.

I guess I'm not the only one thinking about my next move.

Everyone else has their own future to think about, too.

"There's no point worrying about the future, you know."

Correction. I guess one person isn't thinking about that stuff at all.

"You never know what's going to happen next. If you spend all your time worrying about it, you'll never get anywhere, you know? What matters is how you're going to live in the present."

Whoa.

Did Vampy just make a surprisingly deep statement?

Hrmmm. I guess she has a point.

When I lived in the Great Elroe Labyrinth, all I thought about was how to live (or rather survive) from moment to moment, after all.

I mean, I didn't really have time to think about anything else.

Living in the present is important, but I do think it's better to have some idea of what you're going to do once you manage to survive.

Especially for Vampy.

This kid is the only vampire Progenitor in the world, and already crazy powerful at her age.

But she's still a little girl, so I guess she's got plenty of time to think about her future.

Although...the world might not stick around long enough for her to get a chance to grow up.

In the end, I guess no matter how thoroughly you plan for the future, you're still not exempt from the universal rule: Whatever happens, happens.

2 Let's Make Preparations

Time really does fly. It's already been about a year since we started living in the duke's mansion.

Our days have been pretty peaceful aside from Deadbeat's periodic invasions.

After staying in the mansion for six months or so, Mr. Oni enlisted in the demon army with the Demon Lord's help.

I'm sure he has his own reasons for doing things, and he already looks old enough to be independent, so no one really questions it.

Technically he's an infant like Vampy, but since he's a reincarnation, that doesn't count.

If he wants to be an independent adult, I'm certainly not gonna stop him.

He seems to have learned the demon language during his six-month stay in the mansion, too.

Frankly, I wish Vampy would take a few lessons from Mr. Oni on how to be a little more independent.

How's Vampy, you ask? Well, she's driving me nuts.

She's more emotionally unstable than ever, probably thanks to the effects of the Envy skill.

One minute she'll be clinging to me like a kid, then all of a sudden she's mad at me for no apparent reason.

She always seems irritated and won't hesitate to bite people's heads off at the slightest provocation.

Um, figuratively, of course.

I know she's a vampire, but she doesn't actually bite people.

Even Vampy has enough sense not to do that...I hope.

The scary part is, given how she's been acting lately, I wouldn't be surprised if she did start a bloodbath.

The Demon Lord tasked her with picking up the Heresy Resistance skill, but so far it doesn't seem to be having any effect.

Pretty much the only people who can stop her temper tantrums are Mera and me, but Mera's not around right now, so it's become my job to take care of things.

What a pain.

At this point, whenever the maids come running to my room, I just think, *Great, here we go again.*

Luckily, she hasn't caused any major incidents just yet, so for the time being, it's sort of like pacifying a cute kid throwing a fit.

Although her sheer presence has nearly made the maids faint a few times.

Hang in there, maids!

Anyway, aside from minor changes and difficulties like that, my time in the mansion has been fairly peaceful overall.

If you're wondering what I've been doing all this time, I've been working on creating a clone.

I want to make a copy of myself in the vein of my old Egg-Laying skill.

Oh, but obviously, I don't mean I'm trying to literally lay eggs or have babies, okay?

I wouldn't do anything that crazy and X-rated.

Mostly, I've just been making thread, shaping it into a ball, and trying to create a clone inside.

Hmm? What's that?

You say that's not really an egg at all?

Whatever. The details don't matter as long as I get results.

Huh? Am I getting results, you ask?

Heh-heh-heh.

Fine then, I'll just have to show you the fruits of my efforts over the last year!

Take a good look at my very own clone!

Ta-daaaa! Get a load of this adorable creature!

It's a single white spider, sitting in the palm of my hand.

Yes, this lovely little creature is a copy of yours truly!

...Cute, right? Isn't she adorable?

Huh? You want me to quit talking about her cuteness and tell you how strong she is?

...She's cute!

Super-cute, okay?

Come on, just appreciate her cuteness.

...All right, all right. I admit it.

Right now, cuteness is just about all she has going for her.

Is she a clone or just a mini-me? I don't know if she's really worthy of being called a true clone.

Now, since she is technically a copy of me, she can share her senses with me.

Anything my little mini-me sees or hears gets relayed back to me.

But that's really just about all she does. She doesn't have any hidden special features.

Sure, she can bite things and make thread, but none of that is very impressive.

Her thread-making abilities aren't anywhere near as advanced as mine—they're practically on the same level as a normal spider you could find on Earth.

The same goes for her bite. It's not even venomous, so, to be honest, the most it can do is make someone say *ouchie*. It's definitely not strong enough to kill anyone.

I actually think that anyone could kill this spider just by stepping on her.

...What do you think, everyone? This is what I have to show for myself after a year of hard work!

Yeah, yeah, go ahead and laugh!

Grrr. But still, it took a lot of effort to even get this far, okay?

Making a clone from scratch isn't easy, okay?

If you think about it objectively, producing a living thing from a ball of thread is already wild, isn't it?

When you put it that way, it actually sounds pretty cool.

...Even if my creation amounts to nothing more than a cute-yet-useless mini-me!

But look, she has the ability to think independently, Parallel Minds–style, so she definitely has potential.

I just have to hope that she ends up being useful in the future.

So for now, I'm just gonna yeet my little mini-me into another dimension for safekeeping before someone squashes the helpless little thing.

Yeah. I've been using spatial conjuring to store things in an alternate dimension separate from this plane of existence.

There are three major techniques that come to mind when I think of spatial conjuring: teleportation, item box, and dimensional storage.

So this is my take on number three.

My clone-making might not be anything to write home about, but at least my spatial conjuring has noticeably improved.

If it wasn't already obvious from the whole teleportation thing, I clearly have a knack for spatial conjuring.

Ahhh, I'm so talented, it's almost scary!

Except for the cloning thing.

Anyway, I toss that mediocre clone into an alternate dimension.

It's basically a world of my very own creation, where I make the rules.

I can even control the flow of time in there, at least to a certain extent.

So yeah, it's basically a hyperbolic time chamber.

Focus on training in here, okay?

In the alternate dimension, my mini-me gives a little salute with one of its front legs.

As if imitating it, the other clones all salute, too.

Yeah, that's right. Who said I had only one clone?

This storage dimension is practically crawling with them at this point.

They might be weak, but at least they'll have strength in numbers!

...That's my excuse for making so many. The truth is, I kept trying to see if I could produce something stronger, and next thing you know, I wound up with a whole bunch of these small-fry.

Once they grow up, though, I'm sure they'll be super-strong.

So all my efforts haven't been in vain.

They haven't, okay?

I keep telling myself that as I close the door to the storage dimension.

* * *

Anyway, unlike those so-so clones, I've been making pretty decent progress in other areas.

For one thing, spatial conjuring. As you may have guessed from the fact that I can create alternate dimensions now, I've gotten a whole lot better at it.

The speed and accuracy of my teleportation have both improved, and I've developed a slew of new dirty tricks that let me make full use of it.

Frankly, a few of them are so crazy that they might be considered overkill.

So I'm basically all set as far as attack methods go.

My defense, on the other hand, still leaves something to be desired.

I can always teleport away as a last resort, but that won't help me if I get one-hit KO'd by a surprise attack or something.

I've gotten better at using conjuring for physical enhancements, but I still can't bring my defense up to the point where it was before I became a god.

Especially since the effects deactivate if I'm asleep or anything.

The more I think about it, the more I realize how amazing the stats granted by the system were, since it basically provides perpetual body enhancement.

For now, my goal is to catch up to how strong I used to be and figure out how to keep that active all the time.

As it stands, I'm way too vulnerable when I conk out for the night.

I gotta do something to make sure nobody sneaks up and murders me in my sleep.

Not that I foresee that being a problem anytime soon, with the puppet spiders around to guard me.

But still, there's no harm in being careful. I have to take precautions wherever I can.

I'll just keep trying until I figure out a way to do it.

The only problem is, I can't help but feel that simply raising my defense won't be enough to help me in the future.

For instance, high defense won't help you much against my sneaky teleportation attack methods.

And if I can do it, there must be others capable of similar things, as well.

I can't go around assuming that I'm the only one who's special.

Which means I have to come up with a way to deal with attacks that ignore defense.

My teleportation attacks are relatively easy to avoid—you just have to cancel them out.

Planning for anything beyond that would be difficult, mostly because I don't know what else is out there in the first place.

But it's best to assume the worst in these situations.

Now that I know that the system is a crazy-powerful conjuring, I'm starting to think that I should expect the unexpected in this world.

Especially since D can most likely do pretty much anything.

I wouldn't be surprised if she could kill me before I could even realize it.

Scary!

I don't think just raising my defense would be enough to protect me from that.

So what should I do? Well, right now, I'm trying to figure out if I can use egg revival again.

Egg revival is a strategy in which I transfer my consciousness to an egg that I created using the Egg-Laying skill.

Since I was able to use a similar technique to make clones, I'm thinking I might be able to put my actual self into one of those clones, too.

That way, even if my body is mortally wounded, I can still survive.

No reason to fear defense-ignoring attacks once that's all set up again!

But as of right now, those clones are far from perfect.

If I had to transfer myself into a wimpy body that could easily be stomped to death by any random passerby...

...well, that's not a very good idea if I want to live very long.

So I think I could pull it off easily enough, but there's still more work to be done.

Anyway, that's the current state of my work on the fighting side of things. But yes, I've made plenty of other progress, too.

Most importantly, the Evil Eyes.

I've been practicing seeing through things by doing everything with my eyes closed for a while, so now I can do it without even thinking about it.

Which means that I currently have my eyes closed by default.

Now I can't accidentally make eye contact with someone and get gawked at!

Not that I ever made a habit of looking people in the eye in the first place.

Huh? Why, you ask?

Well, you normies might not understand this, but us shut-ins have a really hard time just making eye contact with people.

And holding eye contact while talking to someone is practically impossible.

I know that sounds pretty pathetic, but now all that experience avoiding eye contact has actually come in handy for keeping people from noticing my freaky eyes.

On top of that, since I can see through solid objects now, I'll never turn a corner and crash into someone ever again.

Not that I was really at risk for that stuff in the first place, since I barely ever leave my room!

But still, x-ray vision is pretty handy.

I mean, that's basically every pubescent boy's dream superpower!

I can peek at people's undies anytime I want!

Not that I'd ever want to.

...Hmm? It sounds like I'm not making very good use of this ability, you say?

Th-th-th-that's SO not true!

I'm using the crap out of it, all right?!

Besides, now I see just like when I had Clairvoyance and stuff!

And I can also re-create Evil Eye effects, so now I have super-long-distance Evil Eye attacks.

I still can't use techniques that are directly connected to the system, like Cursed Evil Eye or Sealing Evil Eye, but I can re-create the effects of Inert Evil Eye and Warped Evil Eye without a problem.

Annihilating Evil Eye? That one's dangerous, so I haven't tried it.

But still, if I use Inert Evil Eye to stop an enemy from moving and Warped Evil Eye to twist 'em in space, I can beat most opponents long before they ever get near me.

You could even say that I'm steadily regaining the power I had before I was deified.

I haven't had a chance to test those powers for real, although I'm not sure if that's a good thing or a bad thing.

Hrm. That means it's peaceful, which is a good thing, right?

But still, I dunno… This "peace" has a very temporary feel to it.
Like, there is some serious unrest hanging in the air right now.
The entirety of the demon territory is practically crackling with tension.
The Demon Lord has been conscripting tons of citizens lately.
Demons have a way smaller population than humans, so they don't have a lot of people to spare, since population equals productivity.
With a limited population, there's inevitably lots of different places that end up shorthanded.
And yet, the Demon Lord keeps stealing people from their already diminutive workforce so they can fight in her army. Needless to say, her approval ratings have hit rock bottom.
But the citizens can't rebel against her.
I mean, she's the DEMON LORD.
That makes her a pretty big deal to demons. Like, the biggest deal.
And even if they tried, I doubt they'd stand a chance against this particular Demon Lord.
No matter how united they might be, I can't imagine them ever beating her.
She's strong enough to cause a natural disaster purely by accident.
But most of the demons don't fully comprehend how strong the Demon Lord truly is.
So there are bad feelings all around, and they're reaching a boiling point.
It might not be long before some demons might just try to defeat the Demon Lord and put someone else in charge.
I'm pretty sure there's gonna be a coup d'état soon.
Especially since they've already gathered enough military strength to start an armed revolution.
How do I know that when I'm always holed up in my room, you ask?
Why, espionage, of course.
Since my survivability and battle readiness are on the rise, my next project's gotta be gathering intel.
In war, whoever has the most information has the upper hand.
What are the enemy's numbers?
Where are they located?
Once you know those things, you can plan accordingly.

And if you don't have any idea what the enemy is doing, you're already at a disadvantage.

Put another way, simply being aware of things like that gives you a massive edge.

Knowledge is power, as they say.

So I've been hard at work gathering info.

Where am I getting my information from, you ask?

From my little mini-mes!

Since they're spiders and all, they can walk on walls and ceilings, and being palm size, they can easily be snuck into all kinds of places.

And everything these mini-mes hear and see is relayed to me in real time.

Could anything be more perfect for espionage?! I don't think so!

The only problem is that they're so weak that they're very easily destroyed if someone spots them.

You know how I said they'd die if someone stepped on them?

Well, I was speaking from experience...

But even if they do get killed, I personally don't feel any pain.

And on top of that, no one would suspect that such a small spider was spying on anyone, so it's not like people get paranoid if they find them. At most, they'll just assume it's some new kind of monster or something.

Which means I can replace them as many times as necessary.

Not that it hurts to avoid being found.

Anyway, I've dispatched my mass-produced mini-mes out all over the place.

And just like that, all kinds of information started pouring in.

Everything from rumors among peasants to secret conversations between higher-ups.

I wouldn't say I know *everything* that's going on in the demon territory, but I've obtained a pretty substantial amount of information at this point.

Ideally, I'd like to send clones into the human territories and elf villages and stuff, too, but I can't do that.

I figured it'd be too dangerous right now.

The human territory is ruled by the Church, and the elves are ruled by Potimas.

My poor little mini-mes would be way out of their league.

Besides, the only reason I can use them so freely in the demon territory is because their existence as spider monsters won't necessarily connect them to the Demon Lord or me.

Even if they're found, no one would suspect the Demon Lord or me of spying.

But if Potimas or the Church finds a strange little spider, they'll immediately know what's up.

And then they'll come looking to destroy us.

And the poor little mini-mes will be mercilessly crushed without even gathering any information...

So in order to prevent that from happening, I'm going to hold off on assigning the clones any surveillance missions in the human and elf territories until they're at least skilled enough to avoid being seen or get away safely if they are spotted.

Although I guess I could always let them get caught on purpose and practically declare that we're spying on the enemy just to make them paranoid.

But that's pretty risky, and it'd mean losing a perfectly good clone, so I don't really want to do that.

Even these tiny mini-mes don't come free, you know. I have to provide the proper materials to make their bodies, and it takes time and energy for them to hatch.

I get my supplies for that in the Great Elroe Labyrinth, where the white spiders provide me with plenty of monster corpses.

It's not like I wanna eat monsters anymore, but they're still a plentiful food source that's rich in nutrients!

So be sure to eat a heaping helping of monster meat every day, kids!

Just watch out for poison!

Eat up, little mini-mes, eat up.

Come to think of it, they're still technically a part of me, so it *does* mean that I'm also eating monsters in a way.

At least since they're in spider form, eating monsters doesn't seem to gross them out.

If they were human, I have to imagine they'd go on strike due to the sheer grossness of the food I'm providing them. So that's a near miss.

They're not spiders for any particular reason.

That's just the way they came out naturally. If I tried, I'm sure I could give them human bodies instead.

But if I make them without anything particular in mind, they come out as spiders.

Does this mean that deep in my heart of hearts, I still identify as a spider?

I'm not sure.

But it's not particularly a problem, so there's no need to think about it too deeply, I'd say.

No matter what, it doesn't change who I am on the inside.

Compared to finding out that I'm actually just D's substitute, this is no big deal at all, right?

Besides, human bodies are super-inconvenient!

Why do they only have two legs?!

Obviously, eight legs are gonna be way more stable!

I can barely keep my balance on two.

And since my body-enhancement conjuring is unstable right now, running is a huge pain, too.

It's like my acceleration can hit full throttle, but my brakes don't work.

If I had eight legs, I could find a way to brace myself, but two legs? Forget it.

So I got to wondering if there was anything I could do about it, and what do you know, I found a solution.

While I was busy worrying about the whole situation, I suddenly noticed that my lower body had turned into that of a spider.

I essentially reverted to arachne form.

I don't really know how it happened exactly, but if I just kinda strain my lower body like this—HRRRGH!—I can turn into an arachne at will.

My body is arbitrary as all hell…

As a sidenote, I thought that if I can transform my lower body, then in theory, I should be able to transform my whole body however I want, but it seems like I can only shift into arachne form.

I guess I won't get to yell *This isn't even my final form* anytime soon.

Technically, this arachne transformation is probably some kind of conjuring, but the rune construction or whatever seems to happen subconsciously, like when I make thread. So I don't really know how I'm doing it.

I guess conjuring is a pretty mysterious art, since I can do things like this without even understanding how it works. But I guess it's not any weirder than the concept of magic and conjuring in the first place.

At any rate, I guess that means I have some amount of close-combat capability.

I don't think that's going to happen very often, and in fact I don't really want it to, but it doesn't hurt to have a physical form I can reliably escape in.

I can transform into an arachne in an instant, so as long as I don't get taken out before I know what hit me, I should be able to deal with most things.

Hmm? What am I doing about underwear?

Oh, well, I'm not wearing any, of course.

NOT! What kind of idiot do you take me for?!

Of course I'm wearing underwear.

I just store them away in an alternate dimension when I transform.

I'm not giving any sexy fan service when I transform, thank you very much.

I'm as thoroughly censored as a Sunday-morning anime!

And I've got ways to counter x-ray vision, too, by the way.

I'm always prepared for anything you might throw at me, especially if it's something I can do myself!

Heh-heh-heh.

If you want to sneak a peek at me in some sort of lewd scenario, you'll have to try a lot harder than that!

...Although I hope I don't run into anyone who actually tries to do such a thing.

Serious opponents only, please.

"I'm coming in."

"How about you don't?"

As usual, Deadbeat invites himself to our tea party, and Vampy promptly invites him to leave.

Normally, they'd launch right into sniping at each other from there, but today I actually have some business with Deadbeat, so I'm gonna need them to give it a rest.

Before Vampy can open fire, I raise a hand to stop her.

She stares at me, shocked by my unusual reaction.

Deadbeat looks surprised, too, but then he quickly smirks triumphantly at Vampy.

That childishness is not a good look, if you ask me.

In response, Vampy… Uh-oh. She's scowling and grinding her teeth something fierce.

I've never actually heard that scraping sound come out of someone's mouth so loudly.

Uh-oh. Now her lip's bleeding, too.

That Envy skill is super-scary!

Now, now. Calm down, will ya?

Come on—you're even freaking Deadbeat out now.

At this rate, it's only a matter of time before disaster strikes, so I'd better wrap things up quickly and get Deadbeat outta here.

So without further ado, I hand him a letter.

It's made of my thread and contains my most earnest feelings.

It's not a love letter or anything like that, though.

Deadbeat looks kinda happy, so I feel a little bad, but…it does say "to the Demon Lord" right there on the envelope, y'know?

Ah, he must've noticed that. Now he looks disappointed.

"What the hell is this? You want me to give it to her?"

Yes, exactly. You really can do it if you try, Deadbeat!

I nod an affirmative, and his shoulders slump.

Sorry, pal.

For using you as an errand boy and for getting your hopes up.

But he's always bothering us, so I feel like I'm well within my rights.

Anyway, go on and deliver that now.

Shoo, shoo!

I wave my hand at Deadbeat to hurry, and he trudges out of the room, slouching sadly.

Well, that should make Vampy feel better.

"Don't go giving him the wrong idea like that."

Or not, I guess?!

Vampy's voice is low and dangerous, like something rising out of the depths of hell.

No infant girl should ever sound like that.

Look, Sael and Fiel are clinging to each other and trembling with fear!

Riel?

She's just grinning like an idiot, as usual!

Now, now. Calm down, will ya?

I somehow manage to pacify the sullen bloodsucker, and our tea party comes to an end.

Ugh. I managed to hand off my letter for the Demon Lord, but I feel like I made Vampy's temper even worse in the process.

I thought having her raise the Heresy Resistance skill would work in the long run, but maybe we need to take some more drastic measures.

Vampy tends to get obsessively attached to the people she knows well.

Especially Mera, to an extreme degree.

We've traveled the world together, but we didn't actually meet a lot of other people.

In other words, Vampy doesn't have many friends.

So she gets extra attached to—and dependent on—the few people who are close to her.

Not that I'm one to talk, but I do think Vampy needs to meet some new faces.

I mean, I'm a strong, independent woman who doesn't need friends, but Vampy's just a kid.

Still, maybe that's none of my business.

Vampy will be sent off to the academy soon enough anyway.

I guess that means I'm not the only one making plans for the future.

Interlude THE SLACKER DEMON LORD

As I relax in my office in the Demon Lord's castle, my feet kicked up on the desk, the sound of thunderous footsteps reaches my ears.

They storm right up to my room and burst through the door without so much as a knock.

"It's pretty poor manners to barge into a lady's room without even knocking, don't you think?"

"You call yourself a lady? Yeah, right. What a joke."

It's Balto's younger brother, Bloe, who's not even attempting to hide his disdain for me, as usual.

He's mad that I showed up out of nowhere and assumed the throne instead of his big brother.

But Balto has been perfectly cooperative with me and hasn't made any attempts to rebel. So I guess I'll generously let his baby brother off the hook for his extreme rudeness.

I'm not mad. I'm sooo not mad, okay?

"So. You must've come here for a reason, yes? Balto's not here right now, in case you haven't noticed."

Bloe hates me, so he avoids me as much as possible.

So if he's here now, he must need something from me, or else he's looking for his brother.

"I got sent here to give this to you, all right?"

Bloe stomps up to my desk and raises his hand as if to throw something down on it with all his might, then changes his mind at the last second and places it there gently.

What is this guy playing at?

"Um, okay. Thanks, I guess."

"Mm-hmm."

His voice is lacking its usual fire.

Was there a recent shocking development or something?

Well, I guess it's not like I care how Bloe is feeling.

Looking at the object on my desk, I discover it's an envelope containing a letter.

As soon as I pick it up, I can feel that it's not ordinary paper. Judging by the smooth texture, White must've made it herself.

Now that I know who sent the letter, I open it and skim its contents.

"For real?" I mutter without thinking.

The several sheets of paper in the envelope contain the names of ringleaders who are plotting a rebellion, the head count and composition of their forces, the reach of their influence, how well supplied they are, and other detailed information.

I have no idea how in the world she found all this out or why.

White always manages to blow my expectations out of the water.

"Bloe."

"Hunh?"

As Bloe starts to leave the room, I call out to him.

Incidentally, only a few scant seconds have passed from the moment Bloe handed me the letter to the moment I finished reading it.

So from Bloe's point of view, he handed me the letter and turned to leave, and I stopped him almost immediately.

I'm only able to pull that off thanks to the Thought Super-Acceleration skill, but Bloe doesn't know that, so to him it probably seems like I stopped him without bothering to read the letter first.

Not that I care what he thinks.

"Read this."

Naturally, my demand makes a vein pop in his head, but that's none of my concern.

"Listen, you!"

"Once you've read it, bring it to Balto. And give him a message for me. 'Take care of it.'" Ignoring his blustering, I carry on with my commands. "Demon Lord's orders."

"Tch!"

Bloe grumbles a lot, but he does as he's told. I guess he's a good worker deep down.

As Bloe reluctantly reads the letter, his expression slowly changes from grouchy to utterly serious.

Although his brows stay furrowed the whole time.

"Is this true? You sure?"

Bloe looks doubtful.

But the sheer level of detail in the letter leaves little room for doubt.

As hard as it might be to believe, there's so much proof that it's all but impossible to deny.

Although I'm guessing Bloe is even more amazed because it was White who gave him this letter to deliver to me.

From his perspective, White probably seems like a secluded princess, not a combatant of any kind. She's always holed up in the duke's mansion, so he's not exactly wrong.

In fact, even I don't know how White managed to gather all this vital information, when she never leaves the mansion, or what motivated her to do it.

And if it's a mystery to me, it must be even more confusing to Bloe.

"..."

Bloe walks out without another word, still staring at the letter.

Dude, at least say something.

I *am* technically the Demon Lord, aka your boss.

See, this is his problem. Even if he's a good worker for the most part, he lacks common sense about stuff like this.

No wonder he's not popular with the ladies.

Now that Bloe's gone, I put my feet back up on the desk.

To be honest, I've got nothing to do, so I'm super-bored.

Well, I guess there's plenty of things I *could* be doing if I wanted to, but it's more effective if I don't actually do those things myself, I think.

There are lots of guys like Bloe who despise me, even if most of them aren't actively plotting to revolt.

Especially 'cause I've shown my true strength to only a handful of people, like Balto.

The demon race is a meritocracy. So of course the Demon Lord has to be pretty powerful.

And this power isn't limited to just battle, either.

Balto's political prowess is acknowledged as a kind of power, too, for example.

And the person who's chosen as Demon Lord is usually a well-known, influential demon.

Someone who's been popular since before they became the Demon Lord.

Most people are satisfied with that kind of choice.

But I'm not even a demon, and I'm not very well-known.

Yeah, I guess I'm decently famous as the oldest of the Ancient Divine Beasts, but nobody would draw that connection between me and the legends unless I spread the word myself.

To most demons, it probably seems like some random person of totally unknown strength and origin just showed up out of nowhere and became the Demon Lord.

It's only natural that there's gonna be tons of people angry about that.

And ultimately, that anger fuels the forces White found moving in secret.

So why don't I just show them how strong I am? Because I don't want anyone to flee.

It's one thing to rule with fear, but if you add overwhelming military might to that equation, then it's just going too far.

In theory, I'm strong enough to crush the entirety of the demon race all by myself.

And if push comes to shove, I'm willing to do exactly that.

What would the demon race do if they knew all that?

If they'd simply obey me to save their hides, that'd be perfectly acceptable.

But if they run away, that's a problem.

See, turning the tables on would-be rebels who come after me is a piece of cake.

I'm strong enough to do that without breaking a sweat.

But if they scatter and flee in every direction, I'm screwed.

I don't have the time or the manpower to chase them all down, round them up, and dispose of them.

It might be possible if I used my remaining queens and other offspring, but then the whole demons-versus-humans war would be over.

It'd just be me destroying the demons and then me versus humans.

I'd like to make that a last resort.

In order to go up against the likes of Dustin and Potimas, I want to use the demon race as a breakwater and as sacrificial pawns.

Which is why I want to hide my true power from the demon race as much as possible, while still ensuring that they obey my orders.

The fastest way to do that is to show my true strength only to powerful demons like Balto and Agner and bring them to heel.

If they're following my orders, then their subordinates will automatically obey me as well. Like Bloe, for instance.

Of course, there's still bound to be some people who are discontented about the current state of affairs.

When that anger reaches a breaking point—meaning, when there's a rebellion or something—I'll just show them a small measure of my power, enough to silence any demons who were doubtful.

The plan is to let the dissenters gather into a revolutionary army and then purge them all in one fell swoop.

Once I've wiped them out, it'll prove to everyone else that I'm worthy of standing at the top.

I just have to be careful not to go overboard and scare people off.

It might be hard to strike just the right balance...

Or at least, that's what I was thinking, until White laid the whole secret revolution bare before I even noticed it was happening.

Now we might crush them before I even get a chance to take the stage.

'Cause now we know exactly who and where they are, how strong they are, and how to beat them.

And since I got that information so far in advance, I can launch a preemptive strike whenever I want.

With everything laid out so clearly, you'd have to be the worst commander ever to lose this fight.

Now, even if I wanted to show off my power, I'll just seem like I'm full of myself for showing off when victory's already assured!

What is White thinking, being so thorough that it actually messes up my plans?

Now I don't have anything to do at all.

Ughhh, talk about a pain.

...I'm not sitting around doing nothing by choice, all right?

There's a very good reason I'm not working. If I go around taking care of things without justification, it'll just make the demons resent me even more, so I really have no choice but to dump it all on Balto.

I mean, I played the part of the absentee Demon Lord so well that if I start meddling now, it'll just make things worse.

I'm not slacking off because I *want* to.

I'm not. I swear.

3 Let's Take Action

It's been three days since I sent a letter to the Demon Lord by way of Deadbeat, letting her know that there were signs of a rebellion brewing.

A task force to take care of the rebels has already been formed and dispatched.

Damn, that was fast!

Should you really be making such a snap decision about this?!

Like, doesn't it take more time to prepare for military action or whatever?

I used my clones to find out what was going on, and the answer is: They're pushing themselves quite a bit.

Apparently, the Demon Lord dumped this whole situation on Balto, and he's decided to deal with it by using blitzkrieg tactics.

The rebellion is taking their time gathering supporters and supplies in order to avoid suspicion, so I guess Balto wants to crush them before they finish amassing everything they need.

On top of that, the task force is going to great lengths to conceal the fact that they're getting ready to deploy, all so we can catch the rebels by surprise.

Balto must be planning for a quick, decisive battle.

Well, I guess in his position, he doesn't have much of a choice.

He's supposed to be getting troops ready for the upcoming war against the humans right now, so he can't afford to lose any manpower.

The longer he takes, the more time the rebels have to recruit, so he's better off nipping it in the bud as soon as possible to minimize the losses.

If he's lucky, that might be enough to scatter the remaining rebels before they can concentrate their forces.

But are they really gonna be all right if they attack in such a hurry? What about supplies and logistics?

I know what you're thinking. Who needs that crap in a world with stats and skills, right?!

But war in this world actually follows the same basic logic as Earth, at least to a certain extent.

I mean, these are still flesh-and-blood people fighting, y'know?

They gotta eat or they'll starve, and they gotta sleep or they'll collapse.

Sure, there's stuff like the Exhaustion Nullification skill, but only a handful of exceptional individuals have those kinds of abilities.

If you're tired or hungry, you won't be able to fight very well no matter how high your stats are.

Besides, the stats don't actually make as big a difference as you might think.

Whether it's humans or demons, most of them have stats under 1,000.

In fact, as far as I can tell, people who have even one stat that breaks 1,000 are seen as super-legendary fighters.

It really makes you realize how crazy the Demon Lord's faction is for having several people whose stats easily break 10,000.

So anyway, triple-digit stats are pretty much the norm for your average soldier, which means they can't do anything crazy impressive.

Yeah, they can wear a full set of armor and still run at top speed, but that's basically the best they manage.

You don't really see many people shattering the ground with a single punch, scorching their surroundings to ash with one spell, or any of that stuff you might see in overpowered fantasy stories.

I guess if there were tons of people with those kinds of awe-inspiring powers, fortresses and stuff would lose all meaning, huh?

The fact that fortresses exist means that they're enough to defend against most things, or no one would bother building them.

Although I guess there are some fortresses like this one that have their defenses bolstered with skills and stuff, so they're not really comparable to the fortifications you'd find back on Earth.

Hmm. Lemme think.

I guess if you consider the benefits of stats and equipment and exotic mounts and stuff, warfare here might be around the same level as, like, World War I or so.

Bows and arrows in this world are fairly comparable to guns, and you could probably consider magic as a kind of artillery.

Although, like I said, there are differences, like the defensive power of fortresses and stuff.

Huh? That all sounds pretty impressive to you?

I dunno, it's pretty bottom-tier stuff from where I'm standing.

I mean, think about who I've been hanging out with, will ya?

You've got the Demon Lord, who can cause a natural disaster with her bare hands, and a bunch of other powerhouses who wreak mass destruction with the aftershocks of their attacks alone.

Compared to those beasts, being able to produce artillery-level power with your hands or whatever is small potatoes.

But anyway, to get back to the main subject, war in this world does have certain similarities with war on Earth.

From that perspective, it's obvious that this attack is pretty rushed.

It'd be one thing if they'd been preparing in advance, but when they're deploying out of the blue, it seems kinda crazy.

In war, as in any battle, it's very important to prepare in advance.

Gathering troops, honing their abilities, acquiring equipment, and so on.

And then you've gotta come up with a strategy so that you can maximize their potential on the battlefield.

Sure, stats and skills can cover for shortcomings in those areas to a certain extent, but if you want your troops to perform their best, you've gotta make sure they stay supplied and rested.

The lightning-strike strategy Balto's devised is going to take a toll on those soldiers. Will they be all right?

Well, I guess he wouldn't give the go-ahead unless he figured it would work, but still.

Hrmmm.

Maybe I should check things out again.

The rebel army is currently gathering in a town north of the demon capital.

The soldiers are disguised as civilians to avoid suspicion, entering the town a few people at a time.

And they're bringing in supplies and equipment slowly and carefully, too.

Normally, it would be incredibly challenging to detect their movements.

The rebels probably figured that by the time anyone noticed, they'd have assembled a sizable army and already be on the move before anyone realized what was coming.

Damn. I'm pretty impressive, figuring all that out in advance.

Thanks to my amazing powers of observation, now we have the initiative to make the first move while the rebel army is still preparing.

So it stands to reason that we'd want to attack as soon as possible in order to make the most of that advantage.

Thinking about it that way, I guess this blitzkrieg strategy isn't so bad.

The only problem is whether or not we can actually win with it.

The northern town's defenses aren't particularly formidable.

Most demon towns, or really just all towns in this world, are generally set up to ward off monsters, not people.

That makes sense, since it's typically monsters who threaten people more often than not.

You've gotta be prepared for that or your home will get wiped out.

There are exceptions, of course, but the majority of towns are equipped with defenses to match whatever monsters appear in their area.

The monsters that appear around the rebel town are mostly small to medium animal-type monsters.

They're relatively weak and can serve as food, so hunting them is one of the town's main sources of income.

If anything, they're often attacking more than defending…

Anyway, that means their defenses aren't particularly strong, just the bare minimum to prevent roving monsters from getting in.

So there's no fear of them holing up to weather a siege or anything.

If they try to pull that, it'll be easy enough to break through with a direct assault.

No need to worry about them dragging things out while the revolutionary army assembles in another area.

My hastily acquired knowledge of military strategy says that besieging a well-prepared enemy takes tons of time, and the attackers usually need way more manpower than the defense to have any chance of winning.

Not having to worry about that is a big advantage.

If it's just gonna be a field battle, then the most important factors are the number of soldiers and the skills of the commander.

The soldiers' abilities?

That's important, too, but since they're all demons, there's not gonna be that big of a difference.

Since both sides are the same race and lead the same kinds of lives, their stats are naturally gonna be similar.

Of course, if there was a massive gap in stats, then that could decide the fight before it even begins, but there's only a handful of people with those kinds of stats.

And even those guys only have stats that max out around 1,000.

There's only so much you can do with those kinds of stats.

That means you usually never see whole armies getting crushed by a single person with some unbelievable power or anything like that.

With these kinds of constraints, victory purely comes down to the number of soldiers on each side and the smarts of their respective commanders.

In this case, we're sending out about three times the amount of soldiers as the opponent.

And their commander is Balto.

However, it seems Deadbeat is the one who's actually gonna be leading the charge.

I can't say that doesn't make me a little nervous, but given their overwhelming advantage in numbers, it's pretty unlikely that they would lose.

Balto will be there, too, so he won't let things get out of hand.

My only other concerns are what kind of toll the forced march will have on the soldiers and how reliably they can secure supplies.

They're probably bringing food with them, but I'm guessing they'll only have the bare minimum so that they can move quickly. It probably won't be enough.

And I haven't seen any indication that there are any plans for reinforcements.

Are they really gonna be okay?

You can't fight on an empty stomach, you know!

But when I think about it, I guess that might not be too much of a problem, especially considering where they're gonna be attacking.

I mean, the town to the north makes their living hunting monsters for food.

In other words, there's food all over the place.

If they can secure food on-site, there's no need to lug a bunch of heavy supplies around.

Come to think of it, I guess that was the case in a lot of the Earth's history, too. Pillaging and war often go hand in hand.

...When you think about it that way, war is pretty tragic.

Huh? That's rich coming from someone who eats her slain foes, you say?

Look, that's a totally different situation.

Anyway, I assume Balto's got countermeasures in mind when it comes to dealing with the fatigue of the soldiers, so I don't need to worry about that too much.

Hrmmm?

Wait, does that mean they actually stand a pretty good chance of winning?

Well, they've got plenty of advance information thanks to me, so I guess they'd actually have to be shockingly incompetent to lose in this situation.

Not to mention, three very unusual individuals have snuck into Balto's ranks.

Ael, Mera, and Mr. Oni.

What are you guys doing?

I mean, ever since Vampy sealed Mr. Oni's Wrath skill, his strength is limited to what he can control, so he probably isn't all that out of place among the demon soldiers.

And I guess Mera's safe, too?

No, no, he's definitely out.

Mera's been secretly training to catch up with Vampy, and because he's a vampire and all that, he's a whole lot stronger than your average human.

He was even able to hold his own against Mr. Oni in his Wrath state, so that puts him above most demons, too.

And when you throw Ael, a literal monster, into the mix?

Okay, yeah. It would actually be harder for them to lose at this point.

Great. Nothing to worry about.

...Yeah, right. If anything, I'm even more worried than before.

I guess you could say I'm bugging out a little.

Except technically, spiders aren't bugs.

Okay, that's not that important right now. All that matters is that my spider senses are tingling, warning me that something's wrong.

It's never a good idea to ignore your instincts.

The whole reason I was contemplating Balto's troops' chances of victory in the first place is because I had a bad feeling about it.

My conclusion is that they've basically got this in the bag... But for some reason, I'm still uneasy.

Am I missing something here?

No... At least I don't think so, but you can never be too sure.

I've been gathering information by sending out my clones as spies.

They're palm-size mini-mes, so they can sneak into all kinds of tight spaces and overhear all sorts of things.

If nobody's around, they can even look through documents and stuff.

They're just not very strong.

They're still so weak that if anyone finds them, they could squish my little ones with a single step.

So the priority has been to stay hidden while carefully collecting information.

It doesn't actually damage me at all if one of my clones gets crushed, but I'd hate to see them go to waste after I worked so hard to make them.

Besides, I've managed to get plenty of intel without taking many risks, so I'm fairly satisfied with that.

But...what if something slipped past my information network?

If the rebellion is hiding some huge secret so thoroughly that I didn't even catch wind of it, and it turns out to be a game-changing superweapon?

Logically speaking, it's doubtful the rebels would have such a convenient trump card.

Judging by the numbers alone, Balto's troops have a 99.9 percent chance of winning.

Still, I can't just ignore this gut feeling.

My best bet is to watch over them from the shadows, since it's not like I have anything better to do.

All right, I should get going, then.

Oh, wait a second.

I've gotta tell Vampy that I'm leaving first.

She gets reeeal mad when I disappear without saying anything.

"Excuse me? What do you mean, you're leaving? Don't be ridiculous. Obviously, I'm coming with you."

I have no idea how she reached this conclusion. Could someone please explain it to me in a clear and concise essay format?

Vampy promptly picks up her beloved broadsword and stands next to me expectantly, as if her coming along is a done deal.

Ummm.

Now what?

Honestly, I don't know what's gonna go down, so I'd rather not take Vampy with me, buuut...

"Given the timing of this little trip, you're obviously heading to wherever this so-called rebel army is gathering, right? Merazophis is going to be there as well, so there's no reason for me *not* to go."

Wait a minute. Vampy saw right through me?!

Since when is she smart enough for that?!

Hmm, I guess it's not like she was ever *not* smart...

But still, I can't help but feel that she figured out my plans based on some kind of animal instinct, not by reaching that conclusion through rational thought. Can you blame me for thinking that, though?

Besides, her excuse for feeling entitled to go along is still pretty stupid.

She's coming just because Mera's there, too...?

Um, it's kind of a pain if you come along for such a stupid reason...

"What? Is there some reason I can't come along? A reason you have to go chasing after Merazophis without taking me with you? Hmm?"

Eek!

Excuse me, Miss Vampy, do you know how dilated your pupils are right now?

Don't look at me with that horror-movie expression! You're freaking me out!

All right, fine! You win! I'll take you with me!

As I frantically convey my surrender with various gestures, Vampy finally seems satisfied and resumes packing.

Phew.

This damn homicidal, lovesick, preteen vampire.

C'mon, rein it in. That's too many weird traits in one person.

Besides, it's not like anything would ever happen between Mera and me.

If she reacts like this to *me*, I'd hate to think what she might do if some unfamiliar woman tried to get close to him.

As far as I can tell, nothing like that is going on right now, but who knows what might happen in the future?

I mean, Mera's kind of a catch.

He's strong, has a good personality, and he's easy on the eyes to boot.

If you just ignore the fact that he's a vampire, he's basically the perfect man, right?

Aside from coming with some major baggage in the form of a crazy little girl who will try to murder you if you get anywhere near him!

Poor Mera. He could be popular in theory, but that's probably the worst thing that could happen.

I'd rather not see any bloodshed as a result of Envy's side effects.

Ugh. But I guess I should be more worried about my current situation than long-term stuff like that right now.

If I'm going to bring Vampy, then I'll have to bring the other puppet spiders, too.

They are technically supposed to guard me and Vampy, after all.

Hrmmm. Well, in that case, we should be fine as long as nothing totally crazy happens.

I mean the reason we're going in the first place is because of my baseless instinct that something bad might happen...

So that we can be there to help if it turns out to be true.

Really, it's just as likely that nothing's going to happen at all.

There's no harm in being cautious, but I guess there's no point in being *too* cautious, either.

If something DOES happen, it's every beastie for themselves.

Vampy's the one who insisted on coming along.

Of course, I'll keep an eye out to try to prevent anything like that from going down.

Also, I don't wanna rain on her parade while she's busy packing, but we're not actually leaving yet, okay?

I've got the overpowered method of teleporting whenever I want.

We still have a few more days before Balto's troops reach the northern town that's serving as the rebel army's base.

I fully intend to relax until then, all right?

So fast-forward: Balto and his troops should be arriving sometime tomorrow. Meanwhile, we've already reached the northern town with the help of teleportation.

I decided to come a day early to give us time to conduct some preliminary investigations and stuff.

So why didn't I get here sooner, you ask?

Well, my clones have already done most of the investigating for me, y'see?

We're really only here just in case something totally unforeseen happens.

It's my completely baseless gut feeling, and that's about it.

I figure we might as well take it easy.

So we've been wandering around sightseeing in the town, by which I mostly mean scouting. And boy, is there a lot of activity.

Well, I guess I can't blame them, since there's a small army approaching their town right now.

I'm sure the rebels figured they'd be the ones conducting a surprise attack, so they never would've imagined that they'd find themselves on the receiving end when they're not even done assembling yet.

Now they're busting their butts trying to ready the town for battle.

I guess they're planning on turtling up for a siege, then.

That's a little unexpected. How are you gonna hole up in a place with such weak defenses?

Well, I *thought* they were weak anyway.

But I was forgetting that this is still basically a fantasy world.

They've made a whole ring of walls frighteningly fast with Earth Magic, surrounding the northern town completely.

Not only that, but the walls are well-built, on par with modern architecture back on Earth.

It's an amazing castle, constructed overnight, more or less. Even Hideyoshi would be impressed.

It's purely for defense, though, so I guess it's not as fancy as the historic castles of Japan.

Anyway, they've dispatched their speediest horses to the surrounding areas, telling the other rebels to gather in the northern town ASAP.

Looks like there's gonna be a showdown.

But since this is an unexpected development, they're working their earth mages half to death, so I wouldn't exactly say they're fully prepared.

For one thing, the soldiers seem ready to run away at the drop of a hat.

The townspeople, who weren't informed about any of this, are even more distressed.

They don't have any connection to the rebels, y'know?

Surprise! A rebellion was using your town as their base of operations, and now the Demon Lord's army is coming to destroy them!

Yeah, talk about a shocking discovery.

You can't blame them for freaking out about what's going to happen to them.

But it's not like this town just randomly became the rebel base. The lord of the town is actually a rebel leader.

That's right. The truth is out: The leader of the rebellion is the lord of this town!

Say whaaaat?!

Yeah, okay, it's not actually all that surprising.

You'd have to be either an important big shot or a total idiot to try to seriously consider overthrowing the Demon Lord: the very symbol of the demon race.

Fortunately, it's the former in this case.

Well, it's the latter if you know the whole story, but for demons who aren't aware of the Demon Lord's true strength, of course they're gonna be tempted to rebel against her plans.

The demon race is barely getting by as is, and now the Demon Lord's declaring war on humanity.

If you're a town leader, of course you won't just roll over and be like, *Okay, sounds good.*

A lord has a responsibility to protect their lands and people, after all.

While gathering information around the demon territory, I've discovered that high-class demons—the nobles, basically—are generally not corrupt at all.

That doesn't apply to all of them, of course, but compared to humans, there are way more nobles abiding by the principle of noblesse oblige and properly fulfilling their duties toward the less fortunate.

That's got a lot to do with the meritocracy of the demon race.

See, demons don't get to perpetually keep their noble rank.

If their behavior is deemed improper, their land will be stripped from them in no time at all.

So demon nobles have to actually act accordingly: carrying out their duties, raising their children properly, and so on.

The latter is so that their children don't end up getting the family land confiscated due to lack of a proper upbringing once the current generation retires.

As long as they get their kids a gifted education from a young age, which is usually affordable because of their resources, it should be easy enough to raise an upstanding adult.

And an upstanding adult is less likely to get the family chased off their land.

So for demons, passing down power and ability to their heirs is more important than blood inheritance.

Which means most demon nobles are pretty decent, since they're careful not to raise fools.

By that logic, the lord of this northern town is bound to be a pretty upstanding and dutiful person, too.

In point of fact, he was doing excellent work up until now.

His rebel army was assembling stealthily and quietly, at least until I uncovered the whole shebang and squealed on them.

As soon as he found out the authorities were coming, he made a snap decision to turn the northern town into a fortress.

So he has the influence to gather rebels from all over the land to his banner and the flexibility to make quick, calm judgments as the situation changes.

Talk about excellence.

Well, excellent except for the part where he was stupid enough to pick a fight with the Demon Lord... No, I shouldn't poke fun.

But, uh...he's almost certainly screwed now.

I mean, Balto's got Ael in his army.

Let's not forget, she's a beast whose stats are in the 10,000s.

Walls made out of Earth Magic? To Ael, those are practically thin sheets of paper.

Quite frankly, she could destroy this entire town all by herself.

Strategy and battle tactics fall apart in the face of that kind of strength.

When the difference in power is that insurmountable, it doesn't really matter how excellent your commander might be.

I'm sure the Demon Lord just sent her along to be on the safe side, but, like, this is beyond extreme.

Especially when there are no less than three individuals with that overwhelming level of power in the same place at the same time!

And if you count Vampy and me, multiply that by infinity!

This is just overkill, then another layer of overkill on top of that.

Yeah, I'm not even really making sense anymore, but you get the idea.

And don't you dare say *What idea?* to me right now.

Either way, we just have to hope that nothing happens that would justify sending in Overkill Squad.

How's this gonna play out? I wonder.

"So it begins."

We're sitting in our room at the inn, having a leisurely tea party.

Vampy sips her tea daintily as she makes a deep-sounding comment.

Although there's no real special meaning—the fight has literally just begun, that's all.

How do we know that when we're just sitting in the inn, you ask?

Well, Vampy has Panoptic Vision, so it's easy enough to see what's going on in the area even if we're inside.

The way Vampy's eyes are blankly staring at an empty wall is proof enough of that.

If it was anyone else staring into the distance and saying weird things, you'd probably think they were crazy, huh?

...Okay, everything about Vampy is crazy, so I guess that's not too far off the mark.

Anyway, none of this matters right now.

I use my own Clairvoyance to check on things outside the northern town.

There, Balto's troops have launched their attack on the town.

I've never actually seen this kind of large-scale battle in this world before, so while it might be in poor taste, I gotta admit I'm a little excited.

Huh? What do you mean, I do have battlefield experience?

If you're talking about the thing in Sariella, that wasn't so much a battle as a slaughter.

Besides, this is the first time I get a chance to watch others go at it instead of having to participate myself, so it still counts.

Just think of it like watching a movie, and maybe you'll understand how I feel.

Plus, I'm seeing it in real life, not on a screen, so it'll be even more intense.

According to the many books I read while I was killing time in the duke's mansion, the key to major battles in this world is a category of spells called "grand magic."

There are usually three steps to the skills for any given kind of magic.

With fire, for example, it's Fire Magic, Flame Magic, and Inferno Magic.

To simplify things, we'll call those "low," "middle," and "high."

Each of these magic skills has a different spell for each skill level, right?

We'll call the lower-skill-level spells "lesser," the middle ones "intermediate," and the ones you learn later on "advanced."

Going by this system, the Black Spear spell I frequently used before my deification would be considered a "high-intermediate" spell.

So naturally, "grand magic" refers to high-advanced spells… Ha-ha, nah, I'm just kidding. Apparently, it generally means middle-advanced spells.

Are you wondering what about that is "grand"?

If the answer is yes, then your mind has been poisoned by power creep!

There's practically nobody in this world who can even use high magic in the first place.

Even middle magic is pretty difficult for anyone but the most elite mages, so when most people think of magic, they think of low magic.

When I was throwing around high magic like crazy before I got deified, I was waaay outside the standards of the rest of the world!

From a human perspective, middle magic is already crazy dangerous, and even low magic can easily inflict a mortal wound if it hits you dead-on.

That's just normal, apparently.

So destructive wide-range middle-advanced spells are basically the strongest kind of magic most people can realistically use.

Not only that, but they can't just cast those spells whenever they want, either.

Since humans' meager stats are generally well under 1,000, it's very difficult for one of them to use a middle-advanced spell alone.

That's where the Cooperation skill comes in handy.

Multiple people with the same magic skill can use Cooperation to work together and complete a single spell.

It's basically a team-combo attack! Is that cool or what?

So then the resulting grand magic crushes the enemy forces and causes catastrophic losses!

Except obviously, the enemy isn't just gonna sit there and voluntarily take a thrashing.

Thanks to the effects of Wisdom, my magic-casting speed was super-fast, so I could fire off middle-advanced magic in no time at all. But that was just me.

Since humans have to use the Cooperation skill and work in groups to even stand a chance of casting that kind of magic, obviously they can't do it very quickly, either.

It takes time to construct the spells, and the huge amount of energy it emits practically screams, *HEY, GUYS, WE'RE ABOUT TO USE GRAND MAGIC!*

So when the enemy sees signs of grand magic, obviously they come running to try to put a stop to it.

And casting spells is finicky even at the best of times, so the slightest interruption can easily wreck the whole process.

To sum things up, grand magic can cause huge damage to the opposing troops, but it's far from easy to pull off.

In battle, it's super-important to try to hit the enemy with grand magic while preventing them from using it on your side.

Which means that in a siege, where the defenders are protected and can use grand magic at will, the attackers are at a considerable disadvantage.

How will Deadbeat, who's leading Balto's troops, deal with that situation?

That'll be worth watching.

Oh man, I can't wait.

But as I lay eyes on the battlefield, brimming with anticipation, my expression quickly turns serious as I see the situation unfold.

Um, excuse me?

What's up with this one-sided game?

The walls that the rebel earth mages worked so hard to make are getting blown to bits by a bunch of explosions.

Grand magic?

Yeah, no.

This is all the work of just one person.

As I watch, a single sword goes flying into the wall.

Next thing you know, there's a huge hole there.

Balto's soldiers swarm right in.

The walls might as well not exist.

As you may have guessed, the one responsible for blowing up all these walls is none other than Mr. Oni, with the help of his overpowered magic sword–creating cheat skill.

The skill in question can even create exploding swords.

So bombs, basically.

Which is why the defense walls are going KABOOM.

The swords are powerful enough to blast a hole in the wall, and all you have to do is throw them to cause massive damage, so the rebel army can barely put up a fight.

If it was slow-moving grand magic, at least they could try to stop the casting, but all Mr. Oni has to do is chuck a single sword.

I doubt they have many archers with the skill to shoot the swords out of the sky at high speed, and even if they could, the next one would come flying in a matter of seconds.

Those guys are royally screwed.

Man, Mr. Oni fights dirty.

I thought having his Wrath skill sealed by Vampy would slow him down, but I guess he can still use everything else freely.

Including his magic sword–making skill.

And while losing the Wrath skill means his stats are lower, I remember Vampy saying his physical attack skill in Wrath berserker mode was over 20,000.

And the effect of Wrath multiplies your stats by ten.

Which means even his base physical attack skill is still over 2,000?

That puts him on a fundamentally different level from any ordinary demon.

Stats in the 1,000s, and the cheat-like sword-making skill, which is probably a special reincarnation ability.

He might not be quite as powerful as the likes of Ael or Mera, but he can still hack and slash his way through an army like nobody's business.

Yeah, okay. I was a fool to expect an evenly matched siege battle.

This is the problem with cheaters…

"Tch. What's taking so long? He still hasn't broken through? Is he even taking this seriously?"

Apparently, Vampy isn't impressed by Mr. Oni's efforts.

Wow. He's single-handedly busting down their defenses, and you're still not satisfied?

Also, I thought you hated Mr. Oni. So why are you mad that he's not doing as well as you expected?

I just don't get Vampy at all.

Is this one of those situations? Y'know, where you get mad when your rival lets you down?

What's next? Is one of you gonna start spouting lines like *Now things are getting interesting!* or whatever?

Man, I just don't get these battle-crazy bozos.

Why can't they be peace-loving pacifists, like me?

Hrmmm.

Then again, if this keeps up, I'm not gonna have to do anything after all.

At a glance, there doesn't seem to be any suspicious movement on the battlefield.

Aside from Mr. Oni's rampage, all I see is magic flying back and forth, rebels desperately trying to stave off the soldiers storming the walls, and other scenes you'd expect during a siege.

Although I guess the "magic" part makes this a little less than ordinary.

The rebel army guys in the robes who are lobbing spells seem relatively strong: They might actually be winning this magic shoot-out.

That's partly because they've got walls to protect them, but it also seems like their individual soldiers are pretty powerful.

They're outmatching Balto's magic soldiers in both speed and firepower.

No wonder they're wearing robes: the universal sign for *Look, I'm a wizard!*

But that's the only front where Balto's guys are at a disadvantage. Otherwise, they're busting through the enemy defenses thanks to the holes Mr. Oni made in the walls.

No matter how hard these robe guys try, they're not gonna be able to turn the tide.

In reality, they're only a little strong compared to an overpowered cheater like Mr. Oni.

Hrmmm.

Yeah, pretty sure we're gonna win this.

Maybe I was worried for nothing after all?

Don't get me wrong—nobody would be happier than me if it turns out to be my imagination.

Like, why would I want a feeling of imminent disaster to pan out? Ha-ha-ha.

...It usually *is* right, though, is the thing.

I look away from the battlefield for a moment and focus on a certain other point of interest.

The general of the rebel army is holed up in a room somewhere in the lord's mansion, talking to no one by the looks of it.

He must be freaking out, 'cause he's really babbling.

"So please send reinforcements right away. You can use that teleport gate, can't you? Even a small amount would help. At this rate, the whole town will fall!"

Sweet. Signal intercepted.

Of course, I'm eavesdropping by way of one of my mini-mes, hidden in the area.

Only an idiot would pass up a chance to listen in on the general's communications with one of these convenient little guys.

I've had my clone shadowing him around for daaays.

But since he has such an important role, I guess I shouldn't be surprised that this dude somehow sensed that he was being watched.

He's been extra careful, so I haven't been able to catch him red-handed just yet.

After all, in this world, it's common sense that skills and stuff make it easier to do spying and that kind of thing than it was in our world.

What I'm doing isn't technically a skill, but I am still spying on him with a clone.

He's been vigilant so far, but I guess now that his back's against the wall, he can't afford to worry about that kind of thing.

Anyway, sounds like he's requesting reinforcements.

This "teleport gate" thing sounds important, but what's really got my attention is the thing in his hand.

Pressed against his ear is something that looks exactly like what we'd call a cell phone back on Earth.

A magic tool? Yeahhh, I don't think so.

Yes, there are "magic tools" that can replicate the effects of skills.

To make them, you need a skill called Ability Conferment, which allows you to imbue an object with a skill.

So in theory, that cell phone–looking thing could be a magic tool with the Fartalk skill or something.

Buuut...

That would be a little too convenient, wouldn't it?

Yeah. That can't be anything but an elf-made machine.

It's not made with a skill, but it's at least as powerful as a magic tool, I'm sure.

Only the elves could manufacture something like that.

Which means that most likely, the person he's using that phone to talk to is...an elf.

Yep. We've officially got trouble.

Has there ever been a time when something involved the elves, specifically Potimas, and it *didn't* end up becoming a dumpster fire?

Nope, I don't think so!

I think it's already safe to say that my bad feeling was right on the money.

Ughhh.

I can't help heaving a huge sigh.

Getting involved is a pain, but it'll end up being even more of a pain if I don't do anything.

Guess I better pull myself together and take care of this.

At the moment, there don't appear to be any suspicious characters in town.

That's just based on a quick glance, so I could've missed something, but there certainly weren't any big groups up to no good.

And there didn't seem to be any major baddies mixed in with the defenders, either.

If Potimas decided to really insert himself into this war, even the overpowered Mr. Oni would have a hard time against those far-more-overpowered machines.

Seems safe to assume that Potimas's guys aren't here yet.

Which means my next order of business is the teleport gate that guy was talking about.

A teleport gate is a magic circle imbued with the power of Spatial Magic. It's a kind of tool, not a machine.

You set up linked magic circles in two different places, and it connects them by way of teleportation.

You can go to only a specific place, and you can't move that location, either.

The spell it's based on, Long-Distance Teleport, can take the targets anywhere the mage using it has been to before, so it's a lot less useful by comparison.

But Spatial Magic users are actually really rare, so you can't just put them to work whenever you want. On top of that, teleporting multiple targets at the same time can be pretty taxing depending on the mage's abilities and MP and stuff.

A teleport gate, on the other hand, can be used by anyone as long as it's provided with MP, and it can teleport even large amounts of people.

They have their disadvantages, but teleport gates are very useful when it comes to connecting important locations.

Still, this is kinda weird.

Like I said earlier, there are very few people who can use Spatial Magic.

And you need the Ability Conferment skill to make a teleport gate.

That skill is actually fairly rare, too.

There are more people who can use it than Spatial Magic, for sure, but what about people who can use both? That's gotta be super-duper rare.

How rare? Enough that the ones who do exist are almost always under the strictest of government care.

Talk about a living national treasure.

And even then, they supposedly make only a handful of teleport gates in their lifetimes.

This is all information that I read in books, by the way.

From what I hear, there's no one in the demon territory who can make teleport gates right now.

In fact, a suitable candidate comes along only once every hundred years or so, if even that much.

So teleport gates are convenient, but they're not particularly commonplace.

If they existed all over the place, it'd cause a transportation revolution.

It took our little group a few years just to get from the south of this continent to the demon lands in the north, remember?

If we'd had a teleport gate, we could've covered that distance instantly, which would have changed everything.

...Hmm? Wait a minute.

I could probably make teleport gates, couldn't I?

My spatial conjuring can re-create Spatial Magic, and I did have the Ability Conferment skill before I was deified, so...it's not crazy to assume I should be able to reproduce it, right?

Hrmmm. I don't even need to limit that to teleport gates, do I?

If I wanted to, couldn't I make stuff like magic bags that store items in another dimension, Chim**ra Wing–like escape items that teleport you to a particular place, and stuff like that?

Whaaaat?

Hmm. Okay, let's put that aside for now.

The issue at hand is that the lord here was saying something or other about one of these super-rare teleport gates.

The existence of a teleport gate alone is a huge tactical advantage, so nations always know exactly where they are and keep them under careful control.

If this one's not on the books, does that mean it was made without permission?

And judging by what the lord was saying, it seems connected to someplace in the elf territory.

And this gate is somewhere right inside the town?

Hrmmm.

What to do?

Not only that, but what is *he* going to do?

It's not really much of a question why Potimas would be conspiring with this guy.

Stirring up a rebellion and doing even a little damage to the Demon Lord's side would be enough to make him happy.

The rebels would take the lead and the elves would just help out a little bit on the side.

He probably knows full well they're going to fail, but the elves won't sustain major losses either way.

Knowing Potimas, he'd take any chance he can get to harass the Demon Lord. This sounds exactly like something he would do.

But a surprise attack on the rebels probably throws a big wrench in his plans.

The rebel army is gonna get crushed without causing the Demon Lord any trouble at all.

What would Potimas do about that?

...Maybe he won't do anything?

It would take a lot of effort to recover from this situation now, even for Potimas.

And if he did that, the Demon Lord would know he was involved.

Potimas's goal was probably to work quietly behind the scenes to enable the rebel army, so acting openly here would be less than ideal for him.

He's a huge coward who likes to wait for the perfect opportunity to strike when his enemy's back is turned, y'know?

He won't want to deal with this situation with brute force.

If he was going to take that route, he could've done it by now instead of using roundabout methods like supporting a rebellion.

Putting myself in the shoes of that rat bastard Potimas, his next course of action would probably be...retreat.

At this rate, all he's gonna do is lose a bunch of pawns.

He doesn't mind sacrificing pieces, but I bet he's the type who hates wasting resources for nothing. Still, he won't take a risky gamble when he doesn't stand to gain anything in return.

He's more likely to abandon a sinking ship and try to hide the fact that the elves were ever involved.

Which means his next move is probably demolishing the teleport gate.

They're rare and valuable, but only when both ends are in friendly hands.

If one teleport gate gets captured by the enemy, then they could easily use it to infiltrate whatever's on the other side.

I doubt the teleport gate in this town leads straight to the elves' main base, but it's gotta go somewhere.

If he wants to avoid the risk of that place being attacked, his only choice is to break the teleport gate, wasteful or not.

Looks like they're just going to withdraw on their own without me having to do anything.

The one thing is that Potimas will have to destroy that teleport gate.

He probably doesn't want to do that, so there is the slight danger that he'll pull some last-ditch effort on his way out.

If he does, I'm guessing his target would be Mr. Oni, who's super standing out right now.

All right. I think I've got a good idea of what Potimas might do.

Which means my top priority should be protecting Mr. Oni.

He's definitely strong compared to the demons, but Potimas could still assassinate him.

I've got to give him some cover, or he might be killed.

In the worst-case scenario, Mera or Ael might get hurt, too.

I doubt Ael would get killed, but it's Potimas, so you can never be too careful.

Balto and Deadbeat… Eh, I can afford to lose 'em if I really have to.

Although I'd rather not, since they're important demons and all that.

…Hrmmm, but this isn't all that exciting, is it?

Potimas has given us tons of grief over the years. Wouldn't it be nice to lay the hurt on him for once?

I'm sure his real body is still hiding in a bunker somewhere, so it isn't like I can inflict much in the way of serious damage, but still.

I bet it would piss him off if trying to mess with the Demon Lord backfired really badly.

Yep. Plus, it's no good to be on the defensive all the time.

We gotta keep him on his toes once in a while.

Sooo where's that teleport gate? Oh, found it.

Combining Clairvoyance with x-ray vision, I discover the teleport gate in the basement of the lord's manor.

It's a hidden room, which is why my clones didn't find it.

It doesn't look like it's been broken just yet.

Although I guess it's possible that the one on the other end has been broken, in which case there'd be nothing I can do.

Still, it's worth a try…

Downing the rest of my tea, I stand up.

"Making your move?"

I nod at Vampy's question, then realize I have no idea what I'm going to do about her.

It'd be really dangerous to let her come with me, since I'm about to enter enemy territory and all.

Which means I should ideally leave her here, where she can look after Mr. Oni and company.

The only problem is how to convey that request to her!

I hesitate for a minute, then use Illusion to make an image of Mr. Oni appear on the table.

Heh-heh-heh. Yeah, I've learned some cool new tricks.

Illusion is originally Heretic Magic, but that spell works directly on the target's brain, forcing them to see something that isn't there. This, on the other hand, makes a real image appear in midair, so the underlying principle is totally different.

At first, I tried to re-create the Heretic Magic method, but it was too damn hard, so I switched to this.

Heretic Magic's crazy, dude.

Vampy and the puppet spiders stare at the Mr. Mini-Oni on the table.

Bwa-ha-ha. Pretty awesome, right?

Okay, enough gloating for now. I add a mini-Potimas to the image, attacking Mr. Oni.

Then I add Vampy and company beating Potimas up.

And thus Potimas gets smashed to a pulp and dies. The end.

"Hrmmm, okay. So what are you saying? Potimas is here, and he's after the kid? And you want us to put a stop to that?"

You're quick on the uptake!

I nod again.

"And what are you going to do in the meantime?"

Nrgh. That's too hard to explain.

It's, um, you know.

A lady has to have her secrets.

I press my finger to my lips to avoid the question.

"Excuse me? Are you planning on keeping me in the dark again?"

I guess that's not good enough for Vampy.

Uh-oh. She's already getting mad.

C'mon, really? Is it just me, or are you being way too short-tempered lately?

And also, when did I ever hide stuff from you?

Besides, you really expect ME of all people to give a lengthy explanation right now?

We're not screwed just yet, but it's not like we've got tons of time to drag our feet, either.

If you're gonna make childish demands at a time like this, then *I'm* the one who's gonna get pissed off.

""""...!""""

"Huh? What the—?! What are you doing?! Hey!"

Evidently sensing my anger, the three puppet spiders grab Vampy and scurry away.

She's thrashing around, but they expertly restrain her and run off like experienced kidnappers.

They might look like little girls, but they're spiders on the inside.

Bound and gagged with spider thread, Vampy has no chance of escaping.

I wave at her as they retreat into the distance.

She's glaring at me furiously as she gets carried off, but she's the one who decided to follow me in the first place.

Just take out that stress on the rebels and elves, please.

Once I've waved off the Little Girl Squad, I clear the rest of the tea and snacks off the table.

If I send them to the alternate dimension where I store my clones, they'll happily eat it all for me.

Look, it's not good to waste food.

All righty, that should take care of things here.

As long as nothing crazy happens, the reunited four puppet-spider sisters should be able to tackle just about anything around here.

Plus they've got Vampy, too.

It's about time I get to let loose and strut my stuff.

I teleport myself to the hidden room with the teleport gate.

I've never used a teleport gate before, but I've already confirmed that I can still use magic tools post-deification.

I just have to turn MP into energy and channel it into the power source.

In fact, MP itself is basically a kind of energy.

They're just the same thing with different names, so it's easy enough for me to operate a magic tool.

Which means if I just feed energy into this teleport gate, it should transport me to the gate it's connected to, as long as that one hasn't been broken.

I touch the teleport gate and channel some energy into it.

When I feel it respond accordingly, I'm tempted to smirk like a villain.

I'm not going to, though.

I supply the teleport gate with energy and activate it.

I'm used to teleporting.

But unlike when I do it myself, it feels a little weird this time.

Maybe it's like how you don't get carsick when you're driving, but you might when someone else is behind the wheel.

Come to think of it, being teleported by someone else is like being forcibly thrown to a different space, so I guess it makes sense that it might feel a little weird.

I never realized that, since I've always teleported myself around without a problem.

If I did it a bunch of times in a row, would I start to feel sick?

Well, I guess I could cause that just by messing with space a little.

Anyway, while I'm thinking about that stuff, I arrive at my destination.

"I'll head over there now, but don't expect too much in terms of reinforce… ments…"

As soon as the view in front of me changes, I lock eyes with a man from across the room.

That might sound like the beginning of a love story, but no, we're mortal enemies.

Before my eyes is Potimas, frozen in surprise with a phone-like object held to his ear.

When something unexpected happens, people's thoughts stop for a moment.

I guess Potimas is no exception.

Good to know.

"……"

"……"

Take this! Beat-you-to-the-PUNCH!

"Guh?!"

O I'll Do What I Can

Ever since I first opened my eyes in the demon realm, my life has been very peaceful.

I've yet to experience any inconveniences, in part because I'm staying in a particularly wealthy duke's mansion.

Back in the goblin village, it was all we could do to scrape by from day to day while the warriors put their lives on the line to bring back food for the rest of us.

Compared to that, having easy access to any food or supplies I might need at any time feels unbelievably luxurious.

But I can't keep living off their generosity forever.

After letting Wrath control me and fighting nearly to my death, I'm lucky to have regained my senses and control over my life.

So I want to use the life I've been given to do whatever I can, to the best of my ability.

I enlisted in the army with the help of Miss Ariel, the Demon Lord, to put my power to use.

It seemed like the fastest way to start earning a living, and since my combat strength is all I have going for me right now, it's the perfect occupation.

And so I left my freeloading lifestyle in the mansion behind and went off to join the army.

I'm definitely still strong enough to be of use. Even after Miss Sophia sealed off my Wrath skill, my base stats are apparently still quite high. On top of that, I have the advantage of the magic swords I can make with my Weapon Creation skill.

And the army commander, General Bloe, seems to like me for some reason, so I've been able to fit into the army pretty well.

But there's still one challenge I have to tackle.

"Grand magic. Block, long-distance, throw."

"Grand magic. Block, long-distance, throw."

One of my fellow soldiers says the words slowly, and I repeat them in the same way.

What am I doing? Learning the language.

I'm still a long way from mastering the demon language, which is what everyone speaks here.

I was born in a goblin village.

So naturally, I speak goblin language.

While I was being held captive by Buirimus, I learned human language, too, but demon language is different from either of those.

And it's difficult to serve in the army when I can barely hold a conversation.

There are some demons who can speak human as well, so I can communicate with them, but I should really learn the local language.

During my time in the duke's mansion, the kindly staff tutored me in demon language, so I've reached the point where I can at least follow a basic conversation.

But I still haven't learned all the military jargon.

Since I'm in the army, I need to learn the names of common battle formations, strategies, and things like that.

A few friendly soldiers have been teaching me military terms in demon language whenever we have free time.

I didn't think it would be that easy to memorize them, but I figured I had to start somewhere.

All things considered, I've actually been pleasantly surprised.

"That should do it for today. Seems like you've learned a majority of the most common orders at this point, yeah?"

"I think so."

My fellow soldier addresses me in demon language, and I respond in kind.

My pronunciation still needs work, and I struggle with long sentences a lot more than simple responses.

But as far as listening comprehension goes, I can more or less understand what people are saying, even when some basic military terms are involved.

I'm shocked by the speed of my own learning. This happened when I first picked up conversational words, too.

There are a few factors that have helped me learn demon language in such a short period of time.

One of these is the Memory skill.

As the name implies, it's a plain yet useful skill that improves one's memorization abilities, which is incredibly useful for learning. If you can memorize what the other person is saying word for word, you're already well on the way to becoming more familiar with the language.

My ability to remember things surprises even me.

If my memory had been this good in my previous life, I can't help thinking that tests and classes would've been a whole lot easier.

I was only ever able to speak English to the extent that they taught us in school, but now I'm multilingual, quickly raising my fluency in multiple languages.

I guess you never know what life's going to throw at you.

But those memories of my previous life are also part of the reason I've been able to learn demon language so smoothly.

Knowing different languages, like Japanese and English, comes in handy even in this fantasy world.

Since we learned concepts like "subjects" and "predicates" in Japanese class, then applied those to a grammatically different language like English, I can use that experience to learn these otherworldly languages as well.

Tackling a language without any formal classes really makes me appreciate how advanced the Japanese educational system was.

And the similarities between the demon and human languages are probably the other big reason.

They have similar grammar, and certain vocabulary words overlap as well.

Coincidence? Probably not.

Considering the origins of demons and humans, I'd be willing to bet that they used to share a single language that eventually branched off.

Or maybe a few different languages mixed together and eventually unified into the ones that are around today.

Now that I think about it, the demon language probably has a long and storied history.

"That reminds me, I heard Lord Bloe has been studying the human language in earnest lately. Though I'm told he's not getting very far."

While I was busy musing about the history of languages, the soldier recaptured my attention with a casual remark.

I can't help grinning, since I have a feeling I know what that might be about.

General Bloe must have really hated having to ask Miss Sophia to translate for him.

I won't tell anyone else that, though, since it's a matter of the general's pride.

Besides, that situation was my fault in the first place, and I still feel a little guilty.

"Oh, we're getting close."

My fellow soldier points up ahead.

Following his gaze, I see some sort of wall off in the distance.

"They raised a damn wall. Guess our enemies are hoping to ride out a siege."

Our army is currently on the move.

We're marching toward a northern town, where a rebel army is believed to be hiding out.

And now, there's a wall around the town that was never there before. That's as good as confirming the rumors.

"Looks like this is gonna be a tough battle."

The soldier looks nervous.

I'm actually a little nervous myself, since this is my first battle as part of the Demon Lord's army and my first since my Wrath skill was sealed off.

"Charge! Chaaaarge!"

The captain's voice bellows, nearly drowned out by the sounds of battle and violent war cries.

Tension saturates the air and prickles at my skin until a powerful wave of heat flies toward us as if to sear it away.

It's an inferno, strong enough to burn away life itself.

The soldiers are putting everything on the line in this battle, stealing each other's lives.

Enemy soldiers go down under the sword swings of my allies, and comrades I've gotten to know fall to the ground bleeding, then stop moving entirely.

I never experienced such a hellish sight in my old life.

And yet…

"…Is this all?"

If anyone else had heard the words that slipped from my mouth, I'm sure they would seem very cold.

Maybe coldness is a fitting attitude for the battlefield anyway.

But to me, my own muttered comment sounds a little disappointed.

Even as I process this, my body doesn't stop moving.

I use Spatial Storage, an item box–like Spatial Magic skill, to produce magic swords I've stored inside.

My Wrath skill may be sealed off, but I can still use the Weapon Creation skill I was born with and the countless skills I've learned and honed since.

Along with practicing demon language, I've been raising my Spatial Magic skill level and mass-producing magic swords.

I was worried about whether that would be much use, but now my worries are gone.

I throw one of the swords; it gets lodged in the wall, then explodes.

Because it was magically constructed, the wall looks far sturdier than one might expect from its hasty construction.

But it crumbles under the immense force of my magic sword's blast.

Then my fellow soldiers charge in through the newly created breach, breaking through the enemies' defenses.

I guess my magic swords work well enough here. Actually…instead of "well enough," it might be more accurate to say they're excessive against these opponents.

The destruction of the wall and many of the rebel soldiers behind it is proof enough of that.

…I never expected my simple, mass-produced exploding swords to be this useful in battle.

I guess I'm a lot stronger than I realized.

I did notice some signs during my training in the army, but I didn't think that the difference would be this great.

When making the mass-produced exploding swords, increasing the number I make simultaneously reduces their individual effectiveness.

The strength of the magic swords crafted with my Weapon Creation skill is based on the amount of MP used to create them.

Obviously, the strongest magic sword I can create right now would be made by pouring almost all of my available MP into a single blade.

In comparison, I made the mass-produced exploding swords in my spare time simply because it seemed like a good use of my MP Auto-Recovery skill.

And yet, those casually made objects are playing a huge role in this battle.

The exploding swords aren't weak, of course.

Since they take the potential of a magic sword that would normally be used until it breaks and expend all that latent energy at once by self-destructing, they're quite effective for the relatively modest MP investment.

And it does take time to create them, but unlike magic spells, there's no cooldown period after I use one since I can whip another one out right away. Thanks to this, they can quickly win me the upper hand in battle.

But even with those advantages, I never imagined that my mass-produced exploding swords would be *this* effective.

They couldn't lay a single scratch on the beautiful yet hardy scales of that dragon, and I couldn't even get them in range of that small yet blindingly fast powerhouse of a girl.

Vague memories of battles from when I was a slave to Wrath flash across my mind.

I can't remember every detail, but I do get bits and pieces from time to time.

And I remember the strength of those opponents, too.

Because of those memories, I assumed that having Wrath sealed and my strength considerably suppressed would mean that I was now weak.

But I guess I have to change my perspective on that.

It's not that I'm weak.

They were just too strong.

And in general terms, it appears that I'm more than above average, even in my weakened state.

Since I was so worried about how well I'd be able to fight in my current condition, I guess it's inevitable that I might be a little disappointed by this almost anticlimactic development.

And that's not the only reason I'm disappointed.

I take out another exploding sword, fling it at another wall, and watch it explode.

The wall crumbles, and the rebel army soon concedes more ground.

But they're not just giving up without a fight.

I notice some of my fellow soldiers suddenly suffer desperate counterattacks.

Right in front of me, I spot one of the soldiers who was teaching me words in the demon language on our way here.

He's lying facedown, a blade sprouting out of his back, never to stand up again.

He's dead.

Even in this world, with its RPG-like system, or perhaps *because* of that very system, there's no revival spell to bring people back to life.

Once you die, that's it.

My fallen comrade will never come back to life.

But I'm not as shaken as I thought I'd be.

We literally broke bread together, and he even took the time to teach me, yet my heart is barely moved by his death.

I'm not sure if I should be glad that I don't feel much of anything or disturbed that I've become so unfeeling.

I'm definitely a lot colder than I was in my previous life as a human. Come to think of it, I even had more empathy back when I was living in the goblin village.

Taking a life no longer gives me pause, and I barely feel any shock if someone I know is killed.

It's not that I've abandoned my emotions completely.

I think I've just accepted what it truly means to live in this world.

Although that doesn't necessarily mean that I know what exactly I should be doing.

"I'd better focus on this battle for now and worry about that later."

It's never a good idea to let yourself get distracted in a battle, even if it's lackluster.

Reminding myself of that out loud, I scan the battlefield.

At a glance, it seems like one particular clump of defenders on the wall is putting up a lot of resistance.

Countless spells fly out from behind that section of the wall, causing massive damage to any soldiers who try to approach.

It's immediately obvious that their power and coordination are leagues above the other rebel forces.

Those must be the rebellion's core magic users.

In the other areas, our forces are steadily advancing through the breaches made by my exploding swords.

It's only a matter of time before the walls fall completely.

Rather than continuing to hammer those areas at the risk of harming my allies in the process, it's probably best if I focus on the area they can't get into.

I produce a new exploding sword from Spatial Storage and throw it at the enemy position that's still putting up a fight.

There's a fair amount of distance between us, but with my status and Throw skill level, it should reach without a problem.

But as the sword flies through the air, a spell flies from behind the fortifications to intercept it, and it explodes before it can reach the wall.

Damn. If it had gotten just a little bit closer, the blast would've caused considerable damage to the wall.

But I guess it wasn't a total loss, since now I know that there's a mage over there skilled enough to intercept my exploding swords in midair.

Whoever they are, they must be powerful in their own right.

But there's no way they can measure up to the old mage I encountered in the human realm.

And I've gotten a lot stronger since I met that old mage, so I don't feel very threatened by these mages.

Still, now that my Wrath trump card is off-limits, I can't let my guard down.

It's all too easy to lose your life in this world.

So I have no intention of holding back, even if it ends up being overkill.

I take out two more exploding swords and throw them both at once.

Then, while they're still in the air, I start running toward the wall, pulling out yet another exploding sword while on the move.

It's not easy to use Spatial Storage while moving, but it'd be a waste of the many swords I have in storage otherwise.

Luckily, unlike other Spatial Magic, Spatial Storage is relatively easy to use, so I've managed to master it with practice.

It does still take a while to get the magic swords out, though, so it leaves me open to attack for a moment.

My ultimate goal is to be able to produce magic swords from Spatial Storage as quickly and as easily as breathing, but it'll be a long time before I can accomplish that.

Still, in this situation, I'm not too worried about such a brief vulnerability.

The two swords I threw before are hit with counterfire before they reach the wall.

They must be more cautious after the first throw—even though I threw two swords this time, they shot them down while they were still much farther away from the wall.

But that's all.

They're not coming after me personally as I run toward the wall.

I keep throwing more swords as I get closer.

Producing two swords at once and throwing them as I'm running would be a little too difficult, so I'm just doing one at a time.

That might not seem like much in theory, but the more time passes, the closer I get to the wall and the shorter the distance my swords have to fly.

And a shorter distance means less time before my exploding swords hit their mark.

In other words, there's less time for the mages to shoot them down.

Magic takes time to cast, and it must require a lot of concentration to aim spells at a flying target.

While they have to take the time to carefully cast the spell and aim precisely to intercept my swords on their flight path, all I have to do is throw as soon as I have another sword in hand. It's plain to see that I have the advantage.

I need to use Spatial Storage, too, so it's not a huge advantage, but since the rebel army also has to deal with soldiers besides me, even that small difference can prove fatal.

Sure enough, as I throw more swords, the responding fire slows down, until finally one of them explodes very close to the wall.

It's not a direct hit, but it's close enough that the shock waves leave some faint cracks in the wall.

And I'm sure the rebels fighting inside the walls have taken even more damage.

The blast probably sent a shock wave through the firing ports they were shooting through, and I'm sure hearing an explosion at such close range will affect their ears.

That should cause no small amount of chaos.

It's not a fatal amount of damage, but for mages who need to concentrate on their spells as much as possible, it's definitely a big problem.

And I'm not kind enough to let an opportunity like that slip by unnoticed.

The next magic sword I hurl hits the wall without any interference and explodes.

The wall comes tumbling down, and the rebels who were behind it get caught in the explosion.

By the time the dust clears, I've reached the place where the wall once stood and charge inside, my magic swords made for close combat in each hand.

Unlike the single-use exploding swords, the swords I'm currently wielding were infused with as much MP as I could muster.

There's a flaming sword in my right hand and a sword crackling with electricity in my left.

By feeding MP into them, I can instantly produce fire and lightning attacks at least as strong as the explosions, or stronger, and control those effects at will.

And of course, mages are rarely good at close combat.

My magic stats are actually higher than my physical stats, but that's just a natural result of the huge amount of MP I use for my Weapon Creation skill.

My real strength lies in using the magic swords I create with all that MP to execute attacks more high-powered than magic in close combat, at least by my own analysis.

As long as I can get close enough to the opponent, my victory is all but assured.

I quickly scan my surroundings, ignoring anyone killed in the blast or too wounded to put up a fight, then charge at whoever's nearby who looks relatively healthy.

"Graaah!"

"W-wait?!"

The hooded figures fall beneath my blade, putting up little resistance.

I guess a robe is a reasonable thing for a mage to wear, but it's not like wearing armor in this world lowers the effectiveness of magic or anything.

Some of them are indeed wearing armor under their hooded robes.

But for some reason, they're all hiding their faces.

This strikes me as strange, but I just keep moving forward, slashing all the while.

It's only when I send the head of one of the hooded men rolling to the ground and see his face that I realize who they are.

To be precise, it's the ears that tip me off.

"Elves?"

Unlike humans or demons, the man has long, pointed ears.

From what I've heard, that's definitely a trademark feature of elves.

I don't know a lot of the details, but I do know that the elves are enemies of the Demon Lord, Miss Ariel. I unexpectedly fought some of them myself while I was half-controlled by Wrath.

So why are the elves fighting alongside the rebels here?

I'm not sure what's going on exactly, but it doesn't change my mission.

Defeat the enemy. That's all.

Just then, I hear a voice that stops me in my tracks.

"Iijima!"

It's my name from my old life, the one I thought I'd left behind.

"Please just stop!"

My hand freezes, still raising my sword above my head.

A small figure pushes her way in between me and the hooded man I was about to finish off.

With her hood removed, the person between us looks like nothing more than a little elf girl.

No, that's exactly what she is.

In fact, I think I remember seeing a girl like this when I stumbled upon a band of elves in the human territory and slaughtered them, thinking they were human mercenaries lying in wait to kill me.

And didn't she call my name that time, too...?

I was barely lucid because of Wrath's control, so I had assumed it was an illusion or a daydream, but I guess I was wrong.

"Who are you?"

I point the tip of my sword at the elf girl as I address her in Japanese.

Since she knows my old name, I have a rough idea of what might be going on here.

It's just a question of which one of them she is.

"Okazaki... Kanami Okazaki."

She answers in fluent Japanese.

I can tell from her pronunciation that she must be a native speaker.

Which means...she's the real deal.

A reincarnation from Japan, just like me.

And her name is the same as our class's homeroom teacher.

"...It's been a long time, Ms. Oka. Although this isn't how I would have liked to be reunited."

I keep my sword pointed at my teacher as I speak.

"Wh-why are you doing this?!"

What an absurd question.

"If anything, I think I'm the one who should be asking that question. Why in the world are you supporting a rebel army and interfering with the order of the demons?"

I can't figure out why these elves are helping the rebels, nor why Ms. Oka would be with them.

I guess I do understand why the rebels are angry in theory, but since I know the secret of Taboo, that's little more than a laugh to me.

Miss Ariel is doing what's right for this world.

I'm sure it seems like the height of insanity to those who haven't discovered the truth, but Miss Ariel knows exactly what she's doing and acts with firm conviction and determination.

That's why I'm willing to crush the rebel army without a moment's hesitation.

"I'm...fighting to rescue the reincarnations who have been kidnapped by the Demon Lord."

"What?"

I knit my brow, genuinely confused by what my teacher is trying to say.

Reincarnations, kidnapped by the Demon Lord?

As far as I know, the only other reincarnations in the demon territory are Miss White and Miss Sophia.

But best I can tell, they're both working with the Demon Lord of their own accord, certainly not being held captive.

How did Ms. Oka misunderstand things so wildly?

"You too, Iijima... Please forget about all this and just take my hand. The elves are protecting the reincarnations. Everyone else is there, too... You won't need to do such awful things anymore. So please come with me."

Ms. Oka reaches out her hand to me.

I feel like she just presented me with a lot of important information, but I can analyze all that later.

Right now, there's something I have to say.

"I'm not sure what false impression you're under, but I'm here of my own free will. And I have no intention of taking your hand."

Ms. Oka looks up at me with her eyes widening in shock. Evidently, she didn't expect me to refuse.

"I'm fighting because of my own convictions, not because anyone forced me to. It's what I believe is the right thing to do. I don't feel any shame for my actions."

Ms. Oka shakes her head slowly, as if she doesn't believe what she's hearing. Her face is turning pale.

"Let me ask you a question instead. You said I'm doing 'awful things,' and yet, here you are doing the very same. Can you really reach out to your student with those bloodstained hands, claiming to offer me help?"

At that, her eyes get even wider, and her face loses all color completely.

It's true—by joining the rebel army, that's exactly what she's doing.

The elves in her little unit have caused no small amount of losses to the Demon Lord's army.

I don't know if Ms. Oka herself has been fighting, but judging by her reaction, I'm guessing she wasn't just standing around watching.

She claims she's doing this to protect her former students, yet she's participating in a battle that's claimed the lives of countless unrelated soldiers.

Can you really call that just?

"Ms. Oka."

As I address her in a low voice, her shoulders tremble to an almost comical degree.

"If you can't even deny that, then I most definitely won't take your hand."

Still, even I'm not heartless enough to want to cut down someone I know from my former life.

I guess I'm not quite that determined yet.

Feeling as if I'm in no position to lecture Ms. Oka, I open my mouth to concede the fight.

But then my body is suddenly blown backward.

"Huh?!"

I don't understand what just happened.

But something on my right, from the direction of the wall, must have attacked me.

At least, I assume so from the fact that my right hand is broken, and a dull pain is radiating from the right side of my ribs.

I'd been trying to keep an eye on my surroundings even as I conversed with Ms. Oka.

I would never let my guard down on enemy ground, even if I ran into an old acquaintance.

So if something was able to damage me like this in spite of my caution, they must have sniped me from someplace I couldn't detect them, or else they're considerably skilled.

Either way, whoever it was is definitely a threat!

I manage to right myself in midair and land on my feet instead of falling.

Without even looking, I launch a lightning attack from the sword in my left hand in the direction the attack seemed to have originated, hoping to ward off any follow-up attacks.

As the lightning spreads outward, just as destructively powerful as one of my exploding swords, its light illuminates several hooded figures.

Ms. Oka is shouting something, but it's not in a language I understand.

All I see is the person she protected from me earlier grabbing her from behind and dragging her away. With her small frame, there's nothing she can do to escape from the large man carrying her with her arms pinned behind her back.

To be honest, I don't really want to let her get away, but it doesn't look like I'll have a chance to pursue her.

The hooded figures in front of me seem very different from the elves I was fighting before.

The attack from my lightning sword doesn't appear to have harmed them at all, so they must be pretty powerful.

I could be in trouble here.

Then the hooded people get blown away.

If I wasn't on a battlefield, I would be rubbing my eyes in disbelief.

All of the hooded figures just got sent flying.

Well, that's fine, I guess.

I mean, it isn't, but let's just accept that actually happened for the time being.

The problem is that the culprits who sent them flying are a couple of little girls who don't look much older than Ms. Oka did.

And if my eyes aren't deceiving me, it happened by way of three of the little girls swinging a fourth little girl, tied up in white thread, right into the hooded figures.

...What in the world is going on here?

The sense of danger I felt just moments ago is rapidly replaced by mounting confusion.

"Thaaaaat's enooooough!"

The girl wrapped up in thread wobbles to her feet, shrieking with rage.

In a matter of seconds, the thread gets shredded away to nothing.

Frighteningly enough, that action somehow turns the air around us violently cold.

My breath comes out in white puffs.

The young girl pulls out a broadsword the size of her own body that was strapped to her back.

She looks way more threatening than anyone her size has any right to be.

"Miss Sophia."

It's the unforgettable Sophia, one of my fellow reincarnations.

I have no idea what she's doing here, but I think it's safe to assume that she's an ally.

To be honest, I'm a little relieved.

"Hmm? What's got you looking so beat-up? How embarrassing."

As soon as she notices me, Sophia just sneers scornfully.

Although after what I just saw, I can't help but wonder if I'm really the one who should be embarrassed right now.

But I'm wise enough not to say that out loud.

Over the course of this conversation, the other three girls silently and dispassionately charge after the hooded figures and mercilessly bring them down.

It's so extreme that I almost wonder if they really need to take it that far. The sounds of their strikes resemble explosions more than the expected thuds of kicks and punches.

This quickly went from a surprise attack to an outright slaughter.

The girls' excessive violence continues until you can barely even tell what shape the hooded figures were supposed to be.

"Isn't that going a little overboard?"

It's not that I feel pity for the enemy, but I'm not a big fan of beating a dead horse or, in this case, person. Maybe I shouldn't have said anything, since they just came to my rescue and all, but I couldn't help myself.

"Excuse me? Take a good look and then tell me if you agree with what you just said."

Miss Sophia picks up one of the hooded would-be assailants and holds the body out for me to see.

"Huh?!"

I can barely believe my eyes.

Beneath the hood is not a bloodied corpse but what appears to be the scraps of a machine.

"You've never seen this before? You might say it's the true identity of the elven war machine. If we don't take them down fast, they could pose a very real threat, and you can't be sure they're done for unless you destroy them completely. Now do you understand?"

I had no idea machines like that existed in this world...

Is that even allowed?

No. I guess it isn't.

"Sorry. I had no idea."

I have to acknowledge my own ignorance here.

Now I understand why they had no choice but to literally tear them apart.

"Ew, it leaked on me. Gross."

Miss Sophia flings the humanoid machine away as if she's touched something foul.

As she wipes her hand with a handkerchief, my gaze drifts to the abandoned scrap metal–like remains.

Its body is made primarily of mechanical parts.

But the part Sophia was holding—the head—is leaking some kind of gooey substance.

"I guess they're not completely machine, then…?"

"It's just awful, isn't it?"

I nod wordlessly in response.

To think that someone committed such atrocities without a second thought…

This crosses the line in a way that's almost hard to believe.

Most shocking of all is that the sick bastard who did it is connected to Ms. Oka.

"I can't believe she had the nerve to say that to me when she was working alongside *these* things."

"Hmm? Who?"

"I'll tell you later. It has to do with all of us reincarnations, so I'd like to include Miss White in the conversation, too."

I have to inform them about Ms. Oka.

But first, we have to crush the rebel army.

"All right. Let's wrap things up here, then."

A sinister grin spreads across Miss Sophia's face.

From the bottom of my heart, I am eternally grateful that she and the other girls aren't my enemies.

4 Let's Bring the Pain

Hey, it's me. The person who just showed up out of nowhere and punched Potimas in the face.

Cowardly?

I'll take that as a compliment, thanks!

Talk about playing dirty. Good job, me.

"Lord Potimas?!"

Whoops, guess I don't have time to stand around feeling good about myself.

There's a bunch of sketchy-looking people in hoods gathered around where Potimas just hit the floor.

Several of them seem to be in a panic.

I would be, too, if my boss suddenly got punched in the face.

If anything, what's weird is that the rest of the hooded guys haven't moved an inch.

They seem kinda…I dunno, not very human…ooor alive for that matter.

But they don't seem totally lifeless, which is important.

Actually, I have a pretty good guess as to what these things are. They're not normal elves, that's for sure.

Most likely, they're people who have been turned into cyborg weapons, just like Potimas here.

Seeing a whole bunch of them in one place like this is pretty creepy, though.

Uh, 'scuse me, Mr. Potimas?

Does this little scene mean that you were rather serious about trying to crush us this time?

If he had already gathered this much firepower before the rebel army even finished assembling, that means there would've been even more crazy weapons in that northern town if they had been able to complete their preparations.

Yikes. That was close.

Judging by what Potimas was saying earlier, I'm guessing he wasn't planning on sending this bunch over to help the rebel army.

This is just a guess, but maybe he was planning to go collect the reinforcements he'd sent to the northern town because he found out that we were unexpectedly on the move.

Come to think of it, there was that group of hooded guys at the fortifications who were putting up more of a fight than the rest of the rebels.

I guess those were elves, then.

If there were some cyborgs mixed in among them, like there are in the group here, I can see why Potimas would want to swipe those back before anyone noticed.

Based on the way they were fighting, I'm pretty sure most of them were regular elves, not cyborgs. And a small handful of cyborgs wouldn't be much help once the Demon Lord and I arrived on the scene.

So Potimas probably decided to write this plan off as a failure and recover his troops before he incurred any losses.

In that case, how about I cause waaay more damage than you were hoping to prevent?

The early bird gets the worm!

Or in this case, the early spider.

Now, time to activate Warped Evil Eye!

Warped Evil Eye is a nasty move that twists a targeted space and, in the process, messes up whatever happens to be there.

When I used it as a skill, it took more power to manipulate space depending on the strength of the materials in the targeted area.

In other words, the tougher the object, the harder it was to warp.

But wait!

My new Warped Evil Eye doesn't have any such limitations!

It's twisting the very fabric of space itself, so the makeup of whatever's in the way has nothing to do with it!

In a sense, this attack is one that totally ignores defensive ability.

Once you're caught in my Warped Evil Eye, you're screwed no matter what.

The only negative is that it doesn't have a very wide range.

Anyway, I guess the first order of business is to wipe out the elves who have wills of their own, namely the ones who are panicking over Potimas getting his lights knocked out.

I target the three of them, and next thing you know, they're twisted and crushed into blobs of who-knows-what.

Sweet.

Now let's mess up the rest of these cyborgs before Potimas recovers.

"Anti-Technique Barrier, activate."

Oh shoot. He moved before I had the chance.

Still lying facedown, Potimas activates his barrier, rewriting the rules of the world around us.

Immediately, my vision goes black.

My x-ray vision has been canceled, so since my eyes are closed, I can't see anything.

As soon as I open my eyes, I see the cyborg soldiers turning to face me, their arms transforming into guns.

Oh crap!

I'd better use a body-enhancement conjuring on my feet and JUMP!

Seconds later, a barrage of bullets shoots through the space I was in just a moment ago.

I launch a thread toward the ceiling and swing like a pendulum to put more distance between us.

I assume we're in some kind of building.

The cyborgs chase after me, shooting up the walls and ceiling.

If I get hit by one of those bullets inside Potimas's barrier, even I won't escape without a scratch.

Luckily, maybe because I'm a god now, I can make thread even inside the barrier, and my body-enhancement conjuring works, too.

But as I sort of suspected, that's about all I can do.

None of the conjuring techniques I could use to escape seem to be working.

Grrr! I guess I should have thought things through a little more before I charged in headfirst.

This is a bit of a pickle.

Looking around, I see Potimas standing up and preparing a gun arm of his own.

I shoot a mesh of thread toward him.

Take this! Spider net!

Potimas shoves a nearby cyborg soldier into the flying web to protect himself.

Using your people as shields? Now, *that's* dirty!

But that whole stunt did buy me the time I needed.

While he's distracted, I run up close to the wall, then use that momentum to deliver a flying kick!

My aim was to bust right through the wall and escape outside!

I call this strategy Operation: Get Out of the Barrier's Evil Range (Operation: GOOBER for short)!

With my body enhancement, my powerful kick sticks fast into the wall.

Wait, what? Sticks?

Okay, the wall was a little harder than I expected and now my leg sorta stings, but that's no big deal.

But…sticks?

I'm STUCK?!

I was trying to break through the wall to get outside, and instead I pinned myself perfectly to the damn wall.

Well, this is unexpected!

Then I realize why my foot got stuck and start freaking out a little.

We're UNDERGROUND!

There's no outside beyond this wall! It's just hard-packed earth.

No wonder I couldn't bust out, ha-ha-ha.

Um, this isn't funny!!

I hurry up and yank my foot out, but it's too late.

I feel several bullets sink into my body.

Uh-oh. This ain't looking great.

"Keep at it. Don't stop shooting until she stops breathing."

Ohhh boy, I don't like this one bit.

Nope, nope, nope.

Guess I should've just popped in, punched him, and popped right back out.

Things were going a little too well, so I kinda got ahead of myself.

Well, next time I'll know to quit while I'm ahead.

For now, I guess it's time to give up on this body.

I open up my spatial conjuring to the max and push the barrier back just a little.

Then I connect to another dimension through that little gap.

There's no visible change to my surroundings, so Potimas shouldn't notice.

And even if he did, I doubt he'd be able to chase after me in the ensuing chaos.

As soon as my body gets reduced to Swiss cheese and drops to the ground, the little trap I set up earlier activates.

"What?!"

If you asked a bunch of RPG fans what the strongest attack magic is, I bet at least a few of them would answer: Meteor.

An attack where a massive object comes crashing down from outer space is both simple and super-destructive.

That said, it's a little tough to aim at a precise spot when the starting point is literally space, so I didn't actually start from all that high.

What did I do exactly? Well, I just used spatial conjuring to make a giant rock appear in the air above us, that's all.

From there, I just have to let gravity take over, and the rock'll come crashing down and destroy everything.

If I really wanted to, I could make an even bigger object fall from even farther out in space, but that'd cause an awful lot of damage, so I decided to rein it in.

Like, it's generally accepted that a meteor wiped out the dinosaurs, y'know?

I'm not really looking to finish this planet off here.

I'm not like a certain someone who designed a Meteor weapon that could have literally destroyed the planet during that UFO incident a while back. Not naming any names...Potimas!

But yeah, you can take care of most things if you drop a big enough rock from a high enough place. No need to do anything too crazy.

Thus, the giant rock crashes down and crushes everything, including my Swiss-cheese remains.

Special Chapter The Elf Cackles

Ever since that day, I have been a very busy man.

But I've been busy in a way that I found deeply satisfying.

My plan to engage in a spot of harassment by sending elves to support the rebel demons has ended in spectacular failure.

Ariel somehow caught wind of the rebel army's movements ahead of time and unfortunately attacked them before we could finish our preparations.

I cannot blame the rebel leader for this, as even I had never imagined we would be so swiftly and suddenly detected, then attacked in short order.

Worse yet, and even more embarrassing, my own teleport gate was used against me for a surprise attack.

I lost no less than twenty-seven of the humanoid Glorias I had been preparing.

Recently, thanks to the irritating presence of the Word of God pontiff and the Hero, it's been more difficult to acquire the primary parts needed to create these super-soldiers.

To lose so many of them now of all times was a rather significant blow.

On top of that, since the teleport gate was destroyed, I've been forced to leave Oka in demon lands for the time being.

The option of giving up on her did cross my mind, but it would be even more troublesome if she was to make contact with Ariel and, in the worst-case scenario, begin colluding with her.

Letting her die in a ditch somewhere would be fine, but she knows the location of the hidden teleport gate that leads directly to the elf village, and of course I cannot let that information fall into Ariel's hands.

I'm willing to kill her myself if need be, but if I can recover her alive, that would be preferable.

I formed a rescue team led by elves who can use Quick Teleport.

I attempted to dispatch them to the demon territory, but that wound up being a fool's errand, though not in a bad way.

With Agner's help, Oka and the other survivors were able to escape from the demon realm into the human realm on their own.

This means I now owe Agner a debt, but that's not a particularly major issue.

I've received information that some of the Demon Lord's underlings—in other words, Ariel's pawns—have been causing a fuss at the border between the territory of demons and humans.

That does concern me slightly, but since I was able to recover Oka, I suppose I can let it go.

While Oka was being rescued, I went to inspect the remains of the teleport gate in the human realm that connected to the demon realm.

It had been destroyed without a trace, but I carefully dug up the area.

I just had to see it with my own eyes.

And then I found something.

"Well, now you've done it. Thanks a lot."

Ariel's voice spoke to me, sounding lower than usual.

I was sometimes able to hear her by way of the head of the body double I used during the G-Fleet incident, which she had collected.

Most of its features had already been disabled, but I left the audio- and video-recording functions on when she took it.

It appeared that Ariel knew that, though, so when she was in the room containing the head, she let it record only information that would be of no use to me. Sometimes she would even feed it fake information with the hope of misleading me.

If I took the bait, that was fine.

And if I didn't, it was no loss to her.

I suppose the girl has learned to use her brain at least a little.

But now she's undoubtedly speaking to me directly.

"Don't think this means you've won."

With that, the audio and video cut out.

She must have crushed the head she was speaking into.

"Heh-heh."

A small snicker escapes my lips.

"Heh-heh… Bwa-ha-ha-ha-ha!"

I am indeed cackling aloud, though not all that loudly.

How long has it been since I laughed like this?

How long has it been since my spirits soared the way they do now?

Ariel's bitter words of defeat ring pleasantly in my ears.

I gazed happily at the thing I had found in the teleport gate ruins.

"I finally did it."

It was barely in one piece, but it was undoubtedly White's corpse.

Twenty-seven humanoid Glorias?

The time and effort spent to retrieve Oka?

All of that was a small price to pay.

I'd gladly have given all that and more to finally destroy this creature who has plagued me these last few years.

Truth be told, I was planning to send ten times that number of humanoid Glorias to aid the rebel army.

I was even prepared to lose them all in the process.

All without knowing what the results of the battle might be.

Compared to that, I've now gained a massive victory at minimal cost.

This is a huge blow to Ariel's strength.

Her remaining underlings are still a problem, but they're nothing I can't handle.

And Ariel herself is not my enemy.

Demons? Little more than garbage.

It's undoubtedly safe to lessen my vigilance of Ariel and her ilk.

Which means all I have to deal with now is the movements of the Word of God pontiff.

He's been using the Hero to go around destroying branches of my organization.

But even that hardly matters now.

I killed White.

I don't need to rush to collect more parts anymore.

Besides, I've already collected the majority of those precious reincarnations. That means there's little need to continue using that organization to kidnap children as a cover for my goals.

I can probably reduce the scale of their endeavors now.

My time in the sun has come at last.

It grates on my nerves that the pontiff has interfered with me so persistently, but that is of little consequence now.

If I was to go and slay the Hero who serves him, it would cause trouble for me as well.

Now that the chaotic element known as White is out of the picture, I have nothing to fear from Ariel's camp.

But it would still be foolish to destroy the Hero—the pawn best suited to destroying the Demon Lord.

Especially since the Hero is still young. As soon as a Hero dies, the living human who is best suited to the role in terms of overall strength and personality automatically becomes the new one.

Since a young human with still-developing abilities and strengths was chosen as the Hero, that means there is no human alive older than the current Hero who is better suited for the role.

So if this Hero dies, the next one could very well be an even younger human.

This one is already too young to go up against Ariel, so a younger one would be even more useless.

Thus, I cannot lay a hand on the current Hero, even if it galls me to act as the pontiff has undoubtedly predicted.

I have many other tasks at hand, so once we've collected the remaining reincarnations, I shall withdraw my forces there.

But perhaps I can find another avenue through which to attempt to crush the Word of God religion.

At any rate, the destruction of White, one of the biggest thorns in my side, is a great relief.

As I stand up from my chair to proceed to my next action, my footsteps feel a good deal lighter than usual.

5 Let's Observe a Meeting

Hey, it's me.

What, you thought I was dead?

Well, TOO BAD! I'm totally alive!

How did I survive, you ask?

By using the mini-me revival method I mentioned a while back, DUH.

The mini-mes might seem like clones, but they're basically an extension of my body.

Even if you detach them from the original, aka me, they're still a part of me.

And the "original" is just where my consciousness happens to be residing at the moment. Its makeup isn't actually all that different from that of my clones.

Sure, there's the question of whether it takes the form of a human or a spider, but that's small potatoes.

What's important is the soul inside it, not the details of the physical body.

And I've already transferred that soul from one vessel to another by way of egg revival before I was deified, so I figured there's no reason it wouldn't work now.

So when I was caught in a real pinch, I just ditched the body I'd been using all that time and transferred myself into one of my random clones. Boom! Instant resurrection.

Whew. I've still got plenty of extra lives!

Way more than that old dude in overalls who gets more lives when he eats green mushrooms!

If you see one of me, you better call an exterminator, 'cause there's probably a hundred more where that came from!

So yeah, I basically can't die unless something totally bonkers happens, but that doesn't mean I'm gonna go around using up my extra lives like it's no big deal.

I don't need to remind you that my clones are so weak that a single stomp could crush them.

And since I've lost my main body, that means I had to hop into one of those.

I can't seem to do anything about how weak these clones are at the moment, so I'm doomed to get a lot weaker after I use this revival method.

Although I guess the one small mercy is that I'll return to my original strength if given enough time. All I have to do is get through this inevitable period of weakness.

My palm-size body gets a whole lot bigger over the course of a couple of days, sprouts a human top half from the trunk, and eventually returns to my hard-won human form.

Pretty impressive recovery, or rather "regrowth," if I do say so myself.

It's far removed from any normal creature's healing process, but hey, I am technically a god.

I'm sure this is totally super-normal.

...Then again, that means other gods are probably at least as immortal as I am, which is actually pretty scary.

But I gotta say, this revival period gave me the perfect excuse to avoid a lot of annoying post-battle chores, so maybe it's not so bad.

Yeah. I let Vampy know that I'm more or less fine, but I won't be able to move for a few days, so I basically dumped all the work on her.

That made things a whole lot easier.

The battle in the northern town pretty much ended while I was busy reviving.

Thanks in no small part to Mr. Oni, the mammoth task of capturing an entire town was accomplished in a relatively short amount of time.

The ringleader behind the rebels, the lord of the northern town, was captured, and the rebel soldiers have all been disarmed and gathered in one place.

There are still some rebels from other areas who hadn't reached the northern town yet, but since the place that served as their main base has been thoroughly crushed, they don't have the strength to put up organized resistance anymore.

It's probably safe to say that the rebel army is over and done with.

Now all we need to do is rebuild the northern town and appoint a new lord, and this whole problem will be taken care of.

Okay, those tasks are actually a huge pain, but we can leave all that to Balto.

Once I'm done recovering, I can just stroll back into the duke's mansion like nothing happened.

...But when I did return to the mansion, there was a summons from the Demon Lord waiting for me.

"Oh good, you're here."

After receiving the summons, I headed to the Demon Lord's castle.

There's already a small group of people gathered there in a large room when I enter.

The Demon Lord is sitting at the head of the table, the leader of the rebel army is standing in the middle of the room, and a bunch of other important-looking people are seated around a table facing him.

At a glance, the scene reminds me of a courtroom.

The defendant, the judge, and the jury.

And considering what's about to happen, I guess my impression isn't too far off.

We're having a trial to determine the fate of Mr. Warkis, the leader of the rebel army.

But Mr. Warkis doesn't get a lawyer, and of course, the presiding judge is the Demon Lord herself.

So it's pretty obvious that he's gonna get slapped with a guilty verdict, y'know?

The participants in this more or less rigged trial are all big-name demons.

Sitting closest to the Demon Lord is our old pal Colonel, who serves as the First Army Commander of the Demon Lord's army.

Uh, what's his real name again? Agner, I think.

He's got such a commanding, militant presence that he looks way more dignified than the little girl who's actually the Demon Lord.

Sitting opposite the Colonel is Balto, and right next to him is Deadbeat, who's sitting there grumpily with his arms crossed.

And for some reason, Mera and Mr. Oni are standing behind them.

The rest of the jury is all people I've never met before...but I more or less know who they are thanks to the information I've gathered with my mini-mes.

The first one who grabs my attention is Boobs.

Yeah, I know. Not the classiest nickname.

But can you blame me?!

That's the first thing anyone would notice about her! I can barely tear my eyes away!

Seriously, what the hell? Are those real?

Like, y'know how people normally compare a really big rack to melons or whatever?

I always thought boobs of that caliber existed only in the realm of 2D, so imagine my surprise when I saw them in real life for the very first time.

When they're THAT big, well...it kinda just turns the whole thing into a joke, to be honest.

I can't even bring myself to focus on her face or anywhere else.

Man, it's a good thing I figured out how to use x-ray vision. Otherwise, everyone would know that I'm staring at her boobs.

Anyway, Miss Boobs's real name is Sanatoria.

She might look like a sexy, sultry supermodel with nothing going for her but the aforementioned lethal weapons, but she's the commander of the Second Army of the Demon Lord's forces.

As you may have gathered at this point, all of the army commanders are here.

I imagine they don't have a lot of free time, so since they're all gathered at the same time, you can tell this rebellion thing was a pretty big deal.

The Third Army Commander is a muscle-bound behemoth—the total opposite of Miss Boobs.

He's got a seriously ripped bod with visible battle scars. He's the perfect image of a seasoned combat veteran.

...Buuut you can tell from his wimpy expression that he's bound to be unreliable.

Since he's got the title of commander and all, you know those muscles aren't just for show; he must be really powerful. But the way he's absolutely oozing nervous energy, I can't really take him seriously.

The Gentle Giant's name is Kogou.

Number four is Balto, so we'll skip him.

The Fifth Army Commander is a guy named Darad. To sum him up in a word, he's basically like a foreigner's poor misconception of a samurai.

Okay, that's more than one word, but there's no other way to describe it.

Like, I know he's not actually cosplaying or anything, but for some reason, he looks like a Kabuki actor. And yet, he has the air of a straitlaced warrior about him.

What else would you call it if not a knockoff samurai?

He's probably dead serious about that getup, of course, and it's probably just a coincidence that his hair and outfit happen to come together and make him look that way to me.

Nobody else here ever makes any snarky comments about it.

Maybe it's just because I have memories of Japan?

Either way, my private nickname for Darad is definitely Mr. Samurai.

Moving on, the Sixth Army Commander's nickname is Shota.

Look, I get that demons live longer than humans, so they can look a lot younger than their real age, but this boy still looks especially young, hence my nickname for him.

He's probably an adult, but to me, all I see is a little kid.

There are always people like that, who look impossibly young even when they get older.

I've heard that Japanese people's features seem that way to most foreigners, but in the case of Shota here, his youthful face pairs perfectly with his short stature.

I gotta say, having just one person who looks like a kid among all these adults really stands out.

Huh? The Demon Lord?

Nah, she's an exception. You're not supposed to count her.

Shota's real name is Huey

Which brings us to number seven, and guess what? The Seventh Army Commander is none other than the leader of the rebel army, Mr. Warkis himself.

Seems like most of the rebel army were members of the Seventh Army, too.

So we've got Colonel, Boobs, Gentle Giant, Mr. Samurai, and Shota. Plus the leader of the rebel army.

Geez, talk about a colorful cast of characters!

By comparison, numbers eight, nine, and ten are pretty boring.

The Eighth Army Commander is a sheepish older guy, the Ninth looks like a capable office worker, and the Tenth is a dude who's kinda handsome but looks like the unlucky type.

Sure, they've all got unique characteristics, but they don't stand out much compared to the rest of this rowdy bunch.

And honestly, they don't matter as much.

Sure, they've earned the title of commander, but these three don't actually have their own armies to speak of at the moment.

During wartime, they had proper armies, but since the war with the humans is suspended right now, their forces were disbanded, since the demons don't have a ton of soldiers to spare. While they've technically kept their posts, they're not in charge of anyone at the moment.

So what do these three actually do? Internal affairs, it turns out.

They help run the government along with Balto, who leaves most of his army's affairs in the hands of his little brother, Deadbeat.

Anyway, with all these guys in one room, it's essentially a meeting of all the demon race's big players.

"Over here, White. Have a seat."

The Demon Lord directs me to a chair…right next to her.

Uh, isn't this where someone really important normally sits?

Now all these people I've never met before are staring at me…

Stop it! Don't look at me like that!

I shuffle over as discreetly as I can and have a seat.

"Okay, now that we're all here, let's get started."

The Demon Lord begins the meeting, ignoring my dismay.

That means all eyes turn to the Demon Lord, which means they're *also* looking at the person sitting right next to her, aka me.

Wow, I am super-uncomfortable right now.

"Okay. I'm sure you're all aware by now that Seventh Army Commander Warkis was plotting a rebellion. Although it didn't amount to anything, since our dear White here sniffed out his plans before he could make a move."

On hearing that, most of the eyes in the room move to Mr. Warkis or me.

Just focus on the guy on trial here, pleeease.

"It appears that the rebellion was primarily made up of Seventh Army soldiers, but there were a few members from some other commands, too, apparently. Pretty weird, right?"

Uh-huh. There were soldiers from all over the demon territory.

So it definitely wasn't just Seventh Army soldiers filling out the rebel army.

But we're not sure if those soldiers were acting on their own or sent there by their superiors.

Either way, any of the armies that produced traitors are probably gonna be feeling real uncomfortable right now.

Although since these guys are pros and all, the leaders who had traitors in their ranks are all maintaining perfect poker faces, even while enduring the Demon Lord's accusatory tone.

Oh, actually, Third Army Commander Gentle Giant is kinda sweating it out over there.

"Well, I'll follow up with each force later. Right now, we're here to decide how to deal with Warkis and the Seventh Army."

The Demon Lord looks around at the commanders as she speaks.

But I dunno if that's really a question...

"Although obviously, Warkis is gonna be executed."

Yeah, I figured. He did try to start a rebellion, after all.

"Any objections? Hmm?"

Nobody makes a move to respond to this question, which seems to mostly be a formality anyway.

Even Deadbeat is watching in silence, although he doesn't look too thrilled.

Of course he's not gonna try to stick his neck out for the leader of a rebellion.

"All right. If there are no objections, then that's settled."

Just like that, his death sentence has been decided.

Geez, that was quick.

They sure don't value life all that much in this world.

"Anything you'd like to say to defend yourself, Warkis?" the Demon Lord asks.

"Naturally."

The defendant responds in a surprisingly strong tone.

He's just been marked for execution, but he doesn't seem the least bit shaken.

Is he seriously gonna try to defend himself?

I can't tell if he's being brave or what. Maybe he figures now that he's got nothing to lose, he might as well give her a piece of his mind.

"Any fool who wishes to declare war on the humans without a single thought for the future is unfit to be the Demon Lord. I simply acted accordingly. That is all."

Oh, *wow.*

This guy just insulted the Demon Lord to her face.

Guess he's feeling pretty defiant after all.

"A fool, am I?"

"Certainly. We cannot allow an ignorant brat who doesn't even understand the demon race's plight to continue to wreak havoc with our future."

Daaaamn, tell us how you really feel.

Little do you know, this "brat" is actually a whole lot older than you.

Also, she understands the demon race's plight extremely well; she's simply decided to pit them against the humans anyway.

Hmm... Wait, isn't that worse?

"You call me a traitor. But from my perspective, it is you all, who continue to cooperate with this fool and lick her boots, who are the true traitors to the demon race."

Mr. Warkis glares around the room at the other commanders.

Their reactions vary: Some look away awkwardly, some steadily return his gaze, some keep their thoughts from showing on their faces, and...

Uh, Deadbeat? Why are you nodding along like you totally agree with what he's saying?!

Whose side are you on anyway?!

"Traitors, hmm...?"

Despite Warkis's harsh accusations against the Demon Lord and her commanders, she seems totally unfazed.

In fact, she's even smiling a little as she watches Mr. Warkis, who takes the opportunity to let his passions run even wilder.

"All of you! If you care about the demon race, what better time to act than now?! Surely, it is not too late to cast out this pretender and bring our race back to the proper path?!"

Hmm.

Depending on how you look at it, this moment could be the perfect opportunity to act on their grievances.

The Demon Lord doesn't have a single guard, and everyone here is a powerful military commander.

If the majority of them decided to double-cross her right now, she'd have to fend them all off, with me as her only certain ally.

And several of the armies sent soldiers to aid the rebellion. If that was at the behest of their commanders, that means some of these guys are with the rebels.

They probably didn't have time to make any arrangements beforehand, but they could very well answer Mr. Warkis's call by drawing their weapons right here and now.

...Although whether they'd actually stand a chance of winning is another story.

"Is that all you have to say?"

The first person to break the silence in this powder keg situation is none other than the Colonel.

"Lord Agner?!"

"Warkis. Whatever nonsense you may bluster about, they are naught but the meaningless excuses of a traitor. If you truly care for the demon race, as you say, then all that remains for you to do is take yourself to the chopping block and lay down your head. For a demon to speak out against the Demon Lord is inexcusable. You should be ashamed of yourself."

Ohhhh damn!

The Colonel's got one hell of a presence.

Being recognized as one of the most powerful demons by the Demon Lord herself, he knows his words carry some serious weight.

And now that a big shot like him has shut down Warkis so firmly, the other commanders can't really make any stupid moves, since the Colonel basically just declared that he's siding with the Demon Lord.

It was already an unstable situation where the commanders were mostly stealing uncertain glances at one another, so things could have gone either way, but now that the Colonel's cast the first stone, it's pretty much guaranteed that nobody else is gonna make a move.

I'm sure he spoke up right away knowing full well what effect his words would have, too.

This guy's good.

"But, Lord Agner, you—"

"I care deeply for the demon race, too, of course. But that has nothing to do with this. It does not justify turning against the Demon Lord."

After this unwavering declaration by the Colonel, who holds as much or maybe even more sway in this room than the Demon Lord, Warkis's shoulders sag as if he realizes that he's lost.

Then he looks up at the ceiling and speaks in a quiet but determined voice.

"I still do not believe...that what I did was wrong."

Hmm.

Here I thought this guy was just some small-fry who got used by the elves, but he's got guts.

That sure casts him in a better light than the commanders who supported the rebel army but are now quietly hoping all the blame falls on him.

"Yeah, no. You were wrong, that's for sure." A cold voice cuts through Warkis's bold declaration. "You just don't get it, do you? I mean, seriously."

It's the Demon Lord. She's still smiling as she looks at Warkis, but she seems kind of pissed.

"A traitor against demons? Ugh. You're thinking way too small. How stupid can you get?"

Warkis glares back at her, his eyes brimming with hatred, as she speaks in an unmoved voice.

But before he can open his mouth, she continues, her words low and heavy.

"If you wanna talk treachery, it's you guys who are the real traitors. Against the gods, against the world."

This isn't an Intimidation thing.

The Demon Lord uses the Concealment skill to suppress the effects of her Intimidation skill, so it's not active right now.

Her words are just that compelling.

"You called me a fool, didn't you? But demons are the biggest fools in this whole world. The very culprits who mistreated a god, who violated a taboo, who nearly destroyed this planet, shouldn't go around prattling about their right to live. They have no such thing."

A paralyzing chill runs up my spine.

How much deep-seated hatred does it take to make a voice sound like this?

Maybe I don't know the Demon Lord very well after all.

I always think of her as a good, softhearted person, generous enough to take a former enemy like me under her wing and secretly a font of bottomless kindness.

But that's not all there is to her.

Of course it isn't.

She's a living witness to history.

As the oldest of the Ancient Divine Beasts, she's lived in this world long enough to see the cruelty of man with her own eyes and feel the devotion of a god firsthand.

When I absorbed the soul of Mother, the Demon Lord's offspring, I learned what that truly meant.

Or at least, I thought I did.

But knowing and truly understanding are two different things.

She's not just some good-natured softy.

The countless years she's endured have made the Demon Lord who she is.

Without a doubt, she's the evilest, scariest demon lord to have ever lived.

She's peered into the darkness of this world more than anyone else—enough that it's a miracle she can still dredge up kindness from the depths of her heart.

"Okay, sooo! Let's get this execution started!"

The Demon Lord says this next part in an extra-cheerful voice, as if to hide the darkness she'd let slip into her voice.

...Um, it's even scarier when you say something like that in a cheerful voice, y'know.

Look, the other commanders are totally creeped out!

"Hey, Bloe."

"Hunh?"

True to his nickname, Deadbeat responds to the Demon Lord's summons with a grunt.

Next to him, Balto clutches his forehead. Must be tough having such a pain in the ass for a little brother.

Deadbeat, are you trying to kill your own brother with sheer stress or what?

"Execute Warkis for me."

"Huh?"

Deadbeat gapes dumbly, as if he either doesn't understand the Demon Lord's order or maybe he just doesn't want to understand it.

"Did I stutter? I want you to kill Warkis. Right now."

"Wait, what? Hang on a sec! Why me?!"

Deadbeat stands up so fast, his chair falls over as he responds in a panicked tone.

Yeah, I guess most people would be alarmed if they were suddenly ordered to murder someone.

"Why, you ask? I would think you would understand that better than anyone, no?"

"Huh? No, I have no idea!"

Oh boy. He really doesn't, does he?

I guess this guy is an idiot through and through.

Obviously, the Demon Lord is testing his loyalty.

I mean, Deadbeat makes no secret of the fact that he doesn't like her or her plans.

So she's forcing him to prove his allegiance by killing Mr. Warkis, who actually did rebel against the Demon Lord, with his own hands.

I guess this serves as a warning to the others of what happens to traitors, too.

"Bloe."

"Brother! Come on—help me out here."

Deadbeat seems to have interpreted Balto's saying his name as a lifeline.

"Do it."

But his brother simply tells him to obey the Demon Lord's command.

"Brother...?"

"You have to. Prove your innocence to Her Majesty the Demon Lord. Show that there is no doubt that you would never aid the rebellion."

At this, Deadbeat appears to finally understand what the Demon Lord thinks of him.

Well, yeah. He's always shown an attitude of blatant defiance toward her, and she mentioned at the beginning of the meeting that some of the other armies contributed soldiers to the rebel ranks. It's only natural to put two and two together and guess that Deadbeat might have helped the rebels.

In reality, though, Deadbeat did no such thing.

It was a different commander who aided the rebel army.

And Balto knows that, too.

So I guess if he's telling him to do it anyway, he must have his own opinions about Deadbeat's attitude.

Maybe he thinks that at this rate, Deadbeat might try to start something, too. Or maybe he's worried that the next time something happens, Deadbeat will be the one who gets sacrificed like Warkis to prove a point.

He's definitely the easiest scapegoat, if you ask me. Given his usual attitude, everyone else would just think, *Yeah, I figured as much.*

"Wait a minute, Brother. I know he's being executed, but does that really mean we have to kill him right now? Don't we have to, y'know, interrogate him and stuff?"

Oof, buddy, that is *not* the best look for you right now.

Sure, he's not wrong. There's no real reason to carry out the execution right away, and it'd be a smart move to try to squeeze information out of him first, too.

But by saying that now, Deadbeat will make everyone think that he doesn't want to kill Warkis.

Even though he doesn't actually have any ties to the rebel army, you can't blame people for suspecting him with that kind of attitude.

He probably really does sympathize with Warkis, emotionally speaking.

"Bloe!"

All too aware of this, his brother, Balto, snaps a warning.

If he doesn't shake any suspicions off Deadbeat now, it's possible that he'll be suspected of involvement, too, being his older brother.

"Urk...!"

Hearing the tension in his brother's voice, Bloe appears to realize his own error.

But he's still not moving yet.

"Ahhh, I guess it might be tough unarmed, huh? Here, use this."

The Demon Lord tosses a knife over to Deadbeat; it lands on the table in front of him with a *thud*.

Deadbeat stares at the knife, then raises his head to look at Warkis, who looks back at him in expressionless silence.

"I don't—"

"I'll not be reduced to experience points for this fool!"

Just as Deadbeat is about to speak, Warkis lunges forward with a shout.

He runs over to Deadbeat, grabs the knife, and stabs it downward.

For a moment, no one can move.

No, I guess a few of us probably could, but no one *did*.

I guess I fall in the latter camp.

"For the future…of the demon race…"

The knife sinks deep into Warkis's own stomach.

He then goes as far as slitting his own throat before jabbing the knife into his heart.

I guess since there are stats in this world that make people harder to kill, suicide methods have to be a lot more extreme.

Which makes Warkis's manner of death all the more dramatic.

And, at the same time, heroic.

I always thought that you'd have to be an idiot to take your own life.

If you have the good fortune to be alive, and you decide to give that up of your own volition, there's something wrong with you for sure.

From that perspective, Warkis's actions seem really stupid, too.

But beneath the part of me that feels that way, I also feel the urge to commend him for the way he lived.

Mr. Warkis had convictions and pride.

He didn't just meander through life—he dedicated himself to his principles, to what he believed was right.

But no matter how much pride and conviction you have, you also need the strength to see them through.

And if you have strength but no pride or conviction, you're just violent and dangerous.

Take Potimas, for instance. He's got plenty of power, but he lives without a code, so he's nothing but a plague.

Power and pride.

You gotta have both.

Without the former, you'll just fall on your way to the top, like Warkis, and without pride, you'll just be a pest like Potimas.

Life is tough like that.

But Mr. Warkis stuck firmly to his beliefs until his dying breath.

Taking your own life might not align with my personal beliefs, but I still want to show respect for the way he lived.

"Bloe."

The Demon Lord's voice echoes through the frozen silence of the room.

Bloe, in shock with Warkis's blood splattered over him, looks up in a daze.

"Out of respect for Warkis, I won't press the matter any further today."

Deadbeat grimaces at her detached tone, but before he can say or do anything, Balto pushes his head down and bows alongside him.

"We deeply appreciate your generosity, O Great Demon Lord."

I can't see Deadbeat's expression, since Balto's holding him in a bow, but I wouldn't be surprised if he's grinding his teeth.

"Yeah, yeah. Okay, you can take over as Warkis's successor, then, Bloe."

The Demon Lord delivers this finishing blow to Deadbeat with a wicked smile.

"Release the captured members of the Seventh Army and use them along with your own men. It'd be a waste to execute that many soldiers at a time like this, so we're gonna put 'em to good use."

In other words, she's putting the rebel army in Deadbeat's hands as is.

Deadbeat already resents the Demon Lord, and she's putting him in charge of a bunch of guys who already rebelled against her once before.

Yikes, what an awful combo. Even Balto looks disturbed.

"To that end, you'll be making the northern town your base. So take care of restoration and stuff, too."

"Understood, Your Majesty."

Again, before Deadbeat can protest, Balto speaks up for him.

You can tell he doesn't intend to let his little brother say another word.

"Balto, you'll be in charge of the Fourth Army for now, but I'll probably find someone else to take it over for Bloe soon so you can focus on administration stuff."

The Demon Lord glances over at Mera and Mr. Oni.

Maybe that means they're the top contenders to lead Balto's army.

Ohhh, so that's why they're here. I knew she must've wanted to introduce them to the other commanders for a reason.

"I'm planning to put together a proper army for the Eighth, Ninth, and Tenth soon, too. But I want you guys to keep helping with domestic affairs, so I'll probably make other people the commanders instead. That means you'll lose the title, so your pay's gonna go down, but you're fine with that, right?"

The three army-less commanders nod silently without so much as an unpleasant face among them.

Well, yeah, I wouldn't put my life on the line to complain about a pay cut, either.

"All right, I think that's about it. You're dismissed! Oh, White and you two over there, hang back for a minute."

The Demon Lord breaks up the meeting but gestures for Mera, Mr. Oni, and me to stay.

The Colonel stands up and starts to walk toward Mr. Warkis's body.

"You can leave that there. I'll clean it up later."

At that, the Colonel stops his march, turns on his heel, bows silently to the Demon Lord, and leaves the room without another word. The rest of the commanders file out after him.

Deadbeat looks furious—*You're gonna keep disgracing his body like that?!* is written all over his face—but Balto drags him out forcefully before he can say anything.

Once all the commanders are gone, Mera quietly closes the door.

As soon as he's done, the Demon Lord deliberately opens and closes her mouth.

Just like that, Mr. Warkis's body is gone from the floor, without a speck of blood left behind.

One look at the way the Demon Lord's mouth is munching answers the question of where it went.

She must have used her Gluttony skill to consume the corpse.

If Deadbeat saw this, he'd probably lose his mind, but it's not really like that at all.

My Parallel Mind, the former body brain, fused with the Demon Lord. So I know exactly what that gesture means.

It's probably not clear to anyone else but me, but the Demon Lord isn't eating Warkis's body as a mockery. In fact, it's the opposite.

She's eating him without leaving a single drop of blood as a sign of respect. I know that without a doubt.

As I watch the Demon Lord chewing in silence, there's not a trace of the smirk she wore throughout the meeting. A certain emotion shows through her expression, to the point that you might suspect she was a different person entirely.

She's brimming with sorrow and grim resolve.

"You okay?"

That's right. It's so bad that I actually open my mouth and say something.

The Demon Lord looks so startled by my spoken question that she accidentally swallows what's left in her mouth.

Mera and Mr. Oni stare at me with surprise, too.

H-hey, I talk once in a while, and I worry about others on occasion, too, okay?!

Don't look at me like this is some earth-shattering revelation! It's insulting!

"Pfft!"

The Demon Lord snorts, possibly noticing my annoyance.

"Heh-heh...ah-ha-ha-ha!"

Now she's laughing her head off.

Which only makes me scowl even more.

And Mera and Mr. Oni clearly have no idea how to react.

"Okay, okay. Sorry for laughing. Really. Uh...yeah. Thanks for worrying about me." When she finally catches her breath for a moment, the Demon Lord shares a word of gratitude. "Yeah, I'm okay. Really. I made up my mind to deal with all this a long time ago."

With that, she returns to her usual smile.

I can tell it's not just an act because of the look in her eyes.

...Man, she's strong.

And I don't mean her stats or skills. If anything, that's just the tip of the iceberg.

No, the real source of the Demon Lord's strength is that heart of hers.

She feels guilt for having to box the demon race into a corner like this, but she still has the pride and conviction to stick with it.

She's an incredibly kind person deep down, yet she's resolved to walk the thorny path of a villain.

Even if it means trampling her own conscience, she's got the inner strength to keep going.

Warkis may have had pride and conviction, but he didn't have power.

The Demon Lord has all three of those things, in far greater supply than Warkis ever did.

So what about me?

I've got strength, that's for sure. But what about pride and conviction?

...I've lived a pretty reckless life so far.

Almost everything I've done was to make sure I could stand and face enemies who threatened my very existence, instead of running away.

I've lived my life with pride in my own way...or at least, I thought so.

But looking at folks like Warkis and the Demon Lord, I'm not so sure.

In the end, did I really have any pride and conviction, or have I been living simply to survive?

I wish I could deny that with more certainty, but it's hard when the Demon Lord sets such a shining example. When I see the way she lives her life with such pride and confidence, I can't help but look up to her.

And if I'm looking up to her, that means we're not on the same level, y'know?

I can't help but be drawn to that glow of hers.

"Okay, White. I had you stay back because I wanted to share some information with you. Although the matter in question is a little bit troublesome."

Hmm.

If the Demon Lord's calling it "a little bit troublesome"...doesn't that mean it's actually a pretty big deal?

Mm, I can't think of many things she would be that worried about, though...

If anything, maybe it's those damn elves again? But I've got a decent idea of what's going on there already... In fact, I'm the one who trespassed on Potimas's property.

I crushed the whole base that was connected to the northern town, including Potimas, although it was kind of a draw, since I lost my own body in the process.

But I'm sure that Potimas wasn't the real thing, so he'll probably pop up to bother us again.

I even had the Demon Lord put on a little act so Potimas thinks I'm actually dead.

Sure, there's a chance he might see that as an opportunity to attack us with everything he's got, but knowing Potimas, I don't think that's too likely.

That guy's all about being cost-effective, y'know?

He probably figured he could use the rebel army as a vehicle to deal some damage to us, but since the rebellion came to an abrupt end, and I even crushed a base of his and caused him some major losses of his own, I'm almost positive he's gonna keep to himself for a while.

Plus, since I destroyed his precious teleport gate, he doesn't have a convenient shortcut into the demon realm anymore.

Physical distance is a deciding factor in this world, so it'd be tough for some no-good elf to try to invade a territory located at the far end of the world.

Especially when the Demon Lord's already ordered elves to stay out of demon territory.

So it'd be pretty tough for any elves to get up to no good in the demon territory undetected.

I guess it's possible he had other teleport gates or something, but after this incident, Potimas is probably being extra careful about not letting any information leak.

So if he has any other valuable teleport gates, he'd probably be extra careful not to do anything to draw attention to them... At least, that's my optimistic outlook.

Besides, teleport gates are super-valuable, so I'm sure he doesn't have that many of them lying around.

...Right?

Okay, I guess I'll have my clones investigate just in case.

But overall, that still means that it'd be difficult for elves to get up to anything else in demon lands right now.

Which means the effort involved would far outweigh any possible benefits.

That's the worst possible situation for someone like Potimas, who's obsessed with being cost-effective.

And since he thinks he's killed me, that'll probably satisfy him enough to keep him from going after us too intently for a while.

Although I'm alive and well, thank you very much!

Which means this probably doesn't have anything to do with the elves... So what could the "*troublesome*" topic be?

"We've found a new reincarnation."

Oh, so that's it, huh?

That explains why she wanted to keep it to this group in particular, then.

Mr. Oni is a reincarnation, and Mera has ties to them by way of Vampy.

"I'll remember to tell Sophia about it later, but I couldn't exactly have her come here, y'know?"

Yeah, I guess bringing a literal child to an assembly of military commanders would be a little weird.

"I'll have Wrath take it from here, since he's the one who found out firsthand."

With that, the Demon Lord looks to Mr. Oni.

Hmm? Mr. Oni met a reincarnation?

What? Where?

Thinking about it, when could he possibly have had the time to find a reincarnation? While he was blowing up the rebel army?

Besides, finding another reincarnation might be a troublesome topic for those of us directly involved, but why would the Demon Lord be that concerned about it?

It doesn't really have much to do with her. Why would she call it "*troublesome*"?

Uh-oh. I'm starting to get a really bad feeling about this.

"I met our teacher. During the battle. She was fighting alongside the rebels in the northern town. As one of the elves."

......Huh?

...What?

Whaaaat?!

Interlude BROTHERS

Dragging Bloe by the back of the collar, I quickly stride toward my private room in the Demon Lord's castle, where I often spend my nights.

As the head of a dukedom, I am reasonably well trained, but my stats cannot compare to Bloe's, since he's led armies into real battle.

Which means it would be an easy task for him to escape my grasp if he wished, so the fact that he makes no effort to resist means he must recognize his own failure.

Ideally, I would like him to repent for his actions and make a heartfelt declaration of loyalty to the Demon Lord, but I have known him long enough to be painfully aware that he will do no such thing.

When we reach my room, I fling the door open and shove Bloe inside.

Then I follow him in and slam it shut behind me.

If anyone else was here, they would undoubtedly be surprised to see such a different side of me.

I make a point of interacting with everyone but my closest friends and family as politely as possible.

Normally, I would never even raise my voice, never mind move with such violence.

Fortunately, since we made it here without running into anyone else, my image is still intact. Hopefully.

I took the longest route possible from the meeting room to this location in order to avoid the busiest areas, but it was still a stroke of luck that we didn't encounter anyone at all.

If someone saw me like this, I'm sure word would be all over the castle by tomorrow.

And it's even more imperative that no one hears the conversation we're about to have.

So much so that any mere rumors about me would be insignificant by comparison.

But in my private room, with no one else around, we should be able to speak freely.

"Brother..."

Bloe turns around to look at me with a miserable expression.

I promptly punch him in the face with all my strength.

"OOF!"

Bloe staggers back a step, but he doesn't fall.

He is quite strong, after all. I spend far more time at the desk than on the battlefield, so even my strongest punch won't cause him much pain, given the difference in our stats.

If anything, it's my hand that hurts from punching him.

But that's the least of my worries right now.

"You absolute moron!"

I grab Bloe's collar with my still-throbbing hand.

"Do you have any idea what position you've just put yourself in?!"

"Uhhh, I..."

"You do, don't you?! Don't you dare tell me you don't! You've practically wrapped yourself in the colors of a traitor! If you make one wrong move, it'll be your head on the chopping block!"

"Brother, I—"

"You didn't mean to. Is that what you're going to say?! You idiot! Your feelings aren't important right now! You were already on the verge of being a symbol of anti-demon-lord sentiment thanks to the way you've acted all this time! Nobody else knows what you might be thinking or feeling on the inside, you know. That's why I kept telling you to change your attitude!"

Over and over, every time I saw him, I gave him the same warning.

He refused to listen, stubbornly holding a grudge against the Demon Lord, and now he's reaping his reward.

I roughly let go of his collar, collapsing into a chair.

Bloe stands stock-still, as if at a total loss.

"Why didn't you just execute Warkis like she asked?"

I know full well that Bloe could do no such thing, but the question spills out anyway.

Yes, I understand.

That Bloe sympathized with Warkis's declarations and saw him as a comrade.

That they spent many years side by side, leading their respective armies together.

They were more than comrades. They were friends. It's only natural that he would hesitate when suddenly ordered to put him to death.

And yet, if he had only acted as he was told, things never would've deteriorated this badly.

"Brother, I…I couldn't do it."

"Right. I figured as much."

The Demon Lord knew that full well when she gave him that order.

She wanted to make Bloe her next sacrifice.

No matter what the Demon Lord's policies might be, the majority will never accept her.

So sooner or later, someone was bound to raise the banner of revolt against her.

Warkis just happened to step into the shooting gallery first.

He was a straightforward man, entirely too simple.

That was why he was manipulated and used as the figurehead of the rebel army.

And now Bloe is going to be next.

"Bloe, you're at the top of the list of the Demon Lord's dissenters now. How you actually feel isn't relevant anymore. Even if it wasn't your intention, rebels will start to gather around you. Do you understand what I'm saying?"

"…Yeah."

It's too late to stop this now.

He's been put in charge of the Seventh Army—the former rebel army—and he's already made it clear to everyone that he's not fond of the Demon Lord, either.

That meeting sealed his fate.

Thanks to Warkis's actions, we were able to avoid the worst-case scenario, but it's still evident that Bloe intended to disobey the Demon Lord's order to execute him.

This colossal failure isn't merely a refusal to follow orders; it's also tantamount to a declaration that he sides with the rebel army.

I'm sure the other commanders saw it that way, and the Demon Lord seemed to only encourage that interpretation.

Yes, that's right.

That meeting was a setup.

It was all to establish Bloe as the next anti-demon-lord rebel leader.

There was at least one other commander who really was working with Warkis.

A traitor who put Warkis at the front of the rebellion, supported him from behind the scenes, and was careful not to leave behind any concrete proof.

The real purpose of the meeting was for the Demon Lord to indicate to that commander, or commanders, that Bloe is Warkis's successor.

Whether Bloe actually intends to rebel or not, other rebel forces will begin to flock to his banner.

The Demon Lord set it up that way.

Because it makes things easier for her to deal with.

"Listen carefully. You only have one option now. Find a way to take control of these rebel forces and ensure that they do not revolt. As soon as you fail to contain them, it'll be your head. And not just you. This time, there's sure to be a serious purge."

Bloe gulps, as if he finally understands the position he's in, as well as the immense weight of his failure.

"Why...? How did it come to this?"

That's what I'd like to know.

But there really was no way to avoid this outcome.

Bloe was too convenient a scapegoat for the Demon Lord.

Since he made no effort to hide his animosity toward the Demon Lord, it was all too easy to arrange for him to stand at the front of the rebellion against her.

Even though he never actually rebelled against her. Even though he followed her orders, however reluctantly.

He's the perfect person to serve as the new figurehead of the rebellion. He's also the best candidate when it comes to forcing someone to keep them in check.

But the key issue here is that the Demon Lord isn't actually expecting him to succeed at that for long.

If he can, that's great for her, but it's no skin off her back if he fails, either.

Then she can just wipe out all the rebel forces in one fell swoop.

Either way, the Demon Lord comes out on top.

If Bloe succeeds, she doesn't have to purge valuable soldiers, and if he fails, she can get rid of all her dissenters at once.

Whereas Bloe is stuck between a rock and a hard place, trying to keep the rebels in check while also dutifully obeying the Demon Lord.

If he makes one misstep, he'll plummet off the tightrope and into the abyss. But he has to make it all the way across against all odds in order to live.

I know he made this bed for himself with his constant attitude, but still—why did it have to come to this?!

"Hey, Brother. Is that really the only way?"

"Bloe. Don't say another word. Don't even think it."

I know exactly what he's getting at.

No doubt he's wondering if he couldn't just become the rebel leader for real and overthrow the Demon Lord.

But if it were that easy, we wouldn't be in such dire straits.

"I've told you this countless times. And I'll continue to do so until you finally understand. You do not stand a chance of defeating the Demon Lord. If I may be blunt, even attempting to fight her would be nothing short of suicide."

Bloe's face sours, as if he can't accept the finality of my statement.

But whether he accepts it or not, it's the absolute truth.

Surely, Bloe must at least realize that the Demon Lord is no ordinary person.

I'm sure it's still hard to believe.

It must be dawning on him by now that even if he managed to unite every living demon under one banner, he still wouldn't have the manpower needed to take her down.

I might not have believed it, either, if I hadn't witnessed her power with my own eyes.

No, in fact, I'm sure I wouldn't believe it.

How could anyone accept such a preposterous idea?

"Bloe. What's the single strongest monster you've ever encountered?"

Bloe looks perplexed by my sudden change of subject, but he thinks about it for a moment and responds.

"In a swarm, it's definitely anogratches, but if we're talking a single monster, probably the obrock or the deloombeik."

The anogratch is a monster that lives in the Mystic Mountains.

Also known as "revenge monkeys," they move in large packs. As the name implies, if a single member of their pack is killed, they'll seek revenge.

Even if it means their entire pack will be wiped out in the attempt.

Killing even one anogratch can rapidly develop into a disaster.

If you fight off the swarm that comes after you, that means it becomes necessary to fight even more anogratches. This starts another chain of vengeful rage, and it'll continue until all the anogratches in the swarm are dead.

As if that wasn't bad enough, the anogratches periodically increase their numbers and descend from the Mystic Mountains on a rampage.

Each time they stampede like this, we have to send out whole armies to deal with them.

In that sense, they're more dangerous than any other monster in the demon territory.

The other monsters he mentioned, the obrock and the deloombeik, are a giant bird and a giant beast respectively.

Neither of them has any special abilities, but they move surprisingly quickly for their massive bulk and can easily crush their enemies beneath them.

They are monsters of pure and simple strength, but as such, it is easy enough to deal with them.

They're certainly stronger than anogratches individually, but the real threat of the anogratch lies in the swarm.

Overall, anogratches are definitely the larger threat.

"Would you be able to defeat an obrock or a deloombeik single-handedly?"

"That depends. If I had time to prepare and lay traps and all that, I think I could do it. It'd still be life-and-death, though."

Despite this disclaimer, he looks fairly confident that he could do it.

"So what if you were just on your own, with no time to prepare?"

"Well...probably not."

Bloe hesitates for a moment but admits his likely defeat.

I'm sure he hesitated only because he was reluctant to admit it.

"Then what do you think would happen if a bunch of obrocks or deloombeiks were to attack in an anogratch-size swarm?"

"That'd be a tough battle."

Either one of those monsters is manageable on its own.

Bloe seemed confident that he could defeat one by himself if he was able to set traps and such, and it's possible to hunt them without any casualties if you bring a large enough group.

But what if they showed up in a great horde like anogratches?

Anogratches are far weaker than those other monsters individually, but when they run wild, there are always considerable losses.

If a monster even stronger than an anogratch was to swarm and attack in the same way, the death toll would likely be catastrophic.

It might even be the sort of battle that could spell the end of the demon race.

"Are you imagining it now? But you see, the Demon Lord could wipe out even a swarm of monsters like that without breaking a sweat."

Bloe looks at me skeptically.

Dammit. I've failed.

Everything I'm saying is the truth, but the scale of my example was so large that it must have made it seem unbelievable.

"You don't believe me? It's the truth."

"If you say so, Brother, then I believe you."

But despite his words, Bloe doesn't seem convinced.

"At any rate. Don't even think about doing something as foolish as rebelling against the Demon Lord. The situation you're in now may be horrible, but it could still get worse. I'll do whatever I can to help you. So please just hang in there."

It's true.

This situation is bad, but it's not completely hopeless.
There's still a way to survive no matter how difficult it might be.
"I beg you. I don't want to see you...my family...die."
"Brother..."
Bloe trails off for a moment when I bare my honest feelings.
"...I'm sorry. All right. I'll pull it off."
I have no choice but to believe his determined declaration.

Interlude — The Elder Demon Admits Defeat

"Wait."

After leaving the meeting, I called out to a few of those who were quickly walking away.

I stopped Second Army Commander Sanatoria, Sixth Army Commander Huey, and Ninth Army Commander Nereo.

"What is it, Lord Agner?"

"Surely, I need not speak it for you to understand? Or do you need me to elaborate?"

Speaking for the group, Nereo asks my business, but I doubt anyone would fail to understand why I have gathered this particular set of individuals.

"Hmm. I find it difficult to ascertain what you might want of me."

And yet, Nereo feigns ignorance.

I suspected that he might do as much, so I will simply cut to the chase.

"I ask only that you be aware that you have been knowingly let off the hook. That Her Majesty the Demon Lord already has a knife pressed to all your throats. Be assured that there will be no second chances if you make any furtive moves again. The Demon Lord is not so benevolent as to look after those she has no need for."

Nereo's expression doesn't change, but Sanatoria and Huey tense up ever so slightly.

These three are the commanders who sent troops to the rebel army.

I have no proof, but I am certain of it.

And I am sure the Demon Lord knows as well.

She has set Bloe up as the scapegoat, but only as bait to lure out these three.

If they let their guards down simply because she did not overtly single them out at this meeting and tip their hands soon after, she will destroy them without mercy.

"You are free to heed my warning or ignore it as you wish. But in the latter case, all that awaits you is inevitable destruction. That is all."

Having said my piece, I turn my back on the three of them.

I have given them fair warning.

If they choose to rebel against the Demon Lord anyway, that is their choice. I will not save them.

At any rate, Nereo can do little without an army of his own, and if youngsters like Sanatoria and Huey attempt anything, they will quickly give themselves away.

Even if Nereo advises them, it will not change the outcome.

For the Demon Lord is far more powerful than even I had imagined.

Those three certainly don't stand a chance against her.

Leaving the silent trio behind, I walk away.

In the private room that has been allotted to me in the Demon Lord's castle, I sink heavily into a chair and think.

The topic of concern is my next course of action.

But I suppose there is little more to think about there.

I know that I have no other choice no matter how long and hard I contemplate, yet I cannot help asking myself whether there might be some loophole.

But try as I might, I cannot think of a good plan and ultimately circle back to my original conclusion.

Namely, that there is nothing more I can do.

Damn that Potimas.

I thought he might at least be of a little use, but instead he simply withdrew without doing anything at all.

What a tremendous letdown.

As my thoughts reach this point, I cannot help laughing at myself.

I schemed to entrust our problems to another race, yet now I have the gall to blame them for our failure, even if only in my mind.

Potimas made no blunders.

He was slowly and steadily preparing to strike a single, powerful blow against the Demon Lord.

The fact that we were crushed before his preparations were complete simply means that the Demon Lord outmatched us.

It is I who fell far short for failing to even detect that the Demon Lord was going to take action, never mind preventing her from crushing us.

Ah, I have no choice but to admit it.

I have been defeated, completely and utterly.

My plot to create a clash between the Demon Lord and Potimas that would weaken both sides has ended in total defeat.

I planned everything so carefully.

There wasn't a ghost of a chance that Warkis's rebel army could overthrow the Demon Lord.

I assumed that the Demon Lord would recognize this as well and decide to crush the rebels in order to wipe out her dissenters once and for all.

Then Potimas's unexpected intervention would take advantage of her careless pride and strike.

Nereo, Sanatoria, and Huey.

I spoke to them dismissively, but it meant nothing.

For I am the true mastermind behind the rebel army.

I am sure those three assumed that they were the ones manipulating the rebels from the shadows, but in truth, it was I who guided them into action.

That is how I know it was them, even if I have no proof.

Sanatoria and Huey played right into my hands.

Nereo, too—of the three, he alone seems to suspect there's someone else pulling strings from behind the scenes, but I do not think he has surmised who it is.

He may have an inkling, but I have no doubt his suspicion of me has dropped somewhat after our most recent interaction.

I do not know what Nereo will do now, but it's none of my concern.

At any rate, I made careful preparations during the years that the Demon Lord was traveling in human lands.

I instigated Warkis to form a rebel army, deepened the connection between him and Potimas, and even used my precious Spatial Magic user to create a teleport gate linking us with the elves.

And I did all this without ever letting on that I was leading the way or leaving evidence behind.

I even fine-tuned the amount of soldiers transferred from the other armies so that we would still be able to recover even if the rebel army was wiped out completely.

If the rebel army got too large and was massacred by the Demon Lord, it was a distinct possibility there might be too few demons remaining to keep our race alive, so I proceeded with utmost care.

That is why I kept Nereo and the other colluding commanders in the shadows.

If they had stood at the forefront, and the entirety of the Second and Sixth Armies joined the rebellion, they might have inspired other armies to join them as well.

That could only lead to a massive civil war that would divide the demon race into two—the one thing I had to avoid at all costs.

So I carefully limited the scope of the rebellion to an amount that would not cripple our race if annihilated, and I even tempted Potimas into assisting us.

We had just received the order from the Demon Lord to ban all elves from demon territory, so I went about quietly disposing of the elves on our land.

I then reported their deaths to Potimas as if I knew nothing of how they had occurred.

"Elves have been disappearing without a trace quite frequently in the demon kingdom as of late. Do you know anything about this?"

It was a simple trap to lay.

Potimas was sure to assume from that little information that the Demon Lord was working against him in the shadows.

And when he received a request for assistance from Warkis at that precise timing, he would no doubt consider it the perfect opportunity to strike back.

Potimas despises incurring one-sided losses.

Childish though it may be, he cannot accept anyone else coming out on top.

If he felt slighted by the Demon Lord, he would never miss an opportunity to exact revenge.

But what would happen when the Demon Lord and Potimas clashed? This outcome alone I had to leave to fate.

Such was my pitiful excuse for a plan, which used an outsider, Potimas, to achieve my ends.

If I thought prayer would promise a better outcome, then I would have pleaded with the gods without hesitation.

Thus was my stage so carefully prepared, yet it was destroyed by the Demon Lord before I could even raise the curtains.

I proceeded so carefully, sending my loyal vassals into each army to gather information and manipulate others.

And yet, I did not catch even a whiff of the Demon Lord's movements.

When did she discover the existence of the rebel army?

I do not believe the rebellion failed to act covertly.

There was no reason she should have known of its existence.

Somehow she saw right through it, and without even the slightest warning at that.

Still, if that was the full extent of it, I could accept that the Demon Lord's reach was simply wider than I realized.

But she also discovered that the elves were helping us.

That was my one and only advantage, the trump card that was meant to deal a great blow against the Demon Lord. I took every available precaution to ensure that the elves' involvement did not leak to anyone.

Even if the existence of the rebel army was discovered, I went to great pains to keep her from knowing that the elves were backing them until the last possible moment.

The Demon Lord was undoubtedly aware that a rebellion was bound to occur sooner or later.

So even if she learned of a rebel army's existence, she would not panic.

I assumed that she would simply confront them without a worry.

And that would be the perfect moment to unleash the elves, the one weapon that could potentially reach her.

As long as I kept the elves hidden, it would not matter even if the rebel army was exposed.

And yet, she somehow learned of the elves as well.

Otherwise, how could she have used the teleport gate to conduct an attack of her own on their base?

If anything, perhaps she reacted so quickly *because* she knew the elves were involved.

In the end, the rebel army was quickly subjugated and the elves unable to assist at all.

Ha. What else can one do but laugh?

I tried everything I could.

To overcome a demon lord who possesses overwhelming power...

It was never a sure thing from the very beginning, but the fruits of all my careful labors have only yielded the realization that the Demon Lord is far more powerful and ingenious than I could ever have imagined.

I suppose gaining that knowledge is an accomplishment of sorts, but having my years of delicate planning crushed so completely for such a meager result is beyond discouraging. I can muster only a strange, bitter chuckle in response.

Like it or not, I understand now.

I must admit defeat.

The only available route for the demon race's survival now is to obey the Demon Lord and somehow win against the humans.

We cannot outmatch her strength.

Nor can we outmaneuver her.

The former point alone was enough to put us in check.

I still did my best to find a way around it, but has it amounted to nothing more than struggling in vain...?

No.

I suppose I knew from the beginning that this was the likely outcome.

No matter how crafty Potimas might be, I suspected he would not manage to kill the Demon Lord.

If nothing else, perhaps he could kill her closest associates and delay the war against the humans due to the chaos caused by the rebel army.

Yes, that was the best I could have hoped for.

But now that it's all over, I am painfully aware of what a hopeless aspiration that was.

I cannot defeat her.

All that is left to me now is to show my submission to the Demon Lord in the hopes that I can minimize casualties from needless fighting.

Which is exactly why I gave Nereo and the others that warning.

As of now, it does not seem the Demon Lord intends to dispose of the commanders who supported the rebel army.

If she did, she would have long since done so by now.

Given that the Demon Lord was able to uncover my carefully hidden information about the elves, she undoubtedly knows that those three were involved.

But she appears willing to let them live, as long as they don't do anything foolish.

I guess the only problem left is...me.

I can feel eyes upon me.

My sword is nearby, well within reach, but I force myself not to reach for it.

One by one, I feel the number of gazes on me increase.

Eyes.

Countless glowing red eyes, looking at me.

My door is closed, yet they still peer into this room, ignoring any space or barriers between us.

A swarm of white spiders.

They stare at me from every direction.

What an unsettling sight.

My heart pounds out an alarm.

How long has it been since such a sound reached my ears?

I strive to keep my expression unmoving, to hide the clammy sweat of my clenched fists.

And then a white figure appears before me.

"Welcome. Although I cannot say I hold much admiration for a woman entering a man's room alone."

My greatest concern is to keep my voice from shaking.

I must not show my agitation or my fear.

These may be my last moments, but I have pride of my own that I wish to hang on to.

Or perhaps I simply do not want to embarrass myself in those last moments.

"Ah, but I suppose you are not alone after all."

My lips twitch sarcastically as I look at the swarm of white spiders all around us.

I had to make some sort of joke, or I fear I might have screamed.

"So may I ask what brings you here?"

The person who appeared is the girl they called White, who seems to be the Demon Lord's closest aide.

Eyes.

Perhaps I should be clearer in my language.

This girl herself is the Demon Lord's eyes.

The watchful eyes that captured not only the rebel army's movements but the elves' as well.

Meaning that most likely, she is also aware of what I have done.

Otherwise, she would not have come to see me at this time, in this situation.

The snow-white girl stands in silence.

Her eyes are closed, but the white spiders all around her stare at my face intently, as if seeing for her.

As if they're ascertaining something.

"Orders."

How much time must have passed?

After a moment that seemed both short and infinite, undoubtedly the most uncomfortable moment of my life, the girl finally opens her mouth.

And then she continues in short, halting words, explaining the contents of said orders.

"Is that what Her Majesty the Demon Lord wishes of me?"

I have my doubts about the orders I've just been given.

If the Demon Lord truly gave them, I cannot understand her intentions.

At my inquiry, the white spiders rustle about in a show of displeasure.

My blood runs cold at the threat of them all attacking me at once.

"Really?"

What exactly does her question mean?

Is she asking whether I really need to ask after what she just told me?

Or is she saying to simply follow orders without asking questions?

In this case, I suppose it must be the latter.

For a moment, I turn my gaze upward.

Toward the ceiling—at least in theory, but all I actually see is a swarm of white spiders staring down at me.

It feels as though I'm being told that there is nowhere to run. I cannot help but smile bitterly.

"I admit it. I have been completely and utterly defeated. There is nothing else I can do. And it stands to reason that the loser must obey the victor. I vow on my life to devote everything to the Demon Lord. Use or dispose of me as you please."

I look the girl straight in the face.

"If you do not mean to destroy me here and now, I shall humbly carry out those orders."

I am prepared to be utterly annihilated if it comes to that.

Such is the gravity of my deeds.

"Okay."

But instead, I'm given an almost anticlimactic one-word response.

And as if that word was a signal, the white spiders all around us begin to vanish.

Is this Spatial Magic or perhaps some higher art of which I remain ignorant?

Perhaps it is Dimensional Magic, the evolution of Spatial Magic, which is whispered of in legends?

Even the Demon Lord's subordinates are terrifying monsters.

"Thanks."

With that, the girl disappears as well, so suddenly that I cannot tell when she cast the spell.

All that remains is the sight of my room in its usual state, so ordinary that one might almost suspect that what just happened was a nightmare or illusion.

But my fists, clenched so tightly that they've drawn blood—the only way I was able to keep my composure—remind me that it was all too real.

It appears that even though I had accepted the possible fate of being erased, I still could not help but experience fear at the moment of truth.

I suppose Warkis, who fell so nobly, was a far better man than I.

...In the end, all I accomplished was sacrificing him.

I lost that simple, honest man and have nothing to show for it.

"A fool," he said...

I am far more deserving of that criticism than the Demon Lord ever was.

For I raised the banner of revolt against the Demon Lord, even knowing how wretchedly hopeless such an action would be, and let her brand me as a traitor.

And a fool such as myself has only one path left.

I must become the Demon Lord's dog and do my best to keep as many demons alive as possible.

I will not let Warkis's sacrifice be in vain.

It will be a warning, to prevent the other commanders from attempting any further rebellion.

If there are any signs that such a thing might occur, then I myself will not hesitate to dirty my hands.

Bloe has been given the burdensome role of cleaning up this mess.

Perhaps he dug his own grave with his everyday words and actions, but I do pity Balto.

I will do anything in my power to help those brothers avoid misfortune.

For I must clean up the mess my struggling caused myself.

Since I am being allowed to live, the Demon Lord must have deemed me useful yet.

I must get on her good side by proving that her judgment was correct.

I shall cast aside my honor and pride.

Wretch that I am, I must hang my head, beg forgiveness, and vie for her favor.

Not for my own life but for the continued existence of the demon race.

Difficult though it may be, I must do it.

For that is the only path left open to me.

Thus, I shall begin by carrying out the orders I have been given.

6 Let's File a Complaint

Teacher.

For us reincarnations, that word can refer to only one person.

We were all reborn in this world after an explosion in our classroom.

The class we were in at the time was classical literature.

And the one teaching us at the time was none other than Ms. Kanami Okazaki.

Aside from me, she's the only reincarnation who wasn't a student.

And she ran into Mr. Oni.

That's fine in theory. The problem is the place and circumstances under which they met and, more importantly, our teacher's race.

Mr. Oni found her supporting the rebel army.

That's already a red flag, but on top of that, she was an *elf* of all races?

Elves—yes, the same race as Potimas.

No waaay.

The biggest "no waaay" ever.

That's no good!

If you think about it, or even if you *don't* think about it, that's totally bad news!

The whole thing seems ridiculous, but we can't just ignore it, either.

No wonder the Demon Lord said this situation is *"troublesome"*!

I figured any situation that she'd find troublesome would be related to either the elves or reincarnations, but I never imagined it'd be two for the price of one!

According to Mr. Oni, she got away from him.

While they were talking, elf cyborg freaks attacked him, and she was picked up and dragged away by some other elf.

And our teacher was nowhere to be found among the rebel soldiers we captured.

In fact, there wasn't a single elf among them, period.

They must've all died or escaped.

It seems strange that we didn't manage to capture a single one, so we suspect that the ones who were in danger of being overrun might've killed themselves.

Maybe they were told to die rather than fall into enemy hands?

That sounds like something Potimas would say, all right, but it's even scarier that the elves would actually obey him.

But I guess dead guys aren't really important right now.

Apparently, the surviving elves have regrouped and are trying to escape from demon territory.

Makes sense. They did get to the northern town using the teleport gate, after all.

Now that the other end of that has gone KABOOM thanks to my Meteor, they can't get back the way they came, meaning there's no choice but to escape on foot.

Although even if it was intact, they wouldn't have any way of reaching it with the whole town now under the Demon Lord's army's control.

But one does not simply walk out of the demon territory.

First of all, there's no way a bunch of elves can travel around here without being spotted. They'll have to resupply eventually, so it'd be virtually impossible to escape without interacting with any demons.

I don't know how far word has spread that the elves were supporting the rebel army, but if that piece of information hits the streets, people will be on the lookout.

Thing is, since there's no Internet or anything in this world, information travels pretty slowly.

Which also explains why the elves are moving south so fast: They're planning to run as far as they can before word gets out about them.

But there's still a pretty big distance between the northern town and the border with the human realm.

There's no way they can cross that distance without the help of any demons.

And even if they manage to reach the border, things only get tougher from there.

The demons and humans have been staring each other down at the border for years now.

Their relationship is so bad that anyone trying to cross the border might very well be killed, no questions asked.

Assuming they make it across the border, there's a really good chance they'll get killed by humans.

There are certain parts of the border where it's easier to cross, but they're all guarded by big ol' fortresses built by the humans.

There's no way they're slipping past that.

So why don't they just avoid those areas?

Oh, if only life were so simple.

First of all, we can rule out all the areas with really annoying terrain, the biggest example being the Mystic Mountains that we crossed to get here.

No normal people could ever make it through there alive.

Then there are the places that don't have proper roads but are still theoretically options.

The thing is, there are bandits in those areas.

More specifically, they're basically groups of human government–sanctioned highwaymen.

They kill and steal just like your average bandit, but they actually have permission from the human empire to do this looting.

You wouldn't think a government would want to allow any bandits, but you'd be wrong.

These guys are contributing to their national defense, see: They lie in wait on these backwater roads that the government can't fully control, and they defeat any would-be intruders from the demon realm.

They live around these checkpoints, create moving settlements that search for prey, steal whatever they can from intruders they stumble upon, and even get compensation from the government.

So while they're basically just thugs, they do manage to help secure the border against incursions from the demon realm.

In other words, if the elves try to escape along any of these routes, they'll get shaken down by these government-backed crooks.

Sure, the elves might be able to fight them off, but these guys are surprisingly strong, since they make their living off killing intruders.

I don't know if the exhausted elves will stand much chance of victory after traipsing their way across demon lands.

If they lose, they'll all be killed, and even if they win, I bet they'd take some major losses.

By the way, there'd be no negotiating or anything, either.

These guys are bandits at heart. If they notice prey passing by, they're bound to attack.

It'd be hard enough to convince them to consider a deal, and even if they did manage to get that far, I'm sure any talks would fall apart quickly.

Why, you ask? Because it's these guys' whole job to kill anyone who wanders in from demon lands.

Their country pays them to do it, and they must take some degree of pride in their job.

They're protecting humanity from the demons' invasions, you know?

Even if what they're doing is almost indistinguishable from plain old banditry!

So they'll target anyone and everyone coming from demon territory, elf or not.

Besides, demons and humans don't even look all that different.

No matter who comes out of the demon territory, they're just gonna kill 'em!

Elves?

They came from the demon territory, so they must be allies of the demons, right?

Kill 'em!

That's how it's gonna play out.

What I'm trying to say here is that Ms. Oka and the other elves have a preeeetty low chance of making it out of the demon realm alive.

So low that if you compared it to a pro baseball player's batting average, it'd be insulting to the player!

Not that I care what happens to the other elves besides Ms. Oka.

But unfortunately, we're gonna need them to get out alive as well.

Wouldn't it be simpler to just place Ms. Oka under guard, you ask?

Yeah, I thought about that, too.

But there's a reason we can't do that.

Which means we have to indirectly help Ms. Oka and company get out of the demon territory.

At least, that's the snap decision I came to as I listened to Mr. Oni's information and used a Detection-like technique to track Ms. Oka down.

"So that's the gist of it. What should we do?"

Once Mr. Oni finishes his explanation, the Demon Lord turns to me.

Gotta say, it's pretty impressive that I'd already found Ms. Oka and figured out a plan by the time she asked me that.

"I'll handle it."

I make a quick declaration.

There's no time like the present, so I put my plan into action right away.

First, I need to go to the person I've chosen to escort the elves to the border. The best possible man for the job.

Naturally, that's the lord who's in charge of the demon side of the human-demon border: the Colonel himself.

Boy, that Colonel is a tough customer.

Yep, that's right.

I just put the Colonel in charge of supporting the elves!

Ugh, it was super-hard to explain.

"Elves." "Running from the rebel army." "They'll pass through here." "Heading to the human territory." "Help them."

It took a whole lot of work for me to relay all that information.

Since he responded with a question right away, I wound up giving him a kind of weird answer, but it seems like he accepted that response for whatever reason.

Good on ya, Colonel.

So dependable.

I mean, I put a whole lot of pressure on him, but he never lost his cool.

Pretty crazy.

It definitely seemed like my thinly veiled threat got through to him, so he must be a fairly sharp guy.

* * *

I managed to send the message of *I know you're the mastermind behind the rebel army* without actually saying it out loud, and he understood.

He's certainly a whole lot more useful than the three small-fry he was manipulating.

Compared to them, Mr. Warkis was a much bigger deal.

Heh-heh-heh.

I wouldn't just get my whole squad of mini-mes together to glare at him for no reason, y'know?

It was to convey the message that he's being watched and that we know what he's been up to, too.

Why would I do it in such a roundabout way, you ask?

To reduce the amount of things I actually have to say out loud, obviously.

Please figure it out so I don't have to say it.

That was the earnest wish behind my gesture.

And the Colonel was smart enough to make it come true, so I'm very happy.

In actuality, I'm the only one who knows the Colonel was the mastermind behind the rebellion.

He hasn't left behind a single scrap of proof.

He sent only his most trusted subordinates to infiltrate the other armies and acted through them.

It must have taken years to lay all that groundwork, but you can do that kind of thing when you live as long as a demon.

And he used that groundwork to manipulate several commanders into raising an entire rebel army.

What's really impressive about the Colonel is that not even once did he directly involve himself, and he even managed to make the commanders think they were acting on their own initiative.

I doubt I could pull off anything like that.

It's a delicate art that involves a deep understanding of people's natures, thorough calculations, and an extremely careful balancing act of various moving parts.

When I put it that way, it makes me wonder if even Potimas was manipulated into making a move by the Colonel.

In fact, he probably was. A genius strategist like the Colonel would definitely realize that demons alone can't defeat the Demon Lord.

At least, not without some outside help in the form of Potimas.

The Colonel planned to coerce Potimas into acting under cover of the rebel army's movements and set him up to clash with the Demon Lord.

I shudder to think what would've happened if he had succeeded.

It's a bold move that puts the heart of the plan in the hands of an outsider.

Actually, it's possible that even the demons getting the elves to help them rebuild might have been due to the Colonel's machinations.

Potimas can be surprisingly gullible. If you buttered him up just right, or promised to owe him a debt or something, or suggested that the demons would need more power to fight the humans, he might very well agree to help.

Like, if you really think about it, it'd probably be more efficient to put that energy to work elsewhere, so there's not really any deep reason for the elves to help the demons.

That makes it even more likely that the Colonel might have used his silver tongue to motivate Potimas to send aid.

And if he was able to do that, I'm sure he could get Potimas to support the rebel army, too.

The Colonel's got some frightening abilities, even if they're the kind that aren't reflected in his skills.

If I didn't have the dirty trick known as my mini-me information network, I would never have guessed that the Colonel was pulling the strings.

But it looks like after this little incident, he realizes that there's no point trying to rebel against the Demon Lord. And if someone that talented is going to cooperate with us, they'll be a huge asset.

Bringing him on to our side is certainly a lot more efficient than executing him.

I'll be keeping an eye on him to make sure he doesn't try anything funny, of course.

But yeah, I put the Colonel in charge of helping Ms. Oka and company.

He's probably got ties to Potimas anyway, so it won't seem too unnatural if he helps the elves in secret.

And those elves are in a major pinch right now, so they'll take any help that's offered for sure.

It's not a trap anyway. We're actually helping them, so we really need them to accept it.

At any rate, they'll be safe for the rest of their stay in the demon lands.

I still have to do something about the border, but it'll take a while for Ms. Oka and friends to get there.

And meanwhile, there's something else I have to do.

Namely, I gotta go file a complaint.

I teleport into midair.

And then: It's dropkick time, baby!

But my target must have known I was coming, because there's no one there by the time I come down.

The momentum of my kick sends me crashing into the wall, and my foot goes right through it, getting stuck there.

...I feel like something eerily similar happened to me very recently, but that must be my imagination.

You won't catch this lady dwelling on the past!

"Welcome. I wish you'd enter a little more quietly, though."

The owner of the room admonishes me for my unusual way of making an entrance.

But I ignore her complaint as I pull my foot out of the wall.

What, the cost of repairs?

Like hell I'm paying for that!

Refusing to look at the hole I just made, I come face-to-face with the master of the house.

Aside from the different color scheme, she could be my mirror image.

Needless to say, it's the original to my copy, the creator of the system in the other world: the god called D, who is now staring back at me expressionlessly.

Then she cheerfully turns away and un-pauses her game.

I guess she must have paused it in order to dodge my dropkick.

The sheer level of disrespect drives me mad, so I grab her shoulder, turn her toward me, and lift her by the collar with both hands.

You know, that classic move you see in TV dramas and stuff.

The difference being that my strength is enhanced with conjuring, so I end up lifting D's whole body into the air.

Yeah, I can do stuff like that if I enhance my arm strength with conjuring.

Maybe this'll show you how mad I am!!

But then I hear a weird noise, like a ripping, popping noise, and the weight in my hands suddenly gets a lot lighter.

Huh? I take a look and discover that D's clothes have gotten all torn up.

Oh. Yeah, I guess that makes sense.

D doesn't weigh much, but if you put all the weight of one person on a single piece of cloth, obviously it's gonna rip no matter how light that person is...

And since her clothes ripped, I'm no longer holding up D herself, so she drops down.

With the giant rip in her clothing, you can see all kinds of things, but D's expression doesn't change in the slightest.

If she was to blush a little with embarrassment or something, this could be kind of a cute situation, but since she's completely expressionless, it's more scary than sexy.

This is probably what it'd feel like if you happened to lay eyes on a butt-naked mannequin in the middle of the night.

"C'mon—at least act a little embarrassed."

"I have no reason to be ashamed of anyone seeing my body. I believe I am the most beautiful person in the world, if I do say so myself."

Wow, that was a really narcissistic thing to say so casually.

Uhhh... Well, okay then.

This weird situation is kind of draining me of all my anger.

I heave a sigh, arbitrarily grab some clothes out of the closet, and toss them at D. (Since I have a portion of D's memories in my brain, I know the layout of this room.)

D catches the clothes, strips off her ruined outfit, and changes into the new one.

"Wanna play?"

And THAT'S what she decides to say next.

She's so laid-back that it's taking the wind out of my sails, dammit!

This isn't gonna work. I slump my shoulders, giving up in various ways.

I knew from the start that complaining to D about things wouldn't actually make a difference in the end, since she's so much stronger than I am, but somehow this is going even worse than I thought it would.

It's not even a matter of strength—she just has a way of making you feel like nothing you say matters.

Even if we manage to have a conversation, I always get the sense that I'm not gonna get through to her.

In fact, it's probably impossible, which just proves all over again that normal rules don't apply to D.

Emotionally speaking, I don't know if you could even consider her a living thing.

"No. I came today to file a complaint."

I know it won't accomplish anything, but I still have to do what I came here to do.

"About Ms. Okazaki, I presume. I was actually looking forward to the two of you meeting, so I'm quite disappointed that you wound up learning about her through hearsay. Couldn't you have met in a more dramatic way? If anything, I'd like to file a complaint myself."

"Who cares?!"

Why do you get to have such weird expectations of me and then get weirdly let down when they don't happen?!

I had no idea where Ms. Oka was or what she was doing, so how was I supposed to put on such a dramatic reunion?!

Plus, if I did somehow know beforehand, it wouldn't be dramatic anymore!

People talk about fateful encounters and once-in-a-lifetime meetings and all that, but in reality, that kinda thing doesn't normally happen so dramatically!

While I'm steaming with rage, D reaches for a bag of potato chips next to her and struggles momentarily before she manages to open it.

You've gotta stop being so laid-back already!

I snatch the bag out of D's hands and devour its contents in one bite.

This is a trick I figured out recently: using spatial conjuring to sort of re-create the Demon Lord's Gluttony skill.

Of course, since I've got such a small stomach in this body, I only actually ate a mouthful. I sent the rest to my mini-mes.

Oh man, it's been ages—no, wait, this is actually the first time I've really had potato chips in my life. They're sooo good.

I do have memories of eating them as Hiiro Wakaba, but those were really just fabricated memories D gave me.

In reality, I would never have actually had a chance to eat potato chips in my old life.

You know, since I was a spider.

Her potato chips stolen, D shrugs exaggeratedly in a weirdly American *What am I gonna do with you?* kind of gesture.

Still expressionless, of course.

Ugh, now what do I do? She's really pissing me off.

I want to punch that expressionless face of hers.

"Didn't you come here to ask me why I made your teacher an elf?"

Yeah! Right, that!

I came to file a complaint so D would explain why she made Ms. Oka an elf, of all things!

D is the one who had us all reincarnated in a new world.

In other words, Ms. Oka being an elf is a deliberate choice made by none other than D herself.

Humans and demons are fine.

Even vampires, too, I guess.

Monsters like Mr. Oni and me, well… I guess we'll call that a pitch that's just barely in the safe zone, for argument's sake.

But elves? Elves are definitely out!

We're talking *elves* here, you know? The race that's basically been enslaved by Potimas.

No, in a way, it might even be worse than that. Whether they know it or not, all elves are Potimas's pawns, his puppets.

It's obviously messed up to reincarnate someone as one of those!

"The reason should be obvious. Because it seemed more entertaining that way."

There it is. D's classic excuse for everything.

"Elves play a very important role in that world, you know. So it only seems fitting that at least one of our major players ought to be an elf, don't you think?"

No, I don't!

'Cause anyone who gets born an elf—in this case, Ms. Oka—is just gonna be miserable.

But I guess to someone like D, who uses an entire world as her plaything, a single individual being unhappy doesn't mean much.

If anything, she seems to take pleasure in it.

"And it's all the more entertaining if the elves somehow know about the reincarnations. So in order to keep things extra fun, I gave her a very interesting skill."

I can already tell this skill isn't gonna be anything good.

And boy, am I right on the money.

"The skill I gave her is called Student Roster. It gives her partial information on the other reincarnations."

What?

Whaaaat?!

Wait. Wait just a second.

What does that mean exactly?

Are you telling me Potimas came after Vampy and stuff like that by exploiting that skill?

"I know what you're thinking, and you're right."

Ugh! Are you reading my mind?!

"I'm not reading your mind. I just predicted your thoughts."

True enough, I don't feel any traces of some kind of technique being used.

She must have just figured out what conclusions I would reach, rather than using a mind-reading power.

Although that's plenty scary in its own way.

"Yes. The elf's actions far exceeded my expectations. I never imagined he would manage to gather a majority of the reincarnations."

Huh?

W-w-wait a minute!

What? Wait, run that by me again!

Excuse me? Are you for real?!

I'm so shocked that my vocabulary is failing me, but I can't worry about that right now.

"What do you mean?!"

"Exactly what I said. Although I won't be telling you how he plans to use the reincarnations he's gathered, of course. This is all top secret information that I'm sharing as a kindness to you because of the special nature of our relationship, all right?"

She's leaving out the most important details, but knowing Potimas, whatever he's planning can't be good.

On top of that, she makes it sound like she's being super-nice, as if to say I should be grateful, but I know she's telling me this only because it'll be more amusing this way.

That's just how D is.

"She's a sensible adult, and she feels a certain responsibility toward her students. So what do you think would happen if I gave such a model teacher a Student Roster skill that, for instance, predicted the deaths of her students?"

Ugh! Only an evil god would invent such a ridiculous skill!

If she sees something like that, of course Ms. Oka is going to try to do something to prevent those deaths.

If I were in her shoes, I would just ignore the list. But she's a sensible Japanese woman and a teacher to boot, so she'd make every effort to save her students' lives.

And I can definitely picture Potimas using that to his advantage to plot something nasty.

Dammit.

This is awful. Ms. Oka's situation is even worse than I thought.

In the words of a certain magical girl, that's cruel... That's just too cruel!

But seriously, this is not good.

"So noble, isn't it? She's braving danger to travel all over the world for the sake of her students even though she's in the body of a child herself. And then she's placing the students she's trying to save right in the hands of the last person she should trust. The poor thing."

"Ugh! Damn you!"

That statement puts me past the point of annoyance into straight-up anger.

But just as I raise my fist to strike her—

"Do you have any idea why you're so concerned for Ms. Oka in particular?"

—D's words freeze me in place.

What the hell is she talking about?

That's obvious, isn't it?

"You don't get nearly as bothered when other reincarnations meet with misfortune—is that fair to say?"

That's not...*not* true, I guess.

"No, you don't. Even when you learned that there were other reincarnations, you didn't worry about them unless they happened across your path. The fact that you haven't started searching for them even now that you're a god is proof enough of that. You're willing to lend a hand to the reincarnations you meet, whether it's the vampire or the oni, but that's only within reason. You won't abandon them, but you won't go out of your way to help them, even with all that power of yours. You sympathize with their situations, but you don't get angry on their behalf. So why are you this upset only about Ms. Oka's circumstances?"

Do you really need to ask?

It's because, erm… Wait…why *do* I care so much about her?

Because it seems like a crime against humanity?

No, I can't claim such a high-and-mighty reason.

I'm not even human in the first place, so I don't really have those kinds of feelings.

Like D said, I'm not really that interested in the other reincarnations.

I feel a certain kinship with them, so I try to help them if I happen to see them, but that's about it.

I'm involved with Vampy and Mr. Oni only because we happened to run into each other.

If coincidence hadn't brought us together, I doubt I would've gone out of my way looking for them.

If I hadn't met Vampy back then, and she had gotten killed by Potimas, I would've just thought *Oh, huh* if I found out.

Now, of course, I have a degree of fondness for her, since we've been together for so long, and I'd probably fly into a fit of rage if she got killed.

But that's only because we met and formed a deeper bond.

If a reincarnation I've never met dies, I don't really feel a thing.

And while I technically know Ms. Oka's circumstances now, we haven't actually spoken face-to-face, so I can't say I've met her exactly, much less formed a bond.

And yet, I'm so mad that I came all the way here to complain to D.

It's not just because a reincarnation was born as an elf, landing her straight in the clutches of our sworn enemy Potimas.

If it was anyone but Ms. Oka, I'm sure I would've just been like *Ugh! D's at it again!* but I wouldn't have come running to file a complaint.

No, it's *because* it's Ms. Oka.

I'm here because of her.

"How entertaining. How very, very entertaining. You don't have many memories of being a spider, so in theory, you shouldn't remember any debts or anything of the sort. Perhaps this one imprinted onto your soul? Consider me thoroughly amused."

Yeah, that's right.

I don't really remember much about being an ordinary spider in my previous life.

But if I combine what little I do remember with Hiiro Wakaba's memories, there's one thing I can't ignore.

"Yikes! A huge spider!"

"Oh man, gross. Grab the broom. I'm gonna crush it."

A group of boys came to school and tried to crush me when they spotted my web in the classroom.

Hiiro Wakaba, aka D, simply watched in silence.

"Wait a minute, boooys!"

But then Ms. Oka came rushing over.

"Eeeven this little insect has a soul. It would be cruel to kill it, you know!"

"Oh, come on..."

The male student froze, broom still in hand.

"Listen to me, okaaay? A spider is a good bug, you knooow? They eat the other bad buuugs. Besides, look how cuuute they are!"

"Cute? Yeah, right..."

The boy complained, but he reluctantly heeded Ms. Oka's words.

"None of you better kill the poor thing, either, okaaay?"

"Yeah, yeah."

"Isn't that niiice? Live your life to the fullest, too, okaaay, little spider?"

That's right.

It was because of that incident that I was allowed to live in the classroom.

That's the reason I survived.

Ms. Oka...saved my life.

That memory is one from Hiiro Wakaba's perspective, not a memory from my life as a spider.

But even if I don't remember it, my soul remembers that I owe her a debt.

Which means I have to do something to repay her.

A life for a life.

* * *

"Just as a reminder, anything you might try to do to me won't change your dear teacher's situation, hmm?"

"Yeah, I know."

But it's the principle of the thing.

My fist that I'd stopped just short of impact flies forward and punches D right in the face!

In fact, the punch is so powerful that it blasts her whole head off.

"Do you feel better now?"

But as soon as I withdraw my arm, D's head reconstitutes like time is rewinding itself.

Um, gross!

What kinda freakish recovery method is that?

Even I'm a little grossed out.

And the tiny glimpse of D's magic power that leaked out in the instant of regeneration is more than enough to terrify me.

Her presence is so powerful, it's like she's exuding death itself.

D calls herself an evil god, but honestly, even that doesn't do her justice.

I'm sure she could kill me in the blink of an eye if she felt like it.

Revival through clones? Yeah, that definitely wouldn't matter if D killed me.

In that one instant, that much became perfectly clear.

But the terrifying aura disappears as quickly as it came.

"Oh no. I messed up. I'm sure I must have been noticed just now."

D murmurs something I don't quite understand.

"...?"

"Oh, don't worry about it. Just some personal business."

Well, D has always been mysterious. And if she's telling me not to worry about it, I'm sure doing so wouldn't get me anywhere anyway.

"I'm going to save Ms. Oka."

"Go right ahead. I'm just an observer here. You're free to do whatever you want. I won't force you, and I won't try to stop you, either."

My bold declaration meets with ready approval from D.

Makes sense. As she said, she's just an observer.

She's meddled with me from time to time, but it was usually just to give me a bit of a helping hand.

The biggest example was when she gave me Wisdom, but that basically means that all the other times were little more than some sage advice.

And while she has helped me before, she's never done anything to interfere.

...Not with us reincarnations, at least.

When Güli-güli came to meet me in the Great Elroe Labyrinth, D definitely said something to chase him off.

And she stopped him from getting involved during the UFO incident, too.

So while she claims to be an observer, she's not totally hands-off, either.

I'm sure her promise not to interfere with me is sincere, but that doesn't stop her from messing with anyone else.

"I haven't done much. At the most, maybe I just let a little false information slip into Ms. Oka's Student Roster. Nobody ever said it was all true, but she sure seems to believe it and runs around accordingly. It's really quite something."

I punch D again.

Damn you!

How can anyone be so nasty?!

Her head explodes again, then restores itself in an instant.

"No need to worry. I won't do anything like that from now on. Or I suppose it'd be more accurate to say I won't be *able* to anymore."

"From now on" must mean she's done it before, right?

Should I punch her one more time for good measure?

But what does she mean, she "won't be able to"?

"I've been looking for you."

The answer arrives almost immediately.

It comes from a voice that belongs to neither D nor me.

Turning around, I come face-to-face with a maid.

Wait, a maid?

She smiles pleasantly as she looks at D.

It's weird. She's a graceful, kindly looking traditional Japanese beauty, but her smile seems oddly sinister.

For some reason, the word *mother* comes to mind.

In the sense that you wouldn't dare stand up to her.

She seems like a big-sister type who would put her hand to her cheek and say things like *Oh my!* and *Dear me!* so why is she so darn scary?

Huh, she is a little lacking in the chest department, though.

Uh-oh, I better not think stuff like that.

Gotta hold my breath and make sure Miss Maid's anger doesn't turn on me, too.

"How careless of me. I did so much work to conceal my location only to reveal myself by regenerating just now."

"As usual, you lack the propriety that a top-ranking god should possess. Your latest escapade ends here. You're coming back with me."

Ohhh, so she's here to bring the runaway D back home?

No wonder she has that don't-mess-with-me air about her.

"And what is this thing?"

Miss Maid looks at me.

You're calling me a "thing," huh? I see how it is.

That makes me kinda mad, but I get the feeling I wouldn't be able to beat her...

For starters, I didn't even notice when she got here.

In fact, for such a pretty lady, she has a ridiculously low level of presence.

Conjuring...? No, I don't think so.

I can't detect anything unnatural about her. But somehow her presence is unbelievably faint.

She's probably using some technique I've never even heard of to erase her presence, but the effect is that you could easily lose track of her even when she's right in front of your face like this.

I must be caught in her illusion.

Anyone who can trap me so easily has gotta be strong.

"This is my new toy."

Ugh, and now D's referring to me like an object, too?!

I'm sure she earnestly means it, but that just makes it even more insulting.

"A simple clone...? No, that doesn't appear to be the case. Just what is it, exactly?"

Seriously, could you stop treating people like things?

Okay, I'm actually a spider, but still.

"A special spider mutation. I created her in my likeness to confuse you about where I was, but she exceeded my expectations and became a god."

"...I haven't the slightest idea what you mean."

Yeah, when you put it that way, I don't really get it, either.

To be honest, all I really did was get super-lucky and fall into some truly miraculous situations. Next thing you know, I'm a literal god.

Even I think it's ridiculous when I look back at my own personal history, so I'm sure it's even more confusing to an outsider.

"At any rate, we're going home. You've got a great deal of work piled up."

"I don't want to go home. I don't want to work. I just want to play forever."

Still deadpan, D starts throwing a tantrum.

I hate to say it, but seeing her like this just makes it all the more convincing that she's my original.

"Please don't be so selfish. Who do you think has to manage the underworld in your place when you're not working?"

"Mm."

D points at Miss Maid.

Uh-oh.

Miss Maid is still smiling, but I can practically see a vein popping on her forehead.

"I'm quite busy managing the circles of hell already, you know."

"But it's not like you *can't* do it, right?"

"It's not a matter of whether I can or cannot. I have my duties, and you have yours. Now come along."

Looks like Miss Maid is finally resorting to force.

She grabs D by the collar and starts dragging her away.

Quite a primitive method, if you ask me.

"Sorry, but as you can see, it looks like I won't be able to come back here for a while. Which means I also can't interfere with that world. The system will continue to run with or without my help."

D addresses me evenly as she's dragged away.

"But yes, that means I cannot interfere with the system. Which also means I can't defend it from any potential outside interference, I'm sure."

Whoa!

"Feel free to use anything lying around in this house. You may even find a useful item or two."

What's this?

Some kind of farewell gift?

Well, if she says I can have whatever I want, I'll definitely take her up on the offer.

"Oh right, one more thing. I can't interfere, but I'll still peek in on you from time to time, of course."

Um, okay, didn't really need to know that.

"Yes, I'll be watching over you. So be sure to entertain me, all right? Until next time."

"You won't have time to watch anything, just so you know."

Miss Maid smiles threateningly at D, and they leave the room.

By the time I glance cautiously into the hallway, they're gone.

I guess the world of gods has its own problems, huh?

Sure, I might end up there myself one day, but for now I'll just pray that D works herself to death.

Hmm. Since she revealed her location to Miss Maid by using her power to regenerate her head after I knocked it clear off, I guess you could say I technically landed a hit on her after all.

Ms. Oka, I've avenged you!

Not that that'll change how bad her situation is right now.

It's up to me to do something about that.

I've got to pay back this life debt. Maybe I should even go above and beyond.

...Debt, huh?

Yeah...yeah, I guess so.

When I think about it that way, there's another person I owe.

We were enemies at first, then eventually called a truce, started working together, and even helped each other out.

And when I first got deified and was in a super-weakened state, my former enemy, someone who probably had every right to kill me, took me under her wing and protected me.

I'm already helping her out when I can, but that's not enough to pay back the debt I owe.

Since she saved my life, I have to do something at least comparable in return.

Yeah, that settles it.

I'll save Ms. Oka.

And then I'll save the Demon Lord.
To the best of my ability, no holds barred, life on the line if need be.
That's how you pay back a life debt.
First things first, though, I gotta search this whole house!
Bweh-heh-heh.
A super-special item left behind by D, an actual god!
What am I gonna get? I can't wait to find out!

Interlude The Vampire Servant's Annihilation

Screams punctuate the night.

Deep darkness is illuminated by fire and flames.

In the air, the scent of blood mingles with the unpleasant stench of something burning.

This is truly hell on earth.

After Wrath's explanation, Lady White teleported away somewhere.

It soon became apparent that she would not be returning right away, so we parted ways. The next day, however, Lady Ariel called us back to the same meeting room.

When I arrived, Lady Ariel and Lady White were already there.

"Pardon me. I did not mean to keep you waiting."

"Nah, it's fine, it's fine. I was just getting the details from White here myself."

As I bow my head deeply in apology, Lady Ariel gives me an easygoing wave, and Lady White shows that she is equally unbothered with a small nod.

Lady White's responses are difficult to understand, but recently I've been able to glean her feelings from them a bit more clearly, although there are still plenty of moments when I cannot comprehend her in the slightest.

"All right, White, why don't you tell... Huh? What? You want me to do it? Oh, all right."

Lady Ariel starts to prompt Lady White to explain, but the latter leans over and whispers something in the former's ear.

Since my hearing is enhanced by my vampirism, I can just barely make out her soft voice.

"You explain it."

It was very quiet but clear nonetheless.

How unusual.

Lady White is normally quite taciturn.

This contributes to her aloofness, but after spending a considerable amount of time with her, I have come to suspect that she is simply not fond of speaking.

Her silence is not necessarily a choice but a result of being perpetually tongue-tied.

And yet, she just spoke in a full sentence without any stuttering or hesitation. Not a particularly long sentence, to be sure, but normally Lady White would have stammered even those three words out syllable by syllable, with considerable pauses in between.

...Could she possibly be under the influence of alcohol?

For some reason, Lady White becomes very talkative when she is drinking.

This is not necessarily a bad thing, at least from my perspective: When I was depressed about having become a vampire, Lady White once drunkenly gave me some harsh but encouraging advice.

That conversation is the very reason I was able to keep moving forward and make up my mind to protect my young mistress.

...Although recently, she has become so strong that she may no longer need my help.

"All right, I'll explain, then."

Ah, but now is not the time to get discouraged.

I must listen closely to Lady Ariel.

Although I cannot help but notice that the other member of our party who was here yesterday is no longer present.

"Should Wrath not hear this as well?"

Wrath is another reincarnation, like my young mistress.

He, too, has a checkered past.

Since he has endured a difficult life not unlike the young miss, I privately feel a certain affinity toward him.

Ever since he enrolled in the army alongside me, we have become rather friendly.

As I am his elder, he has requested that I not use any title when addressing him, so perhaps he is more like a younger brother than an equal?

When I was still human, I did have juniors who worked underneath me on my master's staff, but I was young myself and was always at my master's side, so I rarely interacted with the other servants, certainly not enough to consider any as close as siblings.

In that way, this is not such a bad thing.

Certainly, I do have somewhat mixed feelings when I consider that he once tried to kill the young mistress and me, but I can put that behind us, considering the mitigating circumstances.

But presently, Wrath is not here.

"Yeah, Wrath won't be coming this time. I'm sure he'd be all right in terms of strength, but just to be safe. And more importantly, we can't have them seeing his face."

His face? Is there something wrong with Wrath's face?

And then it finally occurs to me.

"Is this related to reincarnations?"

"You got it."

Evidently, Wrath's face is the same as it was in his "past life."

In other words, reincarnations like the young miss can recognize him simply by seeing his face. For instance, when he encountered this "Missoka" character in the battle against the rebel army, she immediately discerned that he was a reincarnation.

"Missoka" seems to be the name of their instructor from their old world.

Since she appeared so recently, perhaps this reincarnation-related discussion has to do with her?

"Does it involve Missoka, perhaps? Oh, but she has already seen Wrath's face, so this must be something else."

Partway through my question, I realized my own folly: Lady Ariel said Wrath's face being seen would be an issue, but Missoka has already seen him.

"Hmm. Well, it's not entirely unrelated. But I guess this is technically a separate matter. But then again, it's not totally separate. If anything, it's actually quite closely connected."

After this vague response, I must admit I'm even more confused.

But Lady Ariel doesn't seem to be joking around. Rather, it appears that she's trying to decide how best to explain.

Unlike Lady White, Lady Ariel prefers to explain important information in great detail.

If no explanation is needed, she'll generally just smile and gloss over the subject, which doesn't appear to be the case this time.

And when she hesitates like this, it's generally because the situation is particularly complicated and difficult to parse.

Fortunately, in cases such as this, if Lady Ariel is given enough time, she usually gets her thoughts in order and elaborates in a way that's easy to understand. I only need to be patient until she's ready.

"Okay, I guess it'd be easiest to start from the beginning."

Sure enough, Lady Ariel hesitates for only an instant before launching into her explanation.

As always, she makes impressive use of the Thought Super-Acceleration skill.

"First of all, about Ms. Oka. As I think you've heard, she's a reincarnation. She's also the only one who was originally an adult, not to mention a teacher. So as we witnessed firsthand, she's been reincarnated as an elf. And her goal is to protect the other reincarnations. It seems that she's under the mistaken impression that I've kidnapped little Sophia—or most likely, Potimas deliberately misled her. This is likely why she risked joining the rebel army. Are you with me so far?"

"Yes."

I've already heard most of this information.

Presumably, she's pausing here because the next part is new information that I haven't encountered yet.

"So she and the rest of the elf squad escaped from that battle. But according to White's investigation, they're heading south toward human territory on foot."

"They seemed determined to engage in rather reckless actions."

"I know, right? But I guess they don't really have any other way out. Anyway, normally they wouldn't stand a chance of escaping like that, but unfortunately, there's a reason we need to get them out alive."

Did I mishear?

Logically, I cannot fathom what that reason might be.

The elves are our sworn enemies, and we clash with them frequently.

They took my master's and mistress's lives, and they targeted the young miss.

The remorse and rage I felt toward the elves that night still burns in my chest even now.

Putting aside my personal grudge for the moment, the elves are undoubtedly an enemy of Lady Ariel as well, so I cannot imagine why she would want to let them live.

If anything, the existence of the reincarnation Missoka among them is a factor, but surely she could be captured and brought back here.

It will be far more difficult to let her escape alive.

"You remember Potimas, right? He shows his face from time to time, but that's not the real Potimas. It's just a different person's body being controlled by him. It's a special power he has. There isn't much point in killing any version of Potimas we run into because it's probably not the real thing."

Learning of this man's secret gives me no small amount of shock.

I had assumed that he was simply controlling one of those "machines" that had no will of its own.

My simple mind is incapable of completely understanding the nature of "machines," but I have at least grasped that they are nonliving things that move nonetheless.

Machines are not creatures but a kind of tool.

The bodies that man uses are mechanical tools made to look like a man, which he controls from afar…or so I thought.

But if those were not manlike machines but in fact men themselves, then… that is beyond repulsive.

"Treating people as tools… He is truly the lowest of the low."

"No kidding."

In other words, he watches from a safe distance while manipulating some poor soul as his puppet?

This man is truly rotten to the core.

"That being said, it's not like he can do that to just anyone. There are some strict requirements involved, so there's no need to worry that someone you know might suddenly get taken over by Potimas without warning—don't worry."

Lady Ariel's words of reassurance only remind me how weak my powers of imagination truly are.

Logically thinking, if he *was* able to assume control over other people's minds without any constraints, that nightmare scenario would indeed be possible. It hadn't even occurred to me.

What if the young miss was taken over by Potimas...?

No, she would not allow herself to be controlled so easily.

But if I myself was to be taken over and this body of mine caused harm to befall the young miss...?

If such a thing was to happen, death itself would not be enough to atone.

The thought only reminds me how wicked that man's power is and how revolting.

Fortunately, though, Lady Ariel assures me that such a thing is not possible.

Even so, I had never even conceived of such a horrifying power.

"The clincher in this situation is that Ms. Oka actually meets those requirements."

Ah, now I see.

So that's the connection.

I was wondering what this man's atrocious ability had to do with our conversation thus far.

"Once Potimas has taken over someone's body, that person might as well be dead. The skills he can use are connected to the soul of the body's original owner, so the soul won't be destroyed. But once Potimas takes over, the original person's own consciousness will never return. They'll spend the rest of their lives as Potimas's vessel."

What a wretched fate.

"So if we were to take Missoka into our care..."

"Yes, I have no doubt Potimas would use her."

An appropriate turn of phrase for a man who treats other people as tools.

I see. That more or less explains why we cannot simply slaughter the elves... But one thing still concerns me.

"But is this not simply delaying the inevitable?"

Even if we let her escape now, the only way to fully solve the problem would be to dispose of that man once and for all. And if Potimas can take control of Missoka at any time, he may well be doing so at this very moment.

I do not think that postponing the issue is a wise strategy.

"Yeah, that's true. But, well, if we do this, it'll probably send the message that Ms. Oka has value as a hostage, so Potimas won't be so quick to lay a hand on her. At least, that's the hope."

Lady Ariel wears a dissatisfied expression as she responds to my concern; it would appear that, like me, she feels it is unwise to let the elves escape.

Which means that this decision must have been made by the other person here: Lady White.

"But apparently, White owes her life to Ms. Oka. She wants to do whatever she can to help her."

As I turn my gaze to Lady White, Lady Ariel clarifies.

So this is the person she owes her life to?

In that case, Lady White must have had a deep connection with this Missoka in their "past lives."

Perhaps it is something akin to what I shared with my master and mistress.

In that case, I can understand why Lady White would wish to save her.

If the young miss was in a similar position, I would undoubtedly do the same.

"If that is the case, then I have no objection to allowing the elves to escape."

"Thank you."

For a moment, the unexpected voice makes me freeze with shock.

Was that...Lady White?

Of course it was. If it was not Lady Ariel, then it must have been Lady White.

But for Lady White to voice her thanks is a truly unexpected occurrence.

Even Lady Ariel is looking at her in surprise.

Lady White, perhaps in an effort to hide her embarrassment, grabs Lady Ariel's face and forcibly turns her head back toward me.

"Um, ow?!"

I hear a dull, rather unpleasant sound from the vicinity of Lady Ariel's neck.

"Wait, huh? That *hurt*? But my Suffering Nullification... What?"

Lady Ariel holds her neck, looking perplexed.

Does this mean she felt pain just now?

Lady White must have somehow inflicted pain on Lady Ariel despite her Suffering Nullification skill.

"Um... Okay, then! Anyway, that's about it for Ms. Oka. Apparently, White's already got things under control, so they'll be safe until they reach the border of the human realm."

Lady Ariel rubs her neck as she continues.

From the sound of things, there must be another matter at hand aside from Missoka.

"The problem is the border and what the humans will do once the party of elves crosses it. White and I are going to take care of the latter. There'll be some negotiations involved, but we'll figure it out one way or another. As for you, Merazophis, I was hoping you could take care of things at the border itself."

This appears to be the main reason I was called here, so I try to focus.

"As you know, the border region between the demon and human lands is a super-dangerous place. Both races are always watching for signs of enemy invaders. With a few exceptions, like the Mystic Mountains where we came through, it's safe to assume that there are eyes just about everywhere. So if a group of elves tries to pass through one of those places...well, you can probably guess what would happen. Oh, by the way, the strength of the remaining elves is average at best."

"I assume they would be annihilated, or at least suffer serious losses."

"Bingo."

It might be a different story if they were using machines, but since Lady Ariel says that they have only average strength, I believe that is not the case.

"See, there are really two kinds of elves. There are the ones we know all too well, the ones who use machines left and right like Potimas. But the other sort isn't aware about the existence of machines—they genuinely believe in the 'world peace' farce that the other elves play into. The group that Ms. Oka is traveling with consists of the latter."

"Well, that's..."

Doesn't that mean the latter kind of elves are being used by the former, oblivious to the truth?

If that is true, I cannot help but feel sorry for them, elves though they may be.

"Yeah, I know. I call them the half-wit elves."

This admittedly cruel name only makes me pity them even more.

"But that's neither here nor there. Anyway, these guys definitely can't get across the border safely by themselves. So White was searching around the border for some kind of solution, and what do you know? She just happened to stumble on some other reincarnations."

At this point, I finally understand how everything is connected.

Certainly, this is related to reincarnations but a separate incident from Missoka's current plight, while at the same time not being entirely unrelated.

It also explains why Lady Ariel had such difficulty explaining the situation.

"Then you wish for me to go and fetch these reincarnations?"

"Nope. Not at all."

Lady Ariel waves a hand to dismiss my assumption.

"No, what we want you to do is go to their village—oh, there's two of them, by the way. So first, go to this human village on the border and kill everyone, 'kay?"

"Um...what?"

I think it's quite understandable that I found Lady Ariel's words so completely incomprehensible that I responded in an admittedly foolish way.

And so I find myself on my way to the border, astride a mount called a fenesist.

It is one of the earth wyrms that once pulled our cart when I was traveling to the demon territory with Lady Ariel and company.

At the time, it was a lesser wyrm called a fenerush, but it has since evolved into a fenesist.

While its constitution is unchanged, its base stats all went up, and it's even learned Earth Magic to help support me, its rider. Although, of course, its stats are still far lower than mine, so I would be better off dismounting to fight alone.

Still, I look forward to seeing how it will grow in the future.

Monsters usually have few skills but have high stats to compensate.

If it continues to level up and evolve, its stats may even surpass my own one day.

The giant creature galloping alongside my mount and me is the other evolved fenerush.

This one became a fenegrad, an evolution that favors pure strength over the ability to support a rider, unlike the fenesist.

The fenegrad's primary weapon is its size.

It is just as strong as it appears, and since it has gone from walking on four legs to two, it has freed up its arms to use as weapons.

Additionally, it is far faster than its sluggish appearance would suggest.

The fenegrad cannot use Earth Magic like a fenesist, but it has the advantage in pure physical strength.

Both of them are irreplaceable comrades who have aided us throughout our journey.

The speed of these earth wyrms made it easy to catch up with the group of elves, and now we are already close to the border.

Once I arrive, all that remains is to do as I have been instructed.

I think back to Lady Ariel's words.

"I'd like to take the reincarnations into our custody, but we can't do that. The problem is mostly the location. Humans who live in the borderlands form tight-knit communities with their friends and family. They won't hand over a couple of their kids if we just ask. In fact, they might cut you down for even suggesting it. The people who live there make the rules. It's extreme to the point where any outsiders are pretty much seen as enemies. Trying to negotiate with them won't make a difference, I'm afraid. Probably best to assume that there's no peaceful way we can retrieve the reincarnations at all. That's likely why Potimas hasn't laid a hand on them, either."

From what I hear, the people who live in the borderlands are akin to bandits.

Apparently, that's not an inaccurate descriptor, but they apply themselves to their trade with the pride that they are protecting their land from demon invaders in the process.

Demons and humans look very similar, so they essentially kill anyone they haven't seen before to be certain.

They've been doing this for generations, which has naturally cultivated a culture that highly values family, scorns outsiders, and is generally reclusive.

They trust their family to be on their side and kill outsiders because they could well be demons.

This seems an outlandish brand of logic to me, but such a lifestyle is tolerated in the borderlands.

"Which leads me to the main points. I want you to massacre the reincarnations' clan for two reasons. One, it'll mean that the elves can get through safely. And two, it'll draw the reincarnations away from that place. Like I said, the border tribes have a strong sense of family. And they don't like to let their family leave. For most people born on the border, that means living their whole lives there. But that would mean that those two reincarnations would die as soon as war broke out."

Lady Ariel is going to start a war with the humans. That is an immutable fact.

And when she does, the demon army will naturally have to cross the border.

And naturally, they'll clash with the humans who live there.

The likely outcome, I imagine, goes without saying.

"Since there's no way for us to peacefully take the reincarnations into custody, we'll crush their colony and leave only those two alive, so they can run away and live freely. If we took them in by force, they obviously wouldn't be thrilled, y'know? So rather than setting ourselves up for trouble unnecessarily, it seems better to set 'em free and let them do whatever they want. I know this seems drastic, but it's the only way to clear a path for the elves while also letting the reincarnations run away instead of involving them in our eventual war. It's killing two birds with one stone...although I guess that's kind of an unfortunate turn of phrase in this case."

Lady Ariel smiled self-derisively.

To me, she appeared to be lamenting that this violent choice was the only way forward.

I'm sure Lady Ariel would have preferred to avoid resorting to this, too.

But in these circumstances, we're left with no other option.

"On top of that, if Ms. Oka was to run into these two reincarnations, it'd just complicate things even further. It's better to take matters into our own hands and lead those two out of her path."

Unfortunately, I've drawn the short straw for this particular task.

It would be cruel to give Wrath a task that would cause his fellow reincarnations to resent him.

This duty required someone to leave immediately and have the strength to wipe out an entire tribe of borderlands humans.

An entire army would have never made it to the border before the elves.

Since I can travel alone, I am well suited for this role.

And my inside knowledge of the circumstances is a factor, too.

The only question is whether I am strong enough to massacre this entire clan.

"You always sell yourself short, Merazophis. Maybe you're not aware of it, since you're surrounded by freaks like us, but to an ordinary human, you're freakishly strong, y'know?"

Those were Lady Ariel's words.

Is that...true?

To be honest, it doesn't feel that way to me.

Since enrolling in the army and training with other individuals, I have indeed come to the realization that I am stronger than I thought.

But still, I wouldn't have claimed myself to be as powerful as my fellows.

I simply do not have the talent.

Certainly, I have spared no effort in my attempts to become strong enough to protect the young miss.

My training with Lady White on our journey was certainly eccentric, but I have continued it in the hopes of getting stronger.

And I have undertaken additional training of my own, as well.

Yet, the gap in strength between the young miss and me has only continued to grow.

I do not think that I have trained any less than my young mistress.

Perhaps it is just that children and adults grow at different rates, but even more so, I feel that the young miss was born with a natural talent that I simply lack.

The young miss is special. She is a reincarnation, a Progenitor vampire, and the daughter of my esteemed master and mistress.

In comparison, I have always been naught but a humble servant.

I was aware that I lacked natural talent long before I became a vampire.

Certainly, I could carry out tasks as well as any other man, but when it came to going above and beyond, I always fell short.

Ever since I was young, I have ambitiously studied many different fields and subjects.

My hard work did expand the breadth of my abilities, but I could never hold a candle to a specialist in any of those fields.

I fell short of the maids when it came to any housework, could barely assist my master in matters of politics, and failed to fend off even a single bandit with my strength as a so-called bodyguard.

I could do many different tasks, but no matter how much I tried, I could never pass a certain threshold.

That is how I have always been.

Even now that I am a vampire, with vastly improved stats, my nature ultimately has not changed.

Perhaps that is why, even when Lady Ariel tells me that I am capable, I have trouble believing her.

"We will reach our destination tomorrow. Let us rest here for tonight."

I stop the fenesist and fenegrad and prepare our camp.

"Tomorrow is sure to be a difficult battle. I'll be counting on you."

I pat the two earth wyrms on the head and give them feed.

Lady White has given me a special bag that can store large amounts of items in a parallel space, so I am able to travel without unwieldy baggage.

It is a magical item made from Lady White's thread.

She handed it to me quite casually, but Lady Ariel sucked in her cheeks when she saw it, so I can only assume that it is worth more than I could possibly imagine.

As always, Lady White is beyond comprehension.

Perhaps she feels obliged to me for helping to look after her when she lost her powers, but she has done far too much for me.

I wish to be of use to her as well, not least so I can strive to repay this impossible debt, but there are few instances in which one such as Lady White would need help from the likes of me.

Since this is one of those rare opportunities, I must complete this task to the best of my ability.

But still, I fear I am not strong enough.

Not by a long shot.

No matter how much effort I put in, they continue to leave me behind.

"Perhaps one day you two will surpass me as well."

I murmur to the fenesist and fenegrad.

The earth wyrms look back at me with confusion, then at each other.

The action brings a smile to my face.

Even if they do surpass me one day, I am sure these clever creatures will continue to serve me, unworthy master though I am.

I cannot predict the future. All I can do is live and fight in the present moment to the best of my ability.

That is the only path forward for one as talentless as I.

No amount of effort can make up for natural talent, but I must continue to try or I lose my right to stand on this stage at all.

The young miss may already have no use for my feeble strength.

But I must at least ensure that I never hold her back.

"Lady Ariel believes I can do this. I must live up to her expectations."

Strengthening my resolve, I focus all my nerve on the battle to come.

"Alarm! We're under attack!"

"There's only one of 'em? We'll teach 'im to look down on us!"

"What the hell?! What is that guy?!"

"Dammit, he's too fast! I can't keep up!"

"Hey, this has gotta be a joke, right? How can a person split in two like that? C'mon! I must be dreaming, yeah? This is just a nightmare, right?"

"Idiot! Pull yourself together!"

"No! I don't wanna die!"

"Get the women and children outta here! We don't stand a chance!"

"Father! Father! This can't be happening!"

"Keep moving or he'll come after you!"

"Shit! You monster! You damn monster!"

"Aaaaargh!"

"Wait, stop! Please! You can kill me—just don't hurt her!"

"Run for it! Run! Please let us go!"

"Ha. That thing's not human or even a demon. It's some *thing* that's shaped like a person."

"You fiend! Agh—!"

"...God help us."

The massacre of the reincarnations' clan is complete.

Part of me is relieved that it went more easily than I expected, though I also have complicated feelings about the fact that relief is my strongest emotion when all is said and done.

Since I vowed to protect my young mistress, I have come to terms with the fact that I am a vampire. I attacked people to drink their blood night after night without hesitation.

I thought I still had a heart despite everything that's happened, but right now I feel calm, even after all this bloodshed.

Is this a sign that I've grown accustomed to such horrors? That my resolve is simply this strong? Or is it that I have become a monstrous vampire down to my very soul?

I do not think there is any way to know the answer.

Certainly, I was always willing to commit any atrocity necessary to protect the young miss.

But in truth, I thought I would feel more conflicted once I was finally put to the proof.

...This is not good.

If my resolve is firm, then that is ideal, of course.

But I cannot allow my heart to harden completely.

I accepted my fate as a vampire in order to continue serving the young miss, but I must not allow myself to turn into a monster on the inside as well.

I would no longer be able to face my master and mistress.

Vampires have no choice but to live differently than humans do.

But I must also endeavor to lead the young miss down a path that would not break her parents' hearts. If she attempts to go astray, I have a duty to correct her.

But how can I admonish the young miss for such things unless I, too, walk a proper path?

...Perhaps it is too late.

I may already be too far removed from humanity in body and soul.

But even if that is the case, I must find a way to live honorably.

My hands are already stained with blood.

Would my master and mistress weep to see me as I am now?

I vowed to live as a vampire.

To live alongside my mistress, even if I must go drenched in blood.

I decided to abandon my humanity but not my principles.

It is no easy task to stay on a path that offers no right answers.

Even so, I must at least continue to walk with my head held high and set an example for the young miss.

"W-wehhh!"

And so I must show no hesitation.

Before me are two children: a young boy protecting a young girl.

Surely, he knows that he stands no chance against me, and yet he attempts to shield her behind his small back—an act I cannot help admiring.

"...Mere children."

I attempt to keep my voice as cold as possible.

That alone is enough to make the girl turn so pale that she looks ready to faint, and the boy's body trembles.

Two women lie in a heap before them.

Most likely, the children's mothers.

They tried to protect their children to the very end.

"Hmph. I've lost interest."

Glancing at them, I act as though the sight of the mothers' sacrifice has convinced me to stay my hand.

Even though in reality, I've already slain many other parents alongside their children.

But I must let these two escape alive, for they are the reincarnations.

Without another word, I turn away from the children, beckon to the fenesist and fenegrad, and move to leave this place.

"Wait!"

But then something unexpected happens.

The boy calls out to stop me.

"Who are you?!"

For a moment, I don't understand what he's asking.

But then I realize he wishes to know my name.

"Merazophis."

Out of respect for the boy's bravery in demanding to know his enemy's identity, I look over my shoulder and give him my real name, hiding nothing.

Then I walk away from them for good.

Lady Ariel said that she wanted to let these children live freely.

But for them, there will surely be no freedom.

Only a life ruled by revenge.

If there is any other path, it will be one in which they support each other.

I was able to prioritize something other than revenge only because I had the young miss.

So I hope that these two will find a similar way forward.

But judging by the boy's look, I doubt that will be the case.

Most likely, that boy will come to stand before me someday.

And when that happens, I shall face him as his enemy.

But I have no intention of deliberately losing.

For I have my own reason to live, my own cause.

For that, I am even willing to stoop to the same depths as the man who is my most hated enemy.

If this boy wishes to choose the path of revenge with me as his target, he had best tread carefully.

I am not strong like that man Potimas.

But I am confident that my unwavering conviction far surpasses his.

Even if this revenge is justified, I will not accept a villain's fate.

If you wish to kill me, then you must surpass me in strength.

I will oppose you with everything I have.

Even if you are a reincarnation with the same powers as my young mistress, I will not lose so easily.

Master.

Mistress.

Perhaps I am already living in a manner that you would frown upon.

Even so, I must continue to live—as a vampire, as myself, no matter how bloodied my hands become.

And I will do this all while protecting the young miss and repaying my great debt of gratitude to Lady Ariel and Lady White.

Interlude Asaka and Kunihiko

My name is Asaka Kushitani.

I was given a name in this world, too, but I have the vague feeling I might never be called by that name again.

The only people who called me that were the people of our clan; my fellow reincarnation Kunihiko Tagawa and I call each other by our original names, after all.

And now that everyone in the clan except for Kunihiko and me is dead, I'm sure I won't be hearing that other name anymore.

For some reason, we were reincarnated.

I don't really understand why.

Kunihiko tells me that this "*isekai* reincarnation" was a popular genre of light novels and stuff, but when I actually experienced it for myself, I thought I was just having a bad dream.

But it was real: I woke up one day as a baby in an unfamiliar world.

It's impossible to accurately describe the distress and confusion I felt back then.

And when I realized that Kunihiko was right there and had witnessed every moment of me bawling my eyes out...well, I almost died of embarrassment.

Still, it was an immense comfort to have a friend close by in the same predicament.

Kunihiko and I were reborn into a clan of bandits.

Reminiscent of Mongolian nomads, they lived in tents, roaming the human-demon borderlands in search of prey. They attacked any demons they found, stole all their belongings, and reported the kill to their empire to receive pay.

A strange kind of legal banditry.

I wanted to get out of such a place as quickly as possible and live a normal life.

Kunihiko always wanted to go on an adventure, but I just wanted normalcy.

I longed to find a safe place to settle down in peace.

But I never imagined this was how we would leave the clan.

"I see one."

"...Yeah."

Up ahead, a town is coming into view.

Our clan was massacred, but fortunately the carriages and horses were left intact.

So after we dug graves and buried the rest of our clan, we packed all the luggage we could into a carriage and set out for the nearest town.

There was no point staying there any longer.

When we reach the town gates, we explain the situation to the guard.

The guard looks perturbed but lets us into town without the usual entrance fee, recommending that we pay a visit to the church.

A church...?

I don't know what we're going to do next, but I suppose we might as well go there for now.

"Heading out on a request, Gotou?"

"Yep."

As our carriage proceeds down the road, I see two men having a conversation nearby.

Kunihiko is looking at them, too.

"...!"

"Huh? Ah! Wait!"

Kunihiko suddenly jumps down from the carriage.

Then he runs up to one of the men and grabs his arm.

"Hunh? Whaddaya want, brat?"

"Gotou! A katana!" Kunihiko shouts. "Are you one of us?!"

"Huh?"

Gotou? A katana?

Looking closer, I see that the man called Gotou has a katana-like sword at his waist.

Then I finally realize what Kunihiko is getting at.

His name is Gotou, and he has a katana.

Could he be Japanese, too?

He certainly doesn't look Japanese, but then again, neither do we.

Maybe he's a reincarnation like we are.

"Uh, what're you talking about, boy?"

But that faint hope is quickly dashed.

Mr. Gotou looks genuinely confused.

Kunihiko tries to speak to him with Japanese words mixed in but still no reaction.

"Please make me your apprentice!"

But even though we know he's not Japanese, Kunihiko still seems to feel strongly about this encounter.

Why would he ask a total stranger to make him his apprentice?

"Erm...wait a sec. What am I supposed to do here, huh? I gotta go take care of a request now, y'know. Uh, what should I do?"

Gotou looks sincerely flummoxed.

But it doesn't seem like he's going to turn his back on us. Somehow, that causes the dam holding back all my feelings to break down, and I suddenly start weeping.

"Huh? Uh...hang on. Don't cry, little girl. It's okay, see?"

Mr. Gotou's kindness as he reaches out to comfort me despite his confusion has a profound effect on me.

Our whole clan was suddenly slaughtered, for unknown reasons.

We didn't know what to do next, so we came to this town, but of course we had nowhere to go.

The moment Mr. Gotou showed us kindness, I felt for the first time like I could still go on.

This is a cruel world, without a doubt, but maybe it's not a total loss after all.

I can't think about any of that right now. I just want to bawl my eyes out all over again.

I'm sure I'll live to regret this embarrassing moment, but right now I can't bring myself to care.

In the end, the guard hears the commotion and brings over someone from the church.

The clergy agrees to look after us for a while.

I'm so grateful.

"I'm gonna get stronger."

"Uh-huh."

"That guy Merazophis must've been a demon, right? I'm gonna get strong enough to beat him one day. I swear."

"Uh-huh."

I don't know if that's actually possible, and all I want is to live in peace without worrying about all that. But even stronger is my desire to not be separated from Kunihiko.

So whatever he decides to do, I'm going to follow him.

But for now, I just want to cry like the child I appear to be.

In their previous lives, they were known as Asaka Kushitani and Kunihiko Tagawa. They were given names in this world as well, but there isn't anyone left who knows them. For this reason, they continue to use their original names. They were born to a clan in the borderlands between the human and demon territories. Their clan was charged with warding off invaders from the demon territory, so they attacked any unfamiliar faces in the borderlands without mercy. As such, they were trusting of other clan members but avoidant of anyone else. Asaka wanted to escape this clan as soon as possible, and Kunihiko hoped to become a knight who would fight demons. The two were childhood friends even in their former lives, and since they grew up together in this world as well, they see each other as irreplaceable partners. The trauma of being the sole survivors of their clan's massacre only strengthened that bond, and they have continued to support each other ever since.

ASAKA & KUNIHIKO

7 Let's Make a Threat

So I went to file a complaint with D, and as a result, D got escorted away by Miss Maid.

I know that sounds like a lot of nonsense, though trust me, I don't really get it, either.

But I guess this means no more meddling from D, so I'm extra free to do whatever I want now!

And I managed to borrow a few items D left behind, too.

...Even if they all seem like gag gifts to me.

Still, uh, they're just as effective as you'd hope literal god-tier items would be, so I'll find a use for them...probably.

I mean, definitely! Yeah!

Anyway, now that I'm back home, I've wasted no time doing some follow-up investigations.

The Colonel's gonna look out for the elves until they reach the border, but there's no telling what'll happen after that.

The Colonel is a big shot, sure, but that's only in demon territory.

Once our guests are in human territory, he can't do squat.

I've got to find a way to keep the elves safe across the border.

The fastest way to do that would be to deal with the borderlands bandits somehow.

Those guys kinda default to *shoot first, ask questions later* mode with strangers.

Honestly, they're a lot scarier than some stupid monsters. I think they deserve their own danger rank and whatnot.

The various bandit groups cooperate really well, too, so if you take too long to crush one, another clan will come running to their rescue.

And once things get that out of hand, the human army will probably come to check out the ruckus, too.

So the only way through is to crush one of the clans as fast as possible.

I'm sure the Demon Lord could've done that when we came here from the human realm, but there was no need to go out of our way to wipe out a whole tribe just to avoid taking a detour.

But in this case, the elves need to get through bandit country somehow.

Which is why I've gotta find a tribe that looks easy to wipe out.

I'm using my real body and my mini-mes to explore the borderlands, and what do you think I find there?

A boy and a girl speaking Japanese.

Hoo, boy. These are definitely reincarnations, huh?

They call each other Kunihiko and Asaka.

Hrmmm. Based on Hiiro Wakaba's memories, that means they're probably Asaka Kushitani and Kunihiko Tagawa, right?

Huh. D said Potimas had collected a bunch of reincarnations, but I guess he didn't get his grubby mitts on these two.

Makes sense, since they're not exactly in a prime kidnapping location.

If you tried any funny business out here, you'd end up making an enemy of most if not all the dangerous clans who live on the border.

Potimas probably knew these two were there but decided it wasn't worth the trouble.

Really, I guess he didn't have much of a choice.

The only way to kidnap these guys would be to crush their entire clan.

I'm sure Potimas could pull that off, but in terms of effort versus potential gain, it probably wouldn't be very cost-effective. And he hates that kind of bargain, so it's no wonder he left them alone.

Ugh, this sucks, though.

Ms. Oka was enough of a problem on her own, so the last thing I needed was to find even more issues to deal with...

But now that I've found them, I can't just ignore them.

I mean, I'd LOVE to ignore them, but that probably wouldn't be good...

If I just leave them there, they'll definitely get killed in the war the Demon Lord's about to start.

We've gotta take them in, or at least move them to somewhere else.

But taking them in would mean we'd have to kill their whole clan first.

Not exactly the best first impression.

We might end up bringing them back here only for them to make it their life's mission to get revenge.

Argh! This is such a pain, dammit!

I wish we could just sweep away their clan and let them figure it out!

...Wait, maybe that would actually work?

In fact, is it just me or is that our only option?

If we leave 'em alone, they're just gonna get killed in the war, and if we try to take them in, their clan will definitely throw down without entertaining any negotiation. There's no peaceful way to resolve this, that's for sure.

So maybe we just need to chase them off, even if it means resorting to violence, and let them figure out the rest for themselves?

Although we'd have to make sure the elves don't try to mess with them, at least.

Yep, that settles it.

Not quite as delicate as my plan to save Ms. Oka, but there's nothing I can do about that.

So I guess we'll crush that clan and then have Ms. Oka and company pass through their recently cleared turf.

Seems like the only workable solution to me, yep.

As for who's best suited to do the actual deed...that'd be Mera, I guess?

I'm sure Mr. Oni could pull it off, but I'd be a little worried about whether or not he's strong enough. And more importantly, it'd be in pretty poor taste to have a reincarnation wholesale murder the families of his fellow reincarnations.

Mera's the perfect man for the job.

...Unless he refuses, but I'll cross that bridge when I come to it.

I don't know what Vampy's planning to do from here on out, but it's not like her servant, Mera, is obligated to help us with all our plans.

This is a massacre, plain and simple, even if we're doing it for a specific reason.

Mera lost his hometown in battle and had his precious masters killed by Potimas, so violence might be traumatic for him, especially if I'm asking him to do it with his own hands. I wouldn't blame him if he refused.

Well, I guess in that case, I can take care of it myself, even if it'd require some extra effort on my part.

That settles the border situation, which only leaves what happens once they get across.

And that's one thing I can't do anything about myself.

I've gotta make an appointment with the person in charge of the human lands, where they'll wind up once they cross the border.

Which means I have to go negotiate.

With the de facto ruler of humanity, no less: the pontiff of the Word of God.

"So that's the plan."

"Oh. Erm… I see."

"What's with the lackluster response?"

Here I am trying to come up with all these extensive plans, but the Demon Lord seems totally unimpressed.

"It's just, uh, I dunno. Y'know?"

"No, I don't. What are you getting at? Just spit it out already."

"Okay, am I the only one who finds that super-annoying coming from someone who normally refuses to say *anything*? In fact, that's exactly the problem! Has your whole personality changed or what? I mean, I know it hasn't, but still! You're not acting weird exactly, but you're not acting normal, either!"

Now she's mad at me for some reason.

"Um, what?"

"Don't 'what?' me! If anything, I'm the one who should be saying that! Since when are you so talkative, huh?! What happened to your usual fake-mysterious silence bit?! Are you drunk or something? You are, aren't you?!"

No, I'm sober.

I don't know why, but lately I feel like I can talk to the Demon Lord without getting nervous.

I mean, she did take in a part of me when she absorbed my former body brain, and bloodline-wise she's basically my grandmother, so we're definitely related in one way or another. It's not that weird to be able to talk to your relatives, okay?!

Although I guess the biggest reason is my own recent change of heart.

But the Demon Lord doesn't know about that, so I guess she's freaked out that I'm blabbering away all of a sudden.

"C'mon! Forget about those minor details."

"'Minor'?!"

"We need to go threa… I mean, ahem. *Negotiate* with the pontiff."

"You were definitely about to say *threaten*, weren't you?! Hello?!"

"Oh, but first I need to ask Mera to go crush that border tribe."

"Damn, girl! You don't listen to anyone, do you?! How crazy can you get?! Not that this is news to me! But still!"

Ignoring the Demon Lord's little tantrum, I get her to summon Mera and have her explain the situation to him.

Huh? Why didn't I explain it myself?

Oh, uh, y'know, I have a fake-mysterious silence thing to uphold…stuff like that…

Anyway, once the Demon Lord reluctantly explains things to Mera, he agrees right away to massacre the tribe.

If he had hesitated at all, I would've taken care of it myself without pressuring him, but apparently, it won't be a problem.

He seems worried about whether or not he can do it on his own, but that's just silly.

Like the Demon Lord says, he tends to sell himself short.

Has he forgotten that even after having his Wrath skill sealed, our Mr. Oni mowed down the rebel army without breaking a sweat?

Well, at any rate, I guess we can consider the border problem solved.

It seems like Mera's figured some things out for himself and overcome various doubts, so I'm sure I can count on him.

That just leaves the Demon Lord and me about to go on our merry way.

For our surprise attack on the Word of God pontiff.

So yeah, here we are.

The pontiff's office in the Word of God headquarters, the so-called Holy Kingdom of Alleius or whatever.

I brought the Demon Lord along and teleported in without an appointment.

Which I guess is probably why the secretary-type people in the room are frozen in fear and these secret service–looking guys whose faces are hidden by cloth have appeared out of nowhere, pointing their weapons at us.

"Stop!"

But just as they look like they're going to charge at us, the pontiff calls them off.

"You're no match for these two, even if you attack en masse. Stand down."

Ooh. Very imposing.

I haven't had much chance to interact with this pontiff guy, but I always thought he was more the type to smile cheerfully while scheming like mad behind the scenes.

Seems like he can drop the good-natured act for moments like this.

"Well? What might I do for you today, Lady Ariel?"

Next thing you know, though, that imposing aura disappears, and he's back to looking like a gentle, friendly old man.

Talk about scary!

Nobody should be able to switch gears that fast.

This old guy's terrifying in a whole different way from the Demon Lord.

He's basically powerless in battle, but he's still got this undeniable presence.

"Oh, no need to be so guarded. We're just here for some peaceful negotiations, honest. I'm not planning on fighting anyone."

"Then please at least come in through the front door in the future. It's not good for my heart, having you appear out of nowhere with no prior warning."

"You say that, but if we tried to come through the front, I'm sure we'd be turned away at best."

"Ha. I suppose so. Being the pontiff is convenient, but it can also be constricting."

The exchange between the Demon Lord and the pontiff seems weirdly laid-back.

Maybe they understand each other well after knowing each other for so many years.

"Well, let's not stand around talking here. How about a little change of scenery?"

The pontiff waves off the still-tense secret service guys, prompting them to back off.

They disappear with a little *poof*, just like ninjas.

Damn, that's cool!

Except that I can still see their every move with my special spider eyes.

"Please, right this way."

The pontiff leads us to a fancy drawing room.

Somehow, there are already servants inside with tea and snacks. I guess one of the not-ninja guys must have given them a heads-up.

His subordinates do what he wants without him even needing to ask.

What amazingly well-trained staff!

The Demon Lord's people are, well, demons, so they're all over the place. And the puppet spiders have such bizarre personalities that they're not exactly model servants. This guy's got it made!

But then again, the pontiff and the Demon Lord are pretty far apart in terms of actual strength, so it makes sense that you'd give the poor guy some kind of handicap in the form of reliable servants.

I'm already imagining the eldest puppet-spider sister vehemently objecting to this train of thought, but I'm sure it's all in my mind.

"Now then, might I ask why you're here?"

The pontiff sits down on a sofa.

Oh man, this thing's soft enough to suck you right in!

Hmph, but it's still not as good as my thread!

"We were hoping you could lend us a hand with two minor difficulties."

The Demon Lord glances at me, makes a face like *Nope, she can't do it,* and starts negotiating herself.

Um, rude?

I know she's right, but still! STILL!

Couldn't she at least have the decency to not let it show on her face?

"'Difficulties,' you say?"

"Yep, that's right. Just a couple of minor incidents that we can't quite take care of on our own."

"I see."

"Knowing how quickly information reaches you, you might already know this, but we had just a tiny bit of trouble in the demon territory recently.

That's all taken care of now, but there were actually some elves on the enemy side."

"Oh?"

"Well, White here crushed most of them, so it wasn't a huge issue. But this is where it gets a little complicated. One of the elves was a reincarnation."

Wait, huh?

The Demon Lord just casually dropped the word *reincarnation*.

"Well, well. That certainly is troublesome."

And the pontiff is acting like he knows exactly what she's talking about.

Um. Okay.

The pontiff already sniffed out the existence of reincarnations, apparently.

And the Demon Lord must've just assumed he would have that figured out already.

And then the pontiff assumed that *she* would assume that, so instead of getting hung up on that or trying to squeeze each other for more info, they're just…continuing the conversation?

Well, I'll be damned.

"Yeah, an elf reincarnation is already a problem in and of itself, but to make things worse, this one has a skill that can provide basic information on all the other reincarnations."

"I see. Damn that Potimas. No wonder he seemed so quick to act."

"Knowing you, I'm sure you're already taking steps to counter Potimas, but as long as he's got this particular reincarnation on his side, he's always going to be a step ahead in that department."

"So you're saying we have to do something about the reincarnation in question?"

A steely glint flashes in the pontiff's eyes.

"Unfortunately, that's where things get even more complicated. That elf reincarnation is actually in the demon realm right now, trying to escape into human lands. And I want you to let her get back to Potimas safely."

At that, the pontiff sinks into a dubious silence.

He lowers his gaze, thinking for a moment.

"And what is the purpose of that exactly?"

Clearly failing to discern a decent explanation himself, he looks up again.

"See, this elf reincarnation saved White's life. We want to rescue her if we can. But Potimas has already infected her, filthy parasite that he is. So we can't lay a hand on her right now, which is why we have to let her go back to Potimas."

The Demon Lord truthfully explains the reason.

At that, the pontiff starts thinking again.

Um, is being honest really the best option here?

My motivation for wanting to save Ms. Oka is super-personal, so I doubt it makes any difference to the pontiff.

From what I've heard about this guy, I wouldn't be surprised if he decided Ms. Oka had to be killed for the sake of humanity.

In fact, that glint in his eye a minute ago is proof enough of that.

"And in exchange, you will defeat the elves, correct?"

"Yes, of course."

Huh?

Um, whaaat?

Back up a sec. Where did that conclusion come from?

And why is the Demon Lord just agreeing like it's no big deal?

Someone clue me in here, pleeease!

"And you have a plan for how to bring Potimas down?"

"I wouldn't be offering this deal if I didn't."

I am so out of the loop right now.

"...Very well. I shall make arrangements to keep anyone from laying a hand on these elves by using the empire branch of the Word of God. I'm sure Potimas will collect them on his own from there."

"Thanks a bunch."

"But you must make good on your word to defeat the elves."

"Of course. I figure it might be about time to put an end to that particular grudge once and for all."

Looks like the negotiations are wrapping up while I'm still totally lost at sea.

"As for the other difficulty, this one's pretty much just icing on the cake, it's so easy. Y'know the clans that live on the border between the demon and human territories? Well, turns out there are two reincarnations there, too. We're gonna have to wipe out their clan to let the elves get through, see. But we'll let the two reincarnations get away, so would you mind taking care of them on your end?"

"What about that is easy? ...Hrmmm. Well, all right. I'll let the local church know about that as well."

"Thanks. You can do whatever you want with those two reincarnations, by the way. Raise 'em as knights to fight demons, use 'em as bait for the elves, whatever. Anything's fine by us."

Uh, wait a minute. "Fine by us"?

That's a pretty bold claim, Miss Demon Lord.

Sure doesn't sound fine to me...

Hrmmm. We are the ones who are gonna wipe out their whole clan, so we don't really have a leg to stand on if we start making demands about how they're treated.

"Hmm. I suppose that will do as a reward in itself, then. This certainly is troublesome, but it's not without benefits for our side, either."

"Great. We're counting on ya, then."

"Yes, I understand."

"I'll probably come by again in the future to consult with you about the whole elf thing. We've got a lot of preparations to finalize first, so try to be patient, yeah?"

"I'm looking forward to it."

Oh. Sounds like we're done here.

What? I didn't contribute at all, you say?

How rude! I enjoyed my fair share of snacks and tea, I'll have you know!

Negotiations? Never heard of 'em.

"Well, we don't wanna overstay our welcome, so we'll be on our way."

"Very well. I hope you'll bring good news next time you pay me a visit."

Once we've exchanged farewells, the Demon Lord gives me the signal to teleport us back.

Then, in the blink of an eye, we're back at the castle.

"Kinda seems like we got stuck with the job of beating the elves. What's going on?"

"Beats me, dammit!"

The Demon Lord responds to my cautious question with a shout.

Um, what?

"Uuugh! How did that happen?! WHY did that happen?!"

The Demon Lord throws up her hands in frustration.

Whaaat? But she agreed to it so naturally.

Or was she just keeping up a poker face because she had no idea what was going on?

"He's always been like this, the bastard! He thinks so many moves ahead that he's already decided what I'm gonna do before I've even figured it out myself! Quit reading so far into things, stupid!"

The Demon Lord seems to be throwing a tantrum.

Seems this isn't the first time something like this has happened between them.

"I mean, not that I have a real problem with defeating the elves. Really, I'd love to bring those guys down if I can."

Heaving a sigh and calming a little, the Demon Lord slumps into a nearby seat.

"The problem is, now that I talked such a big game, I gotta actually come up with a plan to beat them. I'm counting on ya, White."

"Who, me?!"

"Yes, you! It's your fault we wound up in this position in the first place, so take responsibility and figure it out! Got it?"

O-oh.

I guess I can't argue with that.

"Hmm. Ahhh. Okay, I get it. Saving Ms. Oka is what led to the idea of defeating the elves."

"What do you mean?"

The Demon Lord appears to have figured out how the pontiff reached the conclusion that we were volunteering to defeat the elves.

"Well, Potimas has infected Ms. Oka."

Right.

Potimas has the ability to take control of other people's bodies.

The victims lose their own free will for life, and Potimas gets to use them however he pleases.

But he can't do it to just anyone. Only people who satisfy certain conditions are susceptible.

And apparently, Ms. Oka satisfies those conditions.

You wouldn't believe how shocked I was when I saw it for myself.

I mean, Potimas's nasty feelers are wrapped around Ms. Oka's soul.

The Demon Lord keeps using the word *infected,* and I think that fits perfectly. It has a viscerally gross sort of ring to it, y'know?

Yeah, seeing the way Potimas's creepy invisible tentacles are wrapped around Ms. Oka's soul thanks to his weird ability definitely made me want to puke.

Although I guess it's only because I've become a god and can somehow see people's souls.

"The only way to release her from that is to kill Potimas. And killing Potimas basically means defeating the elves. That's why he mistakenly assumed that we were preparing to do exactly that."

Ahhh.

I get it.

It does kinda make sense now that I think about it.

I was only really thinking about how to muddle through the present situation, but if you think about it in the long-term, the only way to truly save Ms. Oka is to kill Potimas once and for all.

That must be what the pontiff assumed we meant when we said we were going to save her.

"Ughhh. If he refused, I was ready to resort to threats, but I'm not even sure who threatened who anymore. We've gotta figure out a way to defeat the damn elves just to hold up our end of the bargain now." Leaning back against the chair lazily, the Demon Lord grumbles.

"But I guess that's one way to settle things. Yeah. Let's do it." I decided to light a fire under the Demon Lord's butt.

If she's truly worried about the fate of this world, she would've had to beat Potimas sooner or later.

And if we want to save Ms. Oka, again, we have to kill him.

So what's the problem?

Sure, I know it's not gonna be easy.

But if we can save Ms. Oka and beat the Demon Lord's sworn enemy, that's two birds with one stone. If anything, there's no reason NOT to kill him.

Besides, with everything he's done, I'm seriously pissed off. It's personal now.

"We're going to crush Potimas."

It's important to declare your intent out loud.

The Demon Lord actually shivers. Oops, I guess I let my anger show a little.

"Not right away, though."

"R-right."

I'm a spider, after all.

When I'm stalking my prey, I always perfectly lay my traps before I go in for the kill.

Which means we've gotta start by gathering more information.

...I better hurry up and power up my clones already.

Interlude A Teacher Wants Only What Is Best for Her Students

"Oka. Are you all right?"

"Yes."

"Don't push yourself too hard."

One of my sharp-eyed companions notices that my breathing has grown slightly heavier and expresses concern.

To adults like them, my body must appear too small, too weak.

As a reincarnation, my mental age is by all accounts that of an adult, but even counting those years, I seem like a child to the long-lived elves.

How many days have we been walking like this?

We joined the army of demons rebelling against the Demon Lord in order to rescue Miss Negishi, who has been captured by that same Demon Lord. Unfortunately, the Demon Lord discovered the rebel army's plans and all but destroyed them with a surprise attack.

We barely escaped with our lives and have been on the run ever since.

Fortunately, demons who sympathize with the elves have helped us on our way, providing us with food and supplies.

They have guaranteed our safety on our journey and even provided us with a place to sleep from time to time.

Thus, our life on the run has not been as hard as one might expect.

But even so, I find my feet dragging.

Due to both physical exhaustion and mental distress.

I keep remembering what Sasajima said to me.

* * *

"I'm not sure what false impression you're under, but I'm here of my own free will. And I have no intention of taking your hand.

"I'm fighting because of my own convictions, not because anyone forced me to. It's what I believe is the right thing to do. I don't feel any shame for my actions.

"Let me ask you a question instead. You said I'm doing 'awful things,' and yet, here you are doing the very same. Can you really reach out to your student with those bloodstained hands, claiming to offer me help?

"If you can't even deny that, then I most definitely won't take your hand."

Sasajima was one-sidedly massacring the rebel army.

I didn't want him to continue to do such awful things, and I pleaded with him to join us and run away.

But he completely rejected me.

He said he was fighting of his own free will.

And then he asked me a question of his own: Could I really extend these bloodstained hands to my student?

I couldn't answer him right away.

In fact, I don't think I could answer him even now.

All this time, I have done whatever it takes to save my students, living with danger as a constant companion.

I have fought against monsters but also against people, as in this most recent incident.

Though this world may distinguish between humans and demons, they all look like people to me.

And yet, I have raised my hand against such people on occasion, even taking lives when I had to.

This rebellion was no exception...

I told myself I had no choice, since it was for my students' sake, but...

"Am I really doing the right thing?"

Sasajima said that he was fighting of his own free will.

I have been doing the same, but I cannot declare that with the same level of pride and certainty that he did.

"Oka. Don't let what he said get to you."

One of my companions reassures me.

But I cannot help thinking about it.

Am I in the wrong?

"Remember, he is an ally of the Demon Lord. Or perhaps he's just been tricked by the Demon Lord as well. I'm sure you know that this demon lord is trying to end the long-standing truce between humans and demons and rekindle the war, right? I hear anyone who objects meets with a terrible fate. You saw that battle with the rebel army, didn't you? The Demon Lord shows no mercy to any who dares defy her. So no matter what someone who follows such an atrocious leader says to you, you can't take it to heart."

"Right… Of course."

Everything I've heard about the Demon Lord makes her sound quite terrifying.

The demon race was finally beginning to recover from the ravages of the old war, and now she's forcing them to fight again.

They say that her reign of terror keeps anyone from speaking out against her for fear of the consequences.

The demon population has severely declined due to the previous war. They don't have enough strength to fight the humans again.

If they go to war, all that awaits their race is certain doom.

Which is why a rebel army rose up in a last-ditch effort to overthrow the Demon Lord.

The elves agreed to back the rebel army not only to aid me but to assist the demon race out of sympathy for their plight.

Surely, the right thing to do is overthrow this tyrannical leader.

So why would Sasajima side with the Demon Lord?

How can he be so proud of his choice to work on the side of evil?

I simply don't understand.

"Was he like that in your world, too?"

"No, not at all. In fact, he was a quiet boy who valued peace."

Sasajima was reserved and didn't stand out much in the class.

He was usually with his friends Ooshima and Yamada, often scolding the former when he goofed off. Sasajima was diligent, quietly attentive, and overall a very good kid.

So why…?

"Then maybe he really has been deceived by the Demon Lord."

Perhaps that is true.

The Sasajima I know would never side with evil.

But Sasajima was clever, too. Would he really be fooled so easily?

The words Sasajima said to me…

His reasons for supporting the Demon Lord…

When I think about these things, I cannot seem to shake a strange unease, like a tiny bone caught in my throat.

As these thoughts continue to torment me, we keep walking, eventually reaching the border between the demon and human realms.

"There's a path through here that will lead us safely to human territory."

This information comes from the member of our party who's been in contact with our demon supporters.

Everyone else looks doubtful.

I can hardly blame them, since this border ought to be the most difficult part of our journey to human lands.

The humans have built fortresses at every major entry point, and smaller paths like these are guarded by human tribes that attack anyone who attempts to come through from demon territory.

How could this route possibly be safe?

"Apparently, the Demon Lord's elite force massacred the human tribe that guarded this passageway."

This explanation clears up our doubts, but the reason is terribly ghastly.

"The Demon Lord seems to be taking steps to prepare for the impending war against the humans."

A murmur runs through the group.

I cannot blame them for being alarmed.

The Demon Lord only just finished fighting the rebel army, but she's already sending out troops to strike at the humans?

"Perhaps the war between humans and demons will start sooner than we expected."

I believed that we still had time before the demons would be ready for war, especially after fighting the rebel army.

But considering how hastily the Demon Lord seems to be moving, perhaps we cannot afford to take our time after all.

"It's terrible that this human clan was slaughtered, but it may also be our saving grace. Let us pass through before we let this chance go to waste."

Thus, we were able to cross the border.

Along the way, we passed through the area where the massacred clan must have lived.

The bloody traces of the battle were still fresh, and a great many graves had been dug there.

...Someone must have taken the time to bury all the slaughtered victims.

We paused for a moment of silence there before moving on.

After we reached the human realms, the rest of the journey went by quickly.

The elves have hidden teleport gates all over the world.

We met up with Potimas and his forces, who had come to find us, and safely returned to the elf village together.

"Well done making it back alive."

Potimas wears the same icy expression as always, but somehow he seems to be in a good mood.

Is he happy about our safe return?

"Oka."

"Yes?"

"Let us take this opportunity to cease gathering the reincarnations for now."

"What?"

For a moment, I don't understand what he's saying.

As the meaning of his words slowly sinks in, I cry out in protest.

"But we haven't rescued all of them yet!"

"Most of those who remain beyond our grasp would be difficult to retrieve."

At that, I look at the Student Roster, the skill I was born with that gives me information on all my students.

However, the amount of information it provides is very limited.

Only their place of birth, whether they are currently healthy, and the predicted time and cause of their death.

And when one dies, their name disappears from the list.

Already there are four lines that have become blank.

Pulling my gaze away from those empty spaces, I look over the rest of the list.

"Of the people we have deduced to be reincarnations based on their place of birth, several of them are nobles. Obviously, we cannot lay a hand on them."

He has a point, I realize.

Out of the reincarnations we haven't retrieved yet, the ones who appear to be Natsume, Yamada, and Ooshima are recognized as royalty or nobility.

Naturally, a royal or noble family would almost certainly refuse to give up their child to a group of strangers.

"As for the rest of them, about half have been identified as well but would be difficult to lay our hands on for political reasons. Since we know who they are, however, it will suffice to keep watch on them from afar."

"Well, yes, I suppose..."

Just as Potimas says, there is not a particular need to physically take in all of them.

As long as we can keep an eye on them.

"And as far as the half we haven't been able to identify, frankly, it would be extremely difficult to continue pursuing leads."

The ones we haven't identified are the two from the borderlands we just passed through and the one who was born in a dungeon called the Great Elroe Labyrinth.

Both are highly dangerous areas, so it would be risky to try to track them down.

"But even so, can't we...?"

"No. We cannot."

I want to continue searching, but Potimas shuts me down in a sharp tone.

"Listen to me, Oka. I cannot allow you to put yourself in any more danger. You realize how easily you could have died in this incident, yes? If you get yourself killed while trying to save your students, then all would be lost. Besides, the other elves who travel with you put themselves at risk, too."

Again, I understand that Potimas is correct.

In this most recent battle, most of the elves involved lost their lives.

Of course, the main goal was to help the rebel army overthrow the Demon Lord, so rescuing my kidnapped students was only ever a side goal.

But searching for my students in a known dangerous area would be my own selfish demand.

Certainly, I cannot drag other elves into almost certain danger for such personal reasons.

"Then at least let me go alone—"

"I told you, no. My decision is final. Throwing a tantrum will not convince me to change my mind."

A tantrum…

Do my strong feelings amount to a tantrum?

"Lord Potimas…could you not consider allowing Oka to do as she wishes?"

"Hmm?"

Just then, one of my companions intervenes on my behalf.

"Oka has done her very best. It would be a shame to let her work end here. We will be happy to continue assisting her. So please!"

"I'll help, too!"

"Me too."

"Oh, thank you…"

The kindness of these elves warms my heart.

But Potimas puts a stop to all of that with a loud sigh.

"…If you must know, I was thinking of dispatching Oka to a certain academy in the Analeit Kingdom."

I blink in confusion at this unexpected declaration.

"Nobles and royalty from various lands are already enrolled there. Including those reincarnations, of course."

My eyes widen as I realize what he means.

"I myself will continue to search for clues as to the reincarnations we have yet to locate. Oka, you are to go to those we have already located and watch over them from close by."

"Yes! Yes!" I exclaim, overjoyed by this kind gesture.

"One 'yes' would suffice."

Perhaps embarrassed, Potimas turns and walks away.

"That's great, Oka."

"It really is."

"If only Lord Potimas would be clearer about these things."

"I heard that."

As my companion pales with an "urk!" and stands at attention, I let out a small giggle. Then I call to stop Potimas.

"Um, wait!"

"What is it?"

Potimas turns back toward me, looking perplexed.

"Until I take up my position at that academy...no, even once I'm there... may I still help all of you somehow?"

Potimas raises his eyebrows, so I continue.

"Everyone has helped me so much, so I want to return the favor somehow. When I saw the battle in the demon realms, I realized just how tragic war really is. I want to make this world a more peaceful place, even if only a little. So please let me help."

I don't know why Sasajima would help the Demon Lord.

But I do know that I strongly object to people fighting each other.

Since the elves' goal is to stop that from happening, I want to contribute to their cause while also returning the favor of helping me look for my students.

"...I shall consider it."

"Thank you very much!"

I clasp my hands together and pray that Potimas will grant permission.

Sasajima...

I still don't understand why you're fighting.

But I'll do my best to live a life that I can be proud of, too.

Someday, if we meet again, I want to be able to say with pride and confidence that I have done what is right.

So please...don't take on any more sins.

Next time we meet, I don't want it to be on a battlefield again.

But if we do meet again in battle and Sasajima hasn't changed his mind, then...

8 Let's Wrap Things Up

Team Send Ms. Oka Home: Mission complete!

Boy, sometimes things really do work out for the best.

Even if we wound up agreeing to defeat the elves somewhere along the way.

It's not like we have to do it right this minute, though. And since it's Potimas we're up against, I think our best bet is to collect a bunch of information, figure out a thorough battle plan, and generally take our sweet time getting completely ready.

This is to save Ms. Oka, after all, and to save the Demon Lord.

Defeating the elves would be a huge help to her, since they're basically like cancer cells to this world. Since the Demon Lord's ultimate goal is to save this world from destruction, she's gonna have to take them down sooner or later.

Hrmmm.

Elves, elves, eeelves.

To be honest, as much as I hate Potimas's guts, I'd never really thought about wiping out all the elves entirely.

I mean, up until pretty recently, my only plan was to just lazily train and study.

How do you lazily train? Sorry, I'm not taking questions right now.

Really, as far as the whole end-of-the-world thing goes, I kinda didn't care that much as long as it could wait until AFTER I leave this planet.

But y'know.

If I really want to help the Demon Lord, that attitude's not gonna fly.

The Demon Lord wants to save the world.

I get the feeling that she's fully prepared to die to achieve that goal.

Sure, the Demon Lord's strong, but there are still limits to what she can do.

Take the elves, for instance. If Potimas gets serious, he might bust out some crazy weapon like that UFO we took down a while back.

Okay, not "might." He DEFINITELY would.

And it'd probably be even worse than that UFO, too.

Like, Potimas himself said that he was ashamed of ever designing that thing.

There's no doubt in my mind that he's invented a much better weapon since then.

And if that's the case, the Demon Lord can't beat him.

She's definitely one of the strongest individuals in the world, but she can't exactly take on a UFO carrying a bomb that could obliterate an entire continent—never mind a weapon even WORSE than that—all by herself.

She can't save this world without getting rid of the elves, but she's got no way of doing that.

That means this is already a mission that's impossible to clear.

So I bet the Demon Lord is planning to do everything she can and then entrust the future of the world to the next generation.

...Little does she know that there won't BE a next generation.

Ughhh.

Man, this world is the biggest piece of crap ever!

Hmph. All right, let's do this.

Dying along the way? Nope, I'm not gonna let that happen.

An eye for an eye, a life for a life.

I swear on my mother's grave that I won't let the Demon Lord die as long as I still breathe.

Okay, *technically* I'm the one who killed my mother, but that's not important right now!

Either way, at this point, I'm gonna see this thing through to the end.

And I'm aiming to make it a happy ending, too.

Just you wait—the epilogue's gonna be the Demon Lord smiling and saying, *Thanks, White! You're the best. I love you sooo much!*

"Um, I'll say *Thank you* for sure, but I dunno about that last part."

"Whaaat?"

"Wow, why do you look so disappointed? Are you interested in me *that* way?"

"Yeah, right."

"Then why is that your idea of a happy ending?"

So yeah, I've been chatting about all this with the Demon Lord this whole time.

"By the way, is it just me, or did you drop a huge bombshell in the middle of your little monologue?"

"What? You mean my undying love for you?"

"Okay, seriously, why do you always have to take it in that direction? Huh?"

C'mon—it's just a joke. Really.

"What do you mean, 'there won't be a next generation'?"

Oh, thaaat bombshell.

I think there's a more qualified person who should explain that, not me.

In fact, considering all the crazy stuff I'm plotting to do from here on out, I should probably have a little chat with this person anyway.

"Okay, let's call Güli-güli."

"Do me a favor and *never* call him that to his face, okay?"

"Don't worry—I won't be able to talk once he's actually here, so it's not a problem!"

"Um, I'd say that's definitely a problem, but whatever."

The Demon Lord sighs and gets up from her chair.

Inspired by the comfy sofa we sat in when we met with the pontiff, I used my thread to create a brand-new, ultra-comfortable chair that's guaranteed to ruin you for life. That's just how nice it is to sit in.

It's definitely not my imagination that the Demon Lord took a little bit longer than usual to get up just now.

I know, pretty awesome, right?

Yeah, I get it. It's tough to get up from a seat that comfy.

The Demon Lord's turning into even more of a couch potato!

"Why do I feel like you're thinking really rude thoughts about me right now?"

"I don't know what you're talking about."

The Demon Lord squints at me for a moment, then shakes her head, shrugs, and starts walking.

I follow behind her to the basement of the castle.

At the bottom of a crazy-long staircase is a small, seemingly empty room.

But while it looks like that at a glance, there's the faint presence of conjuring on one wall.

The Demon Lord places her hand in the center of it.

Right away, the wall disappears like it was never there, and a space around the same size as the original room appears.

...This isn't just a hidden room behind the wall, huh.

The new room is an alternate dimension.

It's just temporarily connected to this reality right now.

So even if you were to break down the wall that was just there, you wouldn't be able to reach this room.

There's a pedestal-like thing in the center of the room, and someone is sitting on top of it.

To sum that person up, it's basically a black lizardman.

No, I guess *draconian* would be more accurate.

They've got a dragon head, but the body is definitely that of a human. They're even wearing a suit and a silk hat for some reason.

"HEY THERE, SIS."

The dragon addresses the Demon Lord in a hard-to-understand voice, like they're forcing their vocal cords to produce humanoid language.

I can't tell from the voice if they're male or female. Do dragon people even have genders?

"Since when are you and I related? My only siblings are the others from that orphanage."

"OH, DON'T BE LIKE THAT. GENETICALLY SPEAKING, WE'RE TECHNICALLY SIBLINGS, NO?"

"Maybe, but it's not like our parents would acknowledge that."

"FWA-HA-HA! FAIR ENOUGH."

I listen to the conversation between the Demon Lord and the draconian in silence.

Obviously, it raises a lot of questions, but it'd probably be rude to ask.

I've got a vague idea of the Demon Lord's early life thanks to the contents of Taboo, but it seems like an invasion of privacy to pry about it.

Everyone's got a few secrets they don't want to talk about.

I'm not exactly eager to tell anyone else about being D's substitute, so I'm not one to judge.

I have no intention of digging into the Demon Lord's past unless she decides to share it with me herself.

"WELL? WHAT BRINGS YOU HERE? OR DID YOU JUST STOP BY FOR A CHAT?"

"Of course not. I wouldn't summon you for no good reason."

"I THOUGHT NOT. BUT LIKE I TOLD YOU BEFORE, THE SWORD OF THE DEMON LORD ISN'T HERE ANYMORE."

Sword of the Demon Lord? Huh?

Hmm, come to think of it, I might've seen something about that in the Taboo information.

It's not like I read the whole thing from start to finish, and now that I've become a god and lost my skills, I can't call that Taboo stuff back up anymore.

But I guess this draconian must've been guarding the sword in question.

So this Sword of the Demon Lord was being kept in a hidden room protected by spatial conjuring—the kind you probably couldn't reproduce with skills, no less.

If it was mentioned in the Taboo information, it must be an important system-related item.

Although it could also be an item D stuck in just for her own amusement.

But wait, it's not there anymore?

Isn't that kind of, like, bad?

"No, I'm not here about that, either. I came to ask you to call Gülie for us."

"CALL MASTER? IS IT AN EMERGENCY?"

"It's not *that* urgent, but there's something we definitely need to ask him."

"ALL RIGHT. JUST A MINUTE."

The draconian's eyes close.

Are they communicating with Güli-güli telepathically or something?

"White, this is the dark dragon Reise. They're one of the oldest of the dragons."

Ooooh.

A dark-attribute dragon, huh?

Plus, if it's one of the ancients, that's the same category as the wind dragon

Hyuvan in the southern wasteland and the ice dragon Nia in the Mystic Mountains.

A dragon like that was guarding this Sword of the Demon Lord?

It's gotta be a super-important item, then.

"What's the Sword of the Demon Lord?"

I lean close to the Demon Lord to mumble a question in her ear.

"It's a weapon that only the Demon Lord can use. I don't know if the rumors are true, but they say it can unleash a blow that could even kill a god, except it can only be used once, basically."

Um, that sounds super-dangerous!

The Demon Lord said it might not be true, but since that name showed up in the Taboo info, it's almost certainly D who made it.

Knowing D, she might've seriously made an item that could kill a god.

And this super-dangerous weapon is just floating around somewhere out in the world?

Are you for real?!

"No need to worry. The Sword of the Demon Lord is practically a single-use item. Once it's been used once, it can't be used again for another couple hundred or maybe even a thousand years. And according to Reise, it's already been used."

Whew. I guess I don't need to worry about anyone trying to use it on me, then.

But...it's already been used?

A weapon that can kill a god. The explosion that crossed a dimension into that classroom to try and kill D. Only the Demon Lord can use it.

Yeah, the pieces all seem to match up.

So D was attacked with an item that she made herself...?

You can't help but feel bad for the reincarnations who got caught up in that explosion, then.

Though in my case, this version of *me* didn't really exist until I was reincarnated here, so I can't really complain.

Anyway, while I'm talking about that with the Demon Lord and stuff, there's a sudden disturbance in space.

Someone's about to teleport here.

Well, not really "someone," since it could only be Güli-güli.

"I heard you wished to speak with me."

As soon as he appears, Güli-güli immediately cuts to the chase, and the Demon Lord responds equally abruptly.

"Yeah. White told me there's not gonna be a next generation? What's that all about?"

At that, Güli-güli's face twists bitterly, and he glares at me for a moment.

C'mon! Don't look at me like that.

All you actually asked me to do last time was to not tell the Demon Lord about that hidden valley beyond the Mystic Mountains, okay?

I didn't mention that part, and besides, it was more of a request than an actual promise anyway, so it's not like I took a vow of secrecy or anything, okay?

Nobody told me that what you really wanted to keep secret was that there's not going to be a next generation after this, okay?

Okay? Okay? Okay.

Güli-güli heaves a sigh, evidently giving up, and starts to explain.

"The people who live in this world are reincarnated in this very same world over and over. Normally, this wouldn't be possible, but the system has warped the natural order of things. And this unnatural occurrence only distorts things further, until eventually the seams begin to tear. The souls of this world's residents are slowly being worn down by the weight of these repeated reincarnations, all because they've been forced to take on unnecessary burdens like skills. If their souls continue to deteriorate, they will eventually be destroyed, which of course means they can no longer reincarnate. And there are signs that this has already begun to occur."

It's like when you wash clothes over and over, until they eventually get too worn down to wear.

If you keep dyeing, bleaching, and re-dyeing them on top of that, they'll wear out even faster.

By that same logic, the souls of people who keep reincarnating are beginning to weaken.

Skills are like the dye: It might look great right after you first add it, but if you keep bleaching it out and dyeing the same piece of clothing over and over again, you'll shorten its life span.

Each time a soul reincarnates, the skills it had in the previous life are ripped away.

Obviously, if you repeat that enough times, the soul's eventually going to break down.

And the signs of that breakdown are already beginning.

The valley Güli-güli wanted to keep secret from the Demon Lord is a place where he protects people whose souls are reaching their limits.

It's like a little sandbox where he keeps out monsters, forbids fighting, and tries to keep people from taking on any more skills, all to try and extend the life spans of their worn-out souls.

After Güli-güli's explanation, the Demon Lord's mood seems heavy.

"Why didn't you tell me?"

"What good would have come of me telling you?"

Both of them fall into a still-heavy silence.

"Tell me the truth. If I keep acting as the demon lord, will I be able to recover enough MA energy?"

"No."

Güli-güli responds right away.

The Demon Lord lowers her head, her shoulders trembling.

She became the demon lord with the willingness to lay down her life to save the world.

With the unshakable conviction that she would do what had to be done, even if it meant reluctantly playing the role of a villain and being hated by all demonkind.

But Güli-güli just said that still won't be enough.

This world is in such big trouble that the Demon Lord's difficult decisions amount to almost nothing.

Yeah, the world's seriously in danger of ending.

To the point where there's no logical way of saving it.

So why not save it in an illogical way?

"Let's just break the system."

Güli-güli and the Demon Lord both look at me incredulously.

Even Reise, who's been listening in silence, turns to stare at me. Although I can't tell what kind of expression that lizardy face is making.

"What do you mean?"

Güli-güli asks what they're probably all thinking.

This world is sustained by the system, so I can't blame them for looking at me like I'm out of my mind for suggesting we destroy it.

But think about it—like, *really* think about it.

The system was made by none other than D.

You know, the super-nasty, self-proclaimed evil god?

That rotten jerk is the one who designed this whole system.

It doesn't make sense to try and tackle it head-on.

No, there's got to be some kind of dirty trick we can use.

Knowing D's personality, I'm sure there's another way out, something hidden in an underhanded way that you could never normally find.

I swore to save the Demon Lord, remember?

So I've been thinking about how to go about saving this world.

And eventually, the conclusion I reached was that we have to break the system.

I swallow and attempt to calm my nerves before speaking again.

With a mega-serious topic like this, even I know that keeping it short because I'm not good with people isn't gonna cut it.

Not when the Demon Lord's fate is riding on this sales pitch.

"The system is a giant conjuring technique that supports this world. It regenerates this ruined planet, distorts the laws of life and death, and grants supernatural powers called skills."

The system is just one big conjuring.

Its main function is to keep this ruined planet alive.

But it also has several other functions.

Honestly, if all you're trying to do is restore the world, you don't really need all that complicated stuff.

The system forces people to be reborn in this world over and over, confining them here.

It encourages them to install lots of soul expansion packs known as skills, then collects those skills when they die and get reborn, turning them into MA energy to help keep the world alive.

Basically: The system is really a machine that uses people as fuel.

But like I just said, if you only want the planet to recover, you don't really need to do it in such a roundabout way.

"Do you know how much energy it takes to keep all the system's complicated functions running?"

The only person who can answer that accurately is probably Güli-güli, since he's a god who can actually use conjuring.

But it looks like what I'm trying to say is getting through to the Demon Lord, too.

"If you used that energy for the restoration instead, would it be enough?" she asks.

The system distorts this world's natural order of death and rebirth, enhances people with the ridiculous conjuring known as stats, and even piles on skills as a way of stripping more energy from souls.

Obviously, operating such a ridiculously complicated conjuring must consume a corresponding amount of energy.

We just need to break down those unnecessary parts of the system, take the energy freed that way, and put all of that into the part that restores the planet.

The system keeps us alive, but now we're gonna kill the system.

Normally, no sane person would even suggest that approach.

But we're talking about D here. I wouldn't put it past her to include such an obscene method that nobody should be able to find or accomplish.

Unfortunately, though, the Demon Lord's only half-right.

"Not in our current state. Not yet."

That's right. When I calculated the amount of energy in the system and compared it to the current state of the planet's disrepair, I determined that it wouldn't be enough to completely restore the planet.

If we break the parts of the system that recover energy, then we won't be able to produce any more energy for repairing the planet, so the restoration will never be complete.

In other words, this secret method will work only once we've saved up enough energy to completely restore the planet.

"We just have to supply the rest."

This world still has skills, a method of producing energy using the power of souls.

We need people to improve their skills, store up more energy and then let the system collect it—in other words, we need them to die.

"I see. Then I guess that doesn't change what I've got to do."

What the Demon Lord has been trying to do is start a war between humans and demons, forcing both sides to improve their skills, and then recovering more energy for the world when they die in battle.

Since we need to get even more energy, this plan still works out great.

The only difference is that while the Demon Lord planned to return that energy to the energy-deficient system in the normal way, I've got different plans for how to use it.

"Wait a minute. That may be possible in theory, but D will never stand by while someone attempts to intentionally break the system."

A protest from Güli-güli.

Makes sense. Since he's technically in charge of maintaining the system as an administrator, he probably can't accept this plan easily, even if he understands the logic behind it.

And I'm sure he thinks that his boss, D, would get mad if we did something like that.

But I can say this for sure.

"That won't be a problem."

I mean, this is D we're talking about, y'know?

She'd have no problem with the system getting broken as long as she thinks it'll be more entertaining that way.

If anything, I kind of suspect that D's been waiting for Güli-güli to make a dangerous move like that, just for the drama of it all.

A crazy plan like breaking the system is possible only for a god like Güli-güli.

If D actually baked that option into the system on purpose, then I think it's safe to guess that she was hoping Güli-güli might go for it.

"But..."

"It'll be fine. I promise."

Besides, now that D's been dragged away by Miss Maid, she can't interfere with us either way.

When the cat's away, the mice will play!

She might get mad later, but I don't care.

And I'm pretty sure she won't anyway.

So I'm just gonna insist it'll be fine.

"But still—"

"To be honest, this is basically because of your negligence as an administrator."

At that, Güli-güli's face falls.

Boy, am I mean or what?

It's true, though! If Güli-güli had done a better job, we wouldn't be in this situation.

Even if saying it out loud makes me the worst, that doesn't change the fact that it's true!

Especially since what I'm suggesting in the first place is that he basically abandon his post as administrator so we can break the system.

"I won't ask you to help. But don't try to stop us."

The biggest obstacle to this plan is the potential of Güli-güli interfering.

The only people in this world who could possibly defeat me right now are the Demon Lord, Potimas, and Güli-güli.

And that last one is the only one who I can say without a doubt is way, way stronger than I am.

If Güli-güli tries to stop us, our plan is doomed.

"HEH-HEH. SEEMS LIKE YOU'VE LOST THIS ONE, EH, MASTER?"

Reise picks this moment to finally speak up.

"I suppose so."

Güli-güli heaves a deep sigh, looking for all the world like an exhausted office worker.

"Very well. I won't try to stop you… No, it's because of my failure that we're in this predicament. I cannot use my power directly for this purpose, but I will help you as best as I can."

He smiles grimly.

Oh? Ohhh!

I would've been happy just to have him agree not to interfere, but he's actually gonna help.

Did my sarcasm work a little too well?

Either way, I'm counting it as a win!

"Oh, for real? Then can you, like, round up a bunch of dragons and wyrms and stuff who can turn into humanoids and make an army?"

The Demon Lord hits him with a massive request right out of the gate.

Whoa! She's totally planning to work not just Güli-güli but even his subordinates to the bone!

Now, THAT'S evil!

She uses everything and everyone she can, puts them all to work, then holes up at home herself.

The ultimate NEET!

"You could be the Ninth Army. I'll strip the current commander of the title and put you in charge instead."

"As you wish. I shall follow your orders, within reason."

Whoa, her unreasonable request actually got accepted.

Seriously? Is an administrator even allowed to take sides in stuff like this?

Well, I guess that just goes to show how indebted Güli-güli feels to the Demon Lord.

"Reise. You come, too."

"OH?"

"If the Sword of the Demon Lord is no longer here, then you need not stay, either."

"I SEE. I'VE GROWN ACCUSTOMED TO THIS SPACE WHERE TIME STANDS STILL, BUT IF YOU BID ME COME, I WILL FOLLOW MY MASTER."

Huh. I guess time is normally stopped inside this room?

That would explain how Reise's been living in this empty space, I guess. If you're frozen in time, unless someone summons the room up like this, you wouldn't need food or anything.

Although, leave it to D to casually conjure up something as ridiculous as a room where time stands still.

Reise's shape begins to change into that of a person, using some kind of technique.

The resulting person form has dark skin and androgynous looks.

The suit and silk hat seem like something a man would wear, but they could just as easily pass for a gorgeous woman.

So even in person form, you don't have a clearly defined gender?!

"Allow me to reintroduce myself. I am the dark dragon Reise. Since I've been living in stopped time for so long, I'm absolutely overflowing with youth compared to the other ancient dragons. You may rely on me whenever you like."

Reise gives this introduction with a crooked grin.

Is it just me, or do dragons tend to have really over-the-top personalities?

Or have I just so happened to meet the weirdest ones?

Also, I guess they can speak normally when they're in humanoid form.

"I shall go and gather dragons and wyrms from each land who can transform. I won't bring all of them here, since they still need to watch over their respective territories, but it should still be a considerable number. Ariel, if nothing else, please make arrangements to receive them before I return."

"Sure."

Oh boy. I can totally tell that the Demon Lord has no intention of doing that herself.

She's probably gonna dump that task on Balto.

Hang in there, buddy.

"Master, I'll accompany you. I'd like to get a fresh look at the outside world."

"If you wish. You were given the unpleasant role of being left frozen in time for so long. From now on, please do as you wish, within the scope of the role you are next assigned."

"Why, thank you."

Reise looks genuinely pleased.

I have no way of knowing how it felt to be alone in a small room where time stands still.

But I doubt anyone would want to do that.

And yet, Reise had no choice, because that was the role they were given.

This world has a way of sacrificing people like that in order to carry on.

That includes the Demon Lord and Güli-güli, too.

I'm gonna destroy that crummy way of life.

"All right, team! Let's save the world!"

The Demon Lord shouts in a deliberately energetic voice.

Since they've found a way forward after being unable to see the light for so long, she and Güli-güli both look more cheerful than usual.

I...

I didn't lie.

If we use the system as compensation, we can get the amount of energy the world needs.

The thing is, breaking the system means getting rid of skills and stats.

Which means they'll be forcibly removed from the souls they've been attached to.

So when we collect all that energy, it'll be especially hard on the souls of people with lots of skills and high stats.

I didn't lie.

If we break the system, we can save the world.

It's just that, in exchange, a ton of the people who live in this world will die.

I just kept that part to myself, is all.

If it means saving the Demon Lord and Ms. Oka, I don't care if I have to sacrifice most of the people of this world to do it.

That's all there is to it.

MONSTER ENCYCLOPEDIA
file.28

DARK DRAGON REISE

LV.82

status

HP
11411 / 11411
MP
11408 / 11408
SP
11399 / 11399

11398 / 11398

Average Offensive Ability : 11394
Average Defensive Ability : 11386
Average Magic Ability : 11401
Average Resistance Ability : 11397
Average Speed Ability : 11242

skill

[Dark Dragon LV 10] [Divine Scales LV 10] [HP Auto-Recovery LV 8] [Magic Power Perception LV 10] [Precise Magic Power Operation LV 10] [MP Rapid Recovery LV 10] [Magic Divinity LV 3] [Magic Super-Attack LV 2] [SP Rapid Recovery LV 10] [SP Minimized Consumption LV 10] [Destruction Super-Enhancement LV 2] [Cutting Super-Enhancement LV 4] [Piercing Enhancement LV 4] [Shock Enhancement LV 5] [Impact Super-Enhancement LV 3] [Dark Enhancement LV 10] [Battle Divinity LV 3] [Energy Super-Attack LV 2] [Heresy Attack LV 10] [Dark Attack LV 10] [Rot Attack LV 4] [Martial Arts Mastery] [Dimensional Maneuvering LV 10] [Kin Control LV 2] [Concentration LV 10] [Thought Super-Acceleration LV 7] [Future Sight LV 7] [Parallel Minds LV 7] [High-Speed Processing LV 10] [Hit LV 10] [Evasion LV 10] [Probability Super-Correction LV 10] [Stealth LV 10] [Concealment LV 10] [Silence LV 10] [Odorless LV 10] [Heatless LV 10] [Emperor] [Detection LV 4] [Shadow Magic LV 10] [Dark Magic LV 10] [Black Magic LV 10] [Abyss Magic LV 1] [Heretic Magic LV 10] [Great Demon Lord LV 2] [Destruction Resistance LV 2] [Cutting Resistance LV 3] [Piercing Resistance LV 2] [Impact Resistance LV 1] [Black Nullification] [Status Condition Resistance LV 9] [Fear Nullification] [Heresy Nullification] [Rot Resistance LV 4] [Pain Nullification] [Pain Mitigation LV 6] [Night Vision LV 10] [Five Senses Super-Enhancement LV 10] [Perception Expansion LV 10] [Ultimate Life LV 10] [Ultimate Magic LV 10] [Ultimate Movement LV 10] [Fortune LV 10] [Fortitude LV 10] [Stronghold LV 10] [Deva LV 10] [Sanctum LV 10] [Skanda LV 10]

A dark dragon who protects the Sword of the Demon Lord. One of the eldest and strongest of the already powerful dragons. Even without transforming, this dragon already has a humanoid form. As a result, they take unusual battle tactics compared with most dragons, using martial arts and magic. Since Reise was essentially sealed away with the Sword of the Demon Lord in a separate dimension, their level and stats are slightly lower than those of the other ancient dragons. However, they have several skills that would be effective even on gods; thus their total battle capability is no less than the others'. A legendary-class monster, assumed untouchable by humans.

Epilogue Thus an Evil God Is Born

We've acquired a powerful ally in Güli-güli.

The path ahead is clear.

We'll initiate the war between humans and demons as planned and acquire a massive amount of MA energy.

Then we'll combine that energy with the energy from dismantling the system and save the planet.

But before that, we need to remove one major obstacle: the elves.

That will help save Ms. Oka, too, so we absolutely have to do it.

In other words, what I need to do now is prepare to both destroy the system and crush the elves.

I've already started preparing for the latter by using my clones to gather information.

Yes, they've finally gotten strong enough that I can safely send them out to spy on the elves.

Basically, their stealth abilities have improved, and they're fast enough now to get away if they're spotted!

...What, you're not impressed?

But it's still a huge improvement from the start, when they could only relay information back to me, right?

These things happen little by little, you know. Slow and steady wins the race.

I don't need to rush things along. If I just keep them moving forward at a regular pace, they'll keep acquiring new abilities.

I'm gonna make even more mini-mes, too, and send 'em out to spy all over the world and gather information from everyone, not just the elves.

The more we know, the better.

Whoever rules the information rules the world!

And at the same time, I'll start increasing my own combat abilities.

If we're going to crush the elves, that means we're finally gonna have a face-to-face showdown with Potimas.

Thus far, we've done battle only with Potimas's clones.

And those had reduced battle capabilities so they wouldn't draw too much attention.

If Potimas gets serious about taking us on, he won't worry about holding back. He'll bust out every last weapon in his arsenal.

Which probably includes anti-dragon weapons, meant for taking on Güli-güli, who probably could've brought down that UFO.

I don't know if a weapon like that could actually beat Güli-güli, but if you're gonna fight a god, you can't half-ass the preparations.

At present, I don't know if a god like me (LOL) would be able to deal with a weapon like that.

I've got to get strong enough to win without a shadow of a doubt.

There's no room for failure here.

It's time to pull out all the stops.

Besides, I'm sure Potimas isn't the only major opponent I'll have to face.

I mean, if we follow my plan, tons of the people who live in this world are gonna die.

I'm sure Güli-güli won't allow that.

If mass death was all that was gonna happen, maybe he'd let me get away with it.

After all, because of the way this system works, people have to die and get reborn to keep the world running.

That's why he's not trying to stop the Demon Lord from starting a huge war with the intention of getting tons of humans and demons to kill each other.

But if we break the system and the souls of the people who die in the process break completely?

When we destroy the system, the skills and stats carved into people's souls will be recovered, which will place a huge burden on those souls.

If you do that to the people in this world whose souls are already weakened, they'll die.

And their souls will get smashed to bits.

If your soul gets destroyed, that means you're dead for good.

You'll never be able to reincarnate again, system or no system.

Once he finds out about that, I'm sure Güli-güli will challenge me.

Will he stand in my way to stop it from happening in the first place?

Or will he witness the massive number of deaths and attack me in a fit of rage?

I don't know, but either way, we're going to clash eventually.

So I've got to get strong enough to beat Güli-güli, too.

If it happens after we've already put the plan in motion, I can just run away with Teleport, but if he tries to stop me beforehand, I'm gonna have to get past him somehow.

'Cause I have my own reasons for why I can't back down.

Now that I think about it, that's a pretty tall order.

But since I've decided to do it, I've gotta tackle it with everything I've got.

...Except that's not all I have to do, either.

Like, that's already enough to make my head spin, but there's one more big thing I have to do.

Remember? I've gotta destroy the system, too.

But of course, I can't literally just destroy the whole thing.

I've gotta leave the part that regenerates the planet and adjust the rest to funnel all the freed energy into it.

Which means I have to get a solid grasp of the entire system and start preparing to dismantle it.

I'm basically trying to meddle with some really delicate conjuring that's part of a gigantic interlocking system, so as you might imagine, it's gonna be crazy difficult.

In fact, this might be even harder than beating Güli-güli.

But still, that's just in a normal situation.

If D actually did leave a secret method in the system to accomplish what I'm planning, then I just need to find that.

Even a god (LOL) like me wouldn't be able to dismantle a giant conjuring that D created and rebuild it from scratch. So I'm gonna put my faith in D's love of entertaining twists and pray that there really is a secret mechanism of some kind.

But either way, I'm gonna have to dismantle the system at some point.

Which is exactly why I'm here right now.

A giant magic circle stretches across the floor in geometric patterns.

It even covers the walls and ceiling with patterns, all glowing faintly in a dreamlike scene.

And at the heart of the magic circle is a single woman.

The woman floats in the air, the magic circle entwined around her like chains that have cut her off from freedom.

It's less like she's floating and more like she's suspended from the ceiling.

And as if that didn't already look painful enough, the lower half of her body is missing, as if it melted away into nothing.

It's a horribly cruel sight.

<Proficiency has reached the required level.>

<Experience has reached the required level.>

<Proficiency has reached the required level.>

A voice reverberates throughout the room.

Her lips aren't moving.

In fact, the voices constantly overlap one another in an endless echo.

Like a dissonant chorus.

Over, and over, and over.

But even so, that voice is unmistakably that of the woman suspended from the ceiling.

It's proof that even now, the people of this world are continuing to level up their skills.

It's the voice that I once called the Divine Voice (temp.), the one believed by the Word of God religion to be the voice of God, the voice that relays notifications from the system.

And the voice isn't all she provides, either.

This woman has been running the system alone here all this time.

She's the core of the giant conjuring known as the system.

This room is the system's center.

Normally, no one would be able to enter this place, but that's nothing my teleportation can't get around.

That said, it's not impossible to get here using other means, either.

It's not in a separate dimension like the small room that contained the dark dragon Reise.

No, this place exists firmly in the reality of this world.

The system wouldn't be able to control all of its delicate mechanisms from another dimension.

Just like how you can't make a call from outside the range of your mobile network.

This place is deep in the Bottom Stratum of the Great Elroe Labyrinth.

That's right, the same dungeon in which I was born.

The entrance to the Bottom Stratum was guarded by the earth dragon Araba, and it was in the Bottom Stratum that Mother made her nest.

And this place is what they were protecting.

The Demon Lord was so desperate to keep it safe that she put her most powerful asset down here to protect it.

But normally, it would be all but impossible to get inside anyway.

The impassable door prevents any trespassers.

Since it protects the center of the system, the door's defense is so high that no amount of assistance from stats would be enough to break through.

And since it's locked up without a key, it's impossible to open.

Even the Demon Lord, who placed Mother here to protect it, has probably never been inside.

"……"

So that's why I brought her here with me.

Buuut maybe that was a bad idea.

This is my first time here, too, so I had no idea it was going to be in this state.

It might've been cruel to let the Demon Lord see it like this.

Silently, the Demon Lord walks up to the woman bound in midair.

Then she stops right in front of her, close enough to touch if she reached out her hand.

As the woman's voice echoes clamorously throughout the room, the Demon Lord stares at her in silence.

"Mother."

Her single murmured word is drowned out by the woman's voice, barely making a sound.

But faint as it was, it still reached my ears.

There's no blood relation between this woman and the Demon Lord.

There couldn't possibly be.

But I'm sure she has her reasons for calling her that, a relationship rooted in their shared history.

I don't know much about the Demon Lord's past.

But I can guess from what she's said before, and from what I learned from Taboo, that she's been alive since before the system was a thing.

Based on that assumption, I figured that the Demon Lord probably knew the woman trapped in this room.

But it looks like their relationship was much, much deeper than I first thought.

Why else would you call a woman who has no blood relationship to you "Mother"?

The Demon Lord continues to gaze at her wordlessly.

Just looking at her, never once reaching out to touch her.

I watch over the two of them in silence.

A long, long time ago...

The world was considerably advanced.

There were machines everywhere that made people's lives easier.

But the people of the past committed a grave error.

They laid their hands on the forbidden power source, MA energy, which was never to be touched.

A certain woman explained the dangers to them and pressed them to refrain from using it, but they paid her no heed.

After all, MA energy could make their lives even better than they already were.

But all that awaited them was destruction.

By the time they had realized their mistake and tried to repent, it was all far too late.

The end was fast approaching.

As they wept in despair, the people beheld a single ray of hope.

A means of saving the world by sacrificing a single woman.

That woman was the very person who had warned them of the dangers of MA energy.

As the people changed their tune and begged her to save them, she nonetheless agreed.
And so she became the sacrifice that would keep the world alive.
The people called her a goddess and worshipped her.
That woman's name was Sariel.
Even now, she is chained up in the center of the system.

The Demon Lord starts to reach out toward the goddess Sariel, then stops and withdraws her hand.
"Lady Sariel... This is too cruel. It must hurt, right? Are you suffering?"
The Demon Lord—the *Demon Lord*—is crying.
I wonder why...?
For some reason, I always thought the Demon Lord couldn't cry.
I thought she was too strong to let anyone see her tears.
And I'm sure that she rarely ever cries, only in truly exceptional situations.
This is obviously one of them.
"But you still won't stop, will you? That's how you've always been, Lady Sariel."
I don't understand her logic, but I'm sure she firmly believes every word she's saying.
"Please wait just a little longer. I... I'll get you out of here, no matter what. I promise. I promise."
Maybe I misunderstood her.
I always thought the Demon Lord was fighting for this world, but it looks like I was wrong.
The Demon Lord has been fighting this lonely battle all these years just to save one person.
Saving the rest of the world is just incidental.
I understand that, because I feel the same way.
But clearly, my commitment isn't nearly as strong as hers.
That much is obvious now.
I have to admit, I'm a little jealous of the bond between the Demon Lord and Sariel.
The Demon Lord turns away and walks toward me, the tears gone from her face.

"Done already?"

"Yeah. I'm more determined than ever now."

Just as she says, the Demon Lord's expression is clear and resolute.

"Thanks for bringing me here, White."

Maybe seeing the goddess Sariel and crying her eyes out helped her let off some steam.

At first I thought I might've been wrong to bring her here, but if it wound up helping her clear up her feelings, I'm glad I did it.

"Uh-huh. Good."

It *was* good.

Not just for the Demon Lord but for me, too.

I swore to stake my life on saving the Demon Lord to pay her back for saving me.

But it looks like my resolve is still a bit lacking.

The Demon Lord has been fighting all alone for the goddess Sariel for so long.

She may have underlings, but she had no friends.

But even now, she keeps on fighting without ever slowing down.

How hard must that have been?

How much determination must that have taken?

In spite of it all, the Demon Lord is still fighting for Sariel even now.

Would I be able to do the same thing?

I don't think so.

I haven't been staking my life on any of this at all.

There's got to be more, so much more, that I can do.

That's what seeing the Demon Lord's attitude toward Sariel made me realize.

And it also made me start to feel, from the bottom of my heart, that I truly want to help the Demon Lord, not just out of any sense of duty.

How could anyone see her like this and not want to help her?

Just look at how hard she's working.

She's been running at full tilt for ages, even knowing that she might drop dead long before she reaches the finish line.

The demon race hates her. The person she wants to rescue is suffering like this. But she's still trying to save the world, even if it's just the means to saving Sariel?

She definitely deserves to be rewarded.

After all that struggle, she's more than earned a happy ending.

No matter what anyone says, I won't accept any ending that doesn't leave the Demon Lord smiling.

I'll happily commit mass murder or anything else if that's what it takes to make it happen.

Saving the world? That's just an afterthought.

I'm saving only who I want to save.

You won't catch me claiming it's for the good of the world or anything like that.

I don't care if most people will call me a villain.

That's not my problem.

As these thoughts cross my mind, I realize that I really am related to an evil god.

D cares only about her own entertainment.

She'll do anything that seems amusing, even if it results in a whole world's destruction.

I'm not quite as cruel as that, but I'm not so far off, either.

I'll do whatever it takes to accomplish my goals.

Why wouldn't I?

I'm not trying to be a hero here, so I might as well play the villain, reaching my goals with whatever nasty tricks I can get my hands on.

I'm graduating from being a plain old god (LOL).

From now on, I'll be an evil god.

The evilest god this world has ever seen, plunging people and elves alike into the depths of horror and despair.

Afterword

Happy New Year! Okina Baba here.

A new year! Volume 10! That's two major milestones for the price of one! Whoo-hoo!

Sorry, I'm being a lot more upbeat than the book you just read right now.

Can you blame me, though? This series has finally broken into the double digits!

Since only the most legendary of novel series make it into the triple digits, actually hitting double digits is something to be proud of, don't you think?

So it's okay if I stick my nose up a little, right?

If my nose gets super-long like a *tengu*?

It was a *tengu*! A *tengu* did it!

Sadly, though, even though there's an oni, there aren't any *tengu* in this series.

Mr. Oni and the vampire duo get plenty of chances to go on a rampage in this volume, though!

But they're fighting for a reason, not just running wild like a *tengu* might.

Especially Merazophis, who goes on a deadly serious spree of violence.

I didn't do this on purpose for the milestone of the tenth volume, but it has a serious tone overall, with a lot of important developments.

There are still funny scenes once in a while, but that's just 'cause, you know, a god of laughter sprinkled those in.

The characters are all going about their business with great import, but this god of laughter keeps on ruining it.

In other words, it's all ~~the author's~~ god's fault!

Yep. I think that about covers it!

Now, let me say some thank-yous.

An enormous thanks to Kiryu for providing wonderful illustrations as always.

Some of the characters' appearances and stuff are actually reverse engineered from Kiryu descriptions. (For instance, Bloe being weirdly unfashionable may have been a Kiryu idea.)

That's just how much power Kiryu illustrations have. Thank you very much.

I also want to thank the venerable Kakashi, who does the manga adaptation.

Volume 6 of the manga comes out on the same day as this book, and it even contains appearances from some of the characters in this very volume, so please check it out.

I want to thank everyone involved in the production of the anime, too.

Unfortunately, I don't have any new anime information that I can share just yet, but it's coming along splendidly.

I hope you'll keep patiently looking forward to the anime's release.

Thank you also to everyone who was involved in bringing this book out into the world, especially my editor, W.

And to all of you who picked up this book.

Thank you so much.